HEARTSTOPPER
A SEXY ROMANTIC COMEDY

LAUREN LANDISH

Edited by
VALORIE CLIFTON
Photography by
WANDER AGUIAR

INTRODUCTION

From Wall Street Journal & USA Today Bestselling Author Lauren Landish.

Roxy Price

After ten months without a date, I'm eager to go to the hottest new ticket in town, Club Jasmine.

I deserve a night of fun. I've worked hard and I finally got a promotion. But for one night, I'm going to let loose.

That's when I see him.

The drop-dead gorgeous Jake Stone.

With his god-like physique, pure blue eyes, and chiseled jawline, he might be the hottest guy I've ever laid eyes on. A total heartstopper.

The man's probably a player. Then again, maybe that's what I need—a man who knows what he's got, knows how to use it, and knows how to make me scream to the heavens.

Screw it. You only live once.

But when I go in Monday morning to meet my new boss, I'm greeted by that same irresistible smile.

And Mr. Stone is making it perfectly clear that *strictly professional* is not in his vocabulary.

Want the deleted scenes? Sign up to my mailing list to receive them!

Irresistible Bachelor **Series (Interconnecting standalones):**
Anaconda || Mr. Fiance || Heartstopper
Stud Muffin || Mr. Fixit || Matchmaker
Motorhead || Baby Daddy

PLAYLIST

Toxic - Britney Spears
Rude Boy - Rihanna
This Is What You Came For - Rihanna/Calvin Harris
Dangerous Woman - Ariana Grande
Power Of Love - Celine Dion
Uptown Funk - Mark Ronson/Bruno Mars
Milkshake - Kelis
Freak Like Me - Adina Howard
Rockabye - Clean Bandit
American Girl - Tom Petty
Up Where We Belong - Joe Cocker/Jennifer Warnes
Do You Really Wanna Hurt Me? - Culture Club
Take My Breath Away - Berlin
I Want It That Way - Backstreet boys

CHAPTER 1

ROXY

"The guys had better get ready," I say, twirling my hair around my finger. I'm riding shotgun down the road with my best friend, Hannah Fowler, in her beat-up Lexus sedan. The windows are rolled down, the wind blowing through the cabin and ruffling our hair as the downtown streets whiz by.

It's been a long time since I've gone out, and boy, have I missed it.

But tonight I'm going to let loose, I vow. *Enjoy myself for once.*

"Why's that?" Hannah asks as she speeds through a yellow light, glancing over at me. With shoulder-length blonde hair, big round cheeks, and eyes that are as blue as they are huge, she looks a lot like Amanda Seyfried, and she's played it up a few times. Equipped with a sense of humor that almost rivals mine, she's basically been my bestie since I struck out on my own. We're inseparable.

I grin, flashing my notorious wink I learned from my big sister, Mindy, and boast, "'Cause I'm about to release the Rox on them!"

"Did I just hear you just say you're gonna gobble all the cocks?" Hannah yells over the roar of the wind.

I laugh. "You know damn well that wasn't what I said!" I got ninety-nine problems and gobbling cock won't be one. If anything, that's on Hannah's menu, considering the tight black number she's wearing that looks like it's been painted on her frame.

Hannah giggles. "Well, it's better than unleashing your deprived vajayjay on some poor man!"

"I can't help it," I say, shaking my head. "You go ten months without sex and see how you feel. Knowing you, they'd have to call the Ghostbusters because you'd have fucked half a dozen men to death."

We share a good laugh and I smile as I let my arm hang out the window, enjoying the night breeze against my skin. We haven't even gotten to the best part of the night and I'm already in a good mood. It's a far cry from the sour, cantankerous pain in the ass I've become lately.

Don't get me wrong—my job at Franklin Consolidated is okay and all, but it's not my first love. The grin slowly fades from my face as I think back to three years ago. I was working the club scene and singing at Trixie's, a local club back home, busting my ass for my big break.

It never came. There were too many rejection letters, too many times I got passed up on auditions. I almost tried out for *X-Factor* but got sick right before with a bad cold, so even that didn't go as planned. Eventually, I set the microphone aside and went back to school. Mom at least had the decency to not say *I told you so* about my short-lived career as a singer. Instead, she gave me encouragement when I said I was moving away to finish up the degree that I'd been putting off.

I don't really know why I moved away. My stepfather, John, has more money than my family could spend in five lifetimes and is more than happy to share it. Champagne, designer dresses, cocktail parties, and vacationing on yachts. I could've had it all, the total deb socialite.

But nepotism is not a life I want for myself. I want to stand on my own two feet like my sister, Mindy. Sure, she ended up marrying a super-handsome, rich stud, but she worked her ass off before that and still does.

Thinking about her, I feel guilt tighten my chest. I haven't talked to her or anyone in my family for months. It's partly because we all lead such busy lives, but I'd argue that Mindy's life is perfect now. She's got a great husband, two adorable kids, and a business of her own that she loves running.

I'm nowhere near there. And I can't help but have this nagging feeling that even if I'm successful in my new career path, I may never get that feeling. So yeah, a night like this is just what the doctor ordered.

"Seriously, though, I need this," I tell Hannah. "We should do this more often."

As a gift to us both, Hannah decided to hit the grand opening of Club Jasmine, a brand new nightclub that's being opened by a couple of rich pricks whose names I don't know. It's supposed to be hot and ritzy. I just want to get to the hot part.

Hannah nods. "I know, honey. You've been working hard for what? Ten months? And already getting a promotion. You need to reward yourself." She shakes her head. "I've been worried about you."

Satisfaction rolls through me. It's about the only positive thing I can say about my job. My hard work has paid off. I've been recognized by the execs, and starting next week, I'm getting promoted, working as an assistant to the new regional president. I'm not his secretary. I'm going to be one of the junior analysts, gathering data and such for him. I can see myself going up the ladder in a couple of years and making big money.

But at what cost? I think to myself. *At this pace, I'll be sitting in a corner office with nobody to come home to, my best years behind me.* The pay might be good, but is it worth giving up the one thing that brings me joy?

Hannah pulls up to a red light, and I force that troubling thought from my mind, checking my makeup in the mirror. I've got dark hair, sparkling hazel eyes, and pouty lips, just like all the women in my family, and I'm pretty enough, I guess. But my spark, that mischievousness that made men weak in the knees, is absent from my eyes.

I need to get back to doing what I love, even if only on the weekends. Screw prioritizing work.

"What you should be worried about is the poor guy who's gonna need a heart monitor when I get done with him," I say, determined to stay upbeat, snapping my lipstick closed.

Hannah gives me a serious look and deadpans. "Is it really that bad? I thought you were just joking at first, but Jesus, Rox, I'm kinda scared. You ever see that movie *Teeth*, with the vagina that grows fangs? I feel like that's you right now."

"Oh, go to hell!" I laugh, but Hannah grins.

"Seriously, maybe we should just call it a night before you get yourself in trouble. I mean, I'm sure you've got something in your drawer at home that will take the edge off."

I laugh. "Sorry, only the real thing will do. I prefer my meat hard, throbbing, and able to spray paint the walls."

Hannah gags. "Gross! Just make sure you use protection. Don't want you to wind up on Maury waiting to hear 'You are the father!' and the crowd going apeshit."

"Okay, Mom. I'll make sure to snag some of his DNA just in case."

We both laugh as she turns a corner, and we see a line of cars stretching up the street.

Despite all my talk, I probably won't even sleep with anyone. I'm just here to have fun, unwind, and relax. And if it comes along with getting to flirt with a cute as fuck guy, I'm all for it. The gears might be rusty, but I bet I can still twerk my ass with the best of them after I get warmed up.

My breath catches in my throat as the club comes into view. It's beautiful. The parking lot is big and well-lit. The building itself looks like anything but a nightclub, with a large fountain out front and beautiful marble steps that are flanked by grand columns leading to the white double-door entryway. There's a long line wrapped around the building, and I can tell the grand opening ceremony is already over as they're just starting to let people in.

I've seen a lot of clubs, but I'm truly impressed with the presentation of this one. Everything I see says the owners sank a lot of money into this place. Honestly, it puts Trixie's, with its neon sign, disco ball in the ceiling, and pink and purple ambient lighting to shame.

There's no room to park in the main lot, so we have to go to the overflow lot down the street, barely finding a parking spot. Getting out, a cool night breeze sweeps the area, causing goosebumps to rise on my skin and excitement to warm my blood. Overhead, the full moon makes me feel like a wolf on the prowl.

Hannah peers at me, looking around my backside. Unlike her, I've opted for a red club dress, one that hugs my curves in all the right places. I got it from Mindy, who had her fair share of good luck in it, so maybe it'll do the same for me. "Damn, girl, your ass didn't look that big when we left home. Did you stuff it with some pads or something?"

I place my hands on my hips and boast, "Girl, seriously? This is all-natural! They write songs about an ass like this!" I start popping my ass, reciting some classic lyrics.

Hannah bends over, grabbing her sides while laughing. "Oh, my God, stop! You're killing me."

"Stop making fun of my bootyliciousness then and let's go!"

Giggling, we make our way to the club, evading people on the street. I see a couple of guys look my way and I feel a little thrill. I don't see anything I like, though, so I keep going until we reach the club and the line that's jam-packed out the building. Luckily for us, Hannah has a reservation for us so we don't have to wait. I'd like to dance sometime before next Tuesday.

We walk past the men in line, and I feel more eyes on me. These men are all dressed well. There are no open shirts and rolled sleeves but rather suits and ties. It must be the club theme for the grand opening. My confidence should grow, but I'm hit by a sudden feeling of anxiety. Am I really ready to rock someone's world or am I just looking for companionship? It's been so long since I've been in the social company of the opposite sex. I don't even know.

From inside the club, the bass of the music thrums against my body as we reach the door. My heart begins to pound. I almost feel like I'm back at Trixie's. Almost. The two handsome bouncers are dressed in fitted suits, their hair cut professionally and their designer sunglasses blocking their eyes. They kinda look like the Men In Black. Whoever is running this place isn't playing around.

"We have a reservation," Hannah says. I don't know how she got it. She's got connections, I guess. Hannah gives her name and the bouncers let us in, pulling the large double-doors wide.

The entire interior is just as luxurious as the exterior. The bar stretches around a good quarter of the large rotunda that makes up the main room, lit up beautifully in blues and dim whites. Out on the floor, beautiful women and men dressed in great suits are already dancing beneath a balcony that overlooks everything. There's a crowd up there, and I bet it's the VIP section from the way things look.

My eyes are pulled to the stage that's set up so that the VIP balcony can watch, and I feel my heart speed up some more. *I want to get up there. I want to feel their eyes. I want their applause. I want to rock this place out.*

"This place is incredible," I finally say. It's no lie, either. Everything, down to the smallest detail, is amazing.

"Isn't it?" Hannah says, perfectly serious. "They really went all out." Hannah's eyes hungrily rove over the crowd. "But less talking and more stalking. Let's hit the bar."

We're not even seated for a full minute before some blonde guy is hitting on Hannah. In my 'lucky' red dress, I feel a little deflated.

My disappointment is short-lived, unfortunately.

"Mind if I have a seat?" asks a voice. I look up into a pale but handsome face.

"Not at all," I say politely.

He sits down beside me and grins, his eyes piercing into me. For some reason, my flesh crawls at his look. It's just a bit off, even if he is hot.

"So where you from?" His voice has a nasal, whiny tone it, and I regret telling him to have a seat.

Somewhere you're not, I want to say, *and hopefully will never be.* The words are on my lips, but I'm not comfortable being rude.

"Summerfield," I say diplomatically. Come on, it's been ten months. I should give the guy a chance. Maybe he's just nervous and he's actually sweet.

He arches an eyebrow. "Summerfield, huh? Where's that?"

I wave my hands nondescriptly. "Off somewhere on the coast."

He chuckles. "It's like that, huh?" He nods at the waiter. "Can I have a Bud Light for my lady friend here?"

"You don't have to buy me a drink," I try to protest. I hate beer.

"I insist" he says firmly, grinning at me. "A beautiful girl like you shouldn't be sitting here alone without a beer."

"Is he the one?" Hannah whispers sarcastically in my ear. I could just kill her. The guy saddled next to her doesn't give me the creeps and remind me of Draco Malfoy.

I mouth *No*, giving her an outraged look.

"Remember what you said. Unleash the Rox!" she jokes.

More like I'm thinking of unleashing The Rock to come lay the smackdown on this dude's ass if he doesn't take a hint.

The beer comes, and Mr. Weird tries to talk me up some more. "So, what do you do?"

"Office stuff, nothing cool," I reply, trying to politely let the guy know I'm not interested. "You'd be bored."

But he's not having it. "Oh, every job seems boring when you're doing it," he says, fiddling with his drink. "Hey, try the beer. It's pretty good."

"Not just yet. I don't want to have to run to the ladies' room all night," I reply. Actually, hitting up the ladies' room might be a good idea. It'd get me away from this guy.

"Oh, I get that. But come on, what could one beer hurt? Hey, if you need to pee, I'll escort you to the guy's room. Nobody'll say anything."

Seriously? Now I don't feel bad. My gut feeling was right. This dude is a creep. As the music changes, I mutter under my breath, "Somebody *please* fucking save me."

CHAPTER 2

"*T*his is gonna be epic," Nathan Scott, my childhood friend and business partner, boasts as the limo we're in rounds the corner. He's seated across from me, dressed sharp as a tack for our big night.

"All the cards have lined up for us," he continues. "We've got a great local band and an assload of local celebrities. We even got that girl who's got like two million Instagram followers because of her ass. That ass and Club Jasmine are going to be in front of two million people by the end of the night. I'm telling you, we've got everything." Nathan claps his hands and rubs them together. "This is going to be huge, Jake. Huge!"

I shift again in my cushioned seat, messing with the cufflink of my shirt. I can't deny the excitement in Nathan's words, but I know you can do all the right things and still have a business fail. So I'm not getting my hopes up too much yet.

The nightclub was his idea, developed right about the time the rumors started about Graham Holdings, the company I work for, buying out Franklin Consolidated. I'd been reluctant to invest at first. But when Nathan laid out the numbers, I was sold. "I'll believe it when I see it," I say.

"Damn, man, can you be any more excited?" Nathan says, peering at me with a scowl. "This is a big day for us."

It's not that I'm not excited, and I usually consider myself calm and collected under pressure, but I'd be lying if I said I wasn't sweating bullets. We poured a lot of money in this thing. In fact, I poured everything I've saved into this.

I need this to succeed.

Especially when I have Sophie depending on me to take care of her, I think to myself. Sophie's my sixteen-year-old sister who was orphaned six years ago when our parents were taken in a car accident.

She wanted to come with me tonight. Of course, she knew she couldn't since she's underage. "You can let me in. I don't even need a fake ID," she'd said, bouncing up and down and trying to look her cutest. Maybe that works when she wants me to let her buy a new skirt on my credit card, but this isn't the same thing.

Still, it makes me smile. I'd done the same shit when I was younger, but I'm not going to let her break off into bad habits.

"See it?" Nathan asks as I'm still silent in my thoughts, his Bronx accent coming on full as he pulls my mind back to the limo. "The fuck? It's all right in front of you. We got the whole fucking world at our feet."

Nathan's lucky that he works independently because he curses like a sailor.

I adjust my collar, rolling my neck. I'm not in a full-on tux, but I'm in a designer suit that I bought just for the club. It's a slightly brighter blue than I'd wear for my day job with a pristine white dress shirt and metallic red tie. Nathan insisted I wear something that 'pops'. "I was just saying there's a still lot of work to do, that's all."

It's easy for Nathan to feel more nonchalant about the whole project. He's a stockbroker who's gotten rich with other people's money, whereas I've had to work for mine. My grandfather lent me a name and a legacy that got me into a good school, but Mom's love of Dad meant a middle-class life. Climbing the corporate ladder has been grueling. I've busted my ass and more than once pulled eighteen-hour days to make sure that I'm in a place of power. I'm going to be the Regional President for the Franklin Consolidated subsidiary, and I plan to do great things with the role.

Still, I've got responsibilities, Sophie being the chief one. The five million I sank into this club could set her up for life. *Could* being the operative word. "We have a long way to go," I say.

"And I have every confidence we'll make back every red cent," Nathan says. "You do too. Otherwise, you wouldn't have signed on."

It's hard to argue. I knew this was a risk, but I don't mind that. I've always been guided by my instincts, and when something looks good, I go for it.

I shrug. "You're right. It's just a helluva few days—our grand opening and this merger. I start in my new position on Monday."

"Oh, what's up with that?"

"I'm being sent to kick a little ass for an underperforming unit." To say it's been underperforming is a mild way of putting it. "I've been told to cut the fat or burn the place down if I have to. I'm not looking forward to being 'that' guy. I know some of the in-house employees are going to hate me."

"Oh, well. Fuck 'em is what I'd say," Nathan says. "You do you."

"Too bad I love my job," I say. "They might hate me for a little while because I'm new, but trust me, they're gonna respect me by next quarter. Those who are left."

"If you say so," Nathan says. "Glad I don't have to do that shit. Making money with other people's money is my specialty. I don't have to work on someone's job. Which is why you should be jumping for this club to succeed. If it goes right, you can retire off all the Benjamins we bank."

I chuckle. "That's the plan," I say, not wanting to tell him what I'm thinking. Truth is, I don't think I'll be satisfied even if this does turn into a huge income generating machine. I can't imagine just retiring right now. I work too much to even imagine what that would be like.

"Speaking of which," Nathan says as the limo rolls up to the sidewalk of the club. There's a good amount of press, and even a few of the VIPs are gathered outside the club. I'm as impressed by it during the day as I know it's going to look once the sun goes down. It was one of the things I insisted on, that our club looked as classy during the day as it will at night.

The crowd applauds as I get out. I shake hands with our local boxing champ and pose with him for a few publicity shots on the red carpet as the crowd builds. Cameras flash, and as the sun touches the horizon behind the club, it's a certified throng.

Nathan and I both adjust our suits, and I wave as we mount the platform in front of the fountain. Nathan pauses, giving me a wink. "It's show time!"

I know we look strange. I tower over Nathan at six foot three while he's a modest five foot six. The cameras are flashing in our faces as soon as we're ready, press calling our names and people in the crowd already chanting for the club.

Our staff strings the big red ribbon across the stairs leading up to the entrance, and I swear that I feel like I'm at a Hollywood premier. When Nathan brings over the special scissors that we're supposed to use for the ceremony, really just painted up hedge clippers, the camera flashes are nearly blinding. I lift my hand, taking the wireless mic from Nathan.

"Thank you all for coming," I start. "I'm not going to say that we're as important as opening a new wing at the university hospital. But I'm proud of the work our team has done, and I'm looking forward to enjoying a few hours relaxing here. Thank you again."

There's polite applause, and I take one arm of the clippers while Nathan takes the other.

A cheer goes up from the crowd as Nathan and I slice through the ribbon, and the two of us lead the VIPs up the stairs and through the doors. It's been awhile since I've been here. I've been so busy setting up my place here in town and getting things settled with my transition to Franklin Consolidated. But seeing it like this, I have to give it to the architects. The place is a dream, with the perfect blend of classic touches that I like along with cutting-edge lighting and styling. It's going to be a unique club for a very long time.

I check out the bar and the stage, then head to the VIP section

overlooking the club just as the doormen start letting in the regular customers.

"This club is amazing," one of the first women through the doors says to Nathan as she comes up to where we are. She's going around and checking everything out I guess.

By the look in Nathan's eyes, I don't think he'd be opposed to taking her home tonight. "Thank you. My partner here helped, of course. But all the heavy lifting was on me," he says to her.

I smirk. Nathan's going to take the credit, huh? "Well, I let you do the heavy lifting since you're closer to the floor. Less distance to move."

The girl chuckles, but Nathan's undeterred. "You know what they say, big things come in small packages. And you're right, having three legs to stand on helps."

I have to chuckle. Nathan is an outrageous flirt, and it works. The girl's eyes flicker down to his crotch before she smiles. Nathan pats the seat on the couch next to him, and she sits down, making me shake my head. He's going to have a fun night.

"Champagne, sir," the waitress says, handing me a glass. She's wearing a form-fitting blouse, a damn near painted-on skirt, and is even some wearing some thick-rimmed glasses, totally playing up the naughty professional vibe of the night. But she's as professional as can be, just like we instructed all of our employees.

It was one of the things I insisted on. While I know Nathan would love to sample what some of the girls could offer him, I won't allow it on my watch. I want to set an example for Sophie, and that means showing her that I can treat my employees with respect. I can be a gentleman. And I want my employees acting with respect too.

"So how much do you think we'll clear tonight?" I ask, getting down to business. One of the local celebs comes up, shaking hands. I return the favor, sending over a bottle of Kristal as thanks for coming by.

"You send more bottles like that? We might break even," Nathan laughs. "We're doing just fine, man. I'll check with the manager before we leave tonight. He'll get me an estimate. But remember, tonight isn't about turning profit. It's about getting rep. We get rep now, and we make bank later."

We chat for another forty-five minutes or so, and I'm amazed as the club fills up. There's no way the folks still outside are getting in for hours unless they've got a reservation.

"Great turnout!" Nathan crows, loving the flow of people still coming through the doors. It's fun, and best of all, authentic.

"It is," I murmur. I have to say even I'm impressed. "It's a weight off my chest . . ."

My voice trails off as I see her walk in. She stands out in the crowd of mostly whites and blacks in a fire engine red dress that hugs her body like it was custom made for her. Long brown hair frames her angelic face, and while I'm too far away to see her eyes, her lips are perfect. The way her cheekbones are shaped, she looks like . . . "An Angel."

"What?" Nathan asks, but I barely hear him as I watch her breathlessly. She goes over to the bar with a girl who's obviously her friend or wingman, and a thread of anger courses through my head as I see some guy come up on her. I grip my glass harder as I

as I look at my savior, and I feel like this night's
ge my life. The stage is almost prepared for the main
d that's hot on the charts and has a fresh sound. I've
forward to it, but now I have another sweet

ke off my anxiety, I poke the guy playfully in the
t a blue leotard under there?"

eyebrow at me, confused but with a grin on his face.
"No, why?"

showed up and saved me from that creep, you must
," I joke. "I'm wondering where you keep the

aking the seat next to me. "Nope, not Superman, but
it to being called the man of steel a few times in

brow. "Modest much?" Looking at him and his cut
ugh, I don't doubt him. That suit can only hide so
ody.

at I had under my suit. I was just telling you. Being
w?" His eyes twinkle, and something tells me he's
joke. I can't help it, I smile. I like a man who can
my sense of humor.

half of my mind is dirty enough to know what he's
. He has balls of steel and a huge, throbbing, steely
e haven't even introduced ourselves and I'm already

r name then, Superman?" I ask.

see him laying on the moves, even though she doesn't seem too
into it.

Nathan waves his hand in front of my face. "Yo, Jake, are you
listening to me?"

I blink rapidly, shaking my head as I turn back to him. "Huh?"

"I said this place is going to change our lives."

"Hold that thought," I say, my eyes and my mind on one thing
only. I toss back the rest of my glass and get to my feet, heading
for the stairs. As I leave the VIP area, I'm not thinking about
Nathan, or money, or even how well our grand opening is going
to turn out tonight. All I can see is the angel in a red dress.

CHAPTER 3

⚮

ROXY

"*S*o, how about we go back to my place?" the guy asks for the second time. Is 'no thanks' somehow going to change in three minutes?

I try to hold back my annoyed scowl. Go back to his place? I'm about ready to splash my untouched beer in his fucking face. I've turned him down for a dance. He's not that bad-looking. I'm sure he could find some girl in here, even with his creepy ass vibe. Why the fuck's he still here with me?

I look around and see that Hannah's deserted me. I can see her over on the dance floor, twerking her ass up against some cute dude. I'm certain he's about five minutes from blowing a load in his slacks with the way she's moving.

I look back over just in time to see Dr. Strangelove pushing the bottle closer to me, like he's trying to remind me that it's there and force me to drink it, but he's gotta learn that there's a lot of scrap in this little body. "Drink up," he says.

That's it. I just can't with this guy.

18

I open my mouth to finally
polite and have made it per
selling. But before the wo
voice behind me speaks u
late. I was busy upstairs."

I spin in my seat to get a
Seriously, I might need a de
as the breath leaves my lur
ever seen under dark hair tl
of the club catch deep wit
sensual mouth, and it's har
and take the rest of him in.

He's tall and broad-should
him perfectly.

Fuck being a heartthrob. I
guy is.

My mouth opens like a fisl
and I'm able to brush off r
along. "No, honey, I was jus
until you got back from tl
flash a smile, not letting th
turn and give Dr. Strangelo
have all of his front teeth?"

My former creepy-ass suito
about ready to fight for his
him a hard look, he gets u
and disappears in the crowd

Relief flows through me an
when I can't see his face any

---

my heartbea
going to cha
act, a rock b
been lookin
distraction.

Trying to sh
chest. "You g

He arches ar
Fuck, he's ho

"The way yo
be Superma
red cape."

He chuckles,
I have to ad
my life."

I arch an ey
physique, th
much of his

"You asked v
real, you kn
biting back
keep up with

But the othe
talking abou
cock. Fuck,
getting hot.

"So what's y

He chuckles as if he's unused to a woman being so direct with him. "Jake," he says. "How about you, Angel?"

"Roxy," I say. I love the way he calls me Angel, even though I feel like anything but right now. Angel definitely sounds better than horny succubus. "And before you ask, yes, I rock hard."

He laughs. "Cheeky, aren't you? I like the name. It's cute."

"Why not sexy? Or hot? I like that better than cute."

"I'd say you have all three covered," he growls lightly, sitting next to me. "I can think of a few more words to describe you too."

A flush comes to my cheeks at his compliment and I'm momentarily robbed of speech. This guy's a silver-tongued devil, and he's got a voice that seems to heat my body every time he speaks.

He nods at my beer. "I don't peg you for a Bud Light girl."

I recover and shake my head, making a face. "I'm not—haven't touched it. I don't really like beer."

He grabs the bottle and sets it in front of him and signals one of the waitresses. "Let's get something new for the lady!"

She comes over and gives him a look like she'd love to take him out back and ride him like a cowgirl. I know Jake has to be used to it though. The man's probably a player. Then again, maybe that's what I need tonight—a man who knows what he's got, knows how to use it, and knows how to make me scream to the heavens. "Something in particular?"

He turns to me, giving me a wink. "She'd like a Sex On My Face."

I gawk, shocked at his forwardness, but the waitress doesn't even bat an eye. And in my mind's eye, I can see myself grinding all over those sexy lips of his. My face turns red at the thought and I push it away. For now. "Of course, sir."

"You didn't have to do that," I say, trusting that I was just ordered a drink and not a room at the Holiday Inn.

"Nonsense, you've got to try it," Jake says with a laugh. "It's one of the house specials."

His persuasive charm just wins me over. The waitress brings back the drink, and at first I think it looks like an iced tea. I take a sip, my eyes widening. "This is good!"

He winks at me. "Told you. Take it slow. I've heard that they can hit hard." He takes the beer and sniffs it, then turns it up, drinking about half of it. "So, how'd you hear about the club?"

"My friend Hannah," I say, pointing her out on the floor. "She told me about it. I needed a night out to relax and have some fun."

And I need a man like you to take care of a certain need, I think to myself.

Jake nods. "Well, you picked the right place. Even for opening night, it's not over the top. This place has class."

"You're telling me," I agree. I think it'll be what makes Club Jasmine popular for a long time. They could pack this place and tear the dance floor up, sure. But the building's got enough inherent class and charm that it'll be a chill spot too. "What about you? What brings you here?"

A slight smirk comes to one of his lips. "I'm friends with one of the owners."

I stare at him as I take a sip of the delicious drink. It's something else he's not letting on to, but honestly, I don't give a fuck. I didn't come here to learn his life history. And I damn sure don't care about his friend. I just can't get over how handsome he is. Those lips look like they could do damage between my legs, and the more I see them move, the more I want to feel them pressed against mine.

He asks me more questions about myself, but I can barely hear or find the focus to answer. I can only focus on his perfect smile. The more he talks, the more I feel like I want him. Even if it is only for a night.

I finish my drink in a hungry gulp and lick my lips in the most seductive manner I can. *Damn, I don't know if that drink was seriously that good or if literally anything would taste amazing right now.*

"I was thinking . . ." I say, running my hand along his arm. Shit, I'm playing the seductress to the hilt. I even have my next line planned, something about how I'd like to have a little more sex . . . on *his* face.

He raises a brow at me, and anxiety twists my stomach as I look into his eyes. I'm suddenly uncertain. He has to get more pussy than animal control. My ego can't take a hit right now.

But looking around the room, I realize one thing. He's the only one I want. If I can't have Jake, I'm going home alone.

I suck in a breath. Fuck it—you only live once.

"Look, would you like to go somewhere?" I cringe. I know I must sound so fucking desperate, like some slutty skank. But isn't that what I came here for? I'm hot and heavy and this guy is doing crazy things to my ovaries just by sitting next to me. I *need* him.

He turns, looking me in the eye. "Direct, aren't we? I can't imagine an angel like you . . ."

I'm shocked when he seems to steel himself. He turns the bottle up and in one gulp drinks the rest, smacking it down on the bar, and growls almost ferally. "Let's go."

He gets up from the seat and I jump to my feet. He puts his hand on the small of my back as he leads me to the back of the club. "Where are we going?"

"Told you, I know the owners. There are . . . private places around here," he says, and I dismiss it. Fuck, I don't care if he takes me into the VIP bathroom. I'll take it right now.

The show is about to start for the band. I'm gonna miss it but I don't care. He takes me through a door and into a hallway. We come up to another door, and like magic, he produces a key to get in. Before I can ask him why he has a key, he's on me like a dog in heat, pushing me up against the wall and devouring my mouth in a hungry, fiery kiss.

Our lips crash together, and he's doing crazy things to my body, his hands roaming over my dress and lighting my skin on fire.

"Take me," I moan, my thighs trembling with need. Ten long months. And if that huge, hard cock pressing against my thigh is any indication, I want it right fucking now.

"Not here," he half-moans, half-slurs in lust, stepping back and taking me by the hand. He leads me down the darkened hall to a room. He opens the door and turns on the light. It's a medium-sized room with a bed and some rugs in the center. What the fuck is a bed doing back here?

But I don't care about that. I want him.

He's back on me again, and we're kissing, his hands tugging on my dress. With every inch of my skin that's exposed, the fire in my stomach grows as I feel all the sexual frustration start to boil over.

"I'm gonna give you a night to remember," I growl in his ear as I pull off his shirt. "You'll never forget Roxy."

Damn, call the exorcist. I don't know what's wrong with me. It's like the devil himself has possessed my body.

I rip off his shirt with an animalistic snarl. The air freezes in my lungs when I see the hard abs of his stomach. He wasn't fucking lying about being the man of steel. The rest of him has to be pure perfection.

"Your tits are amaaazing," he says, his slur growing, his hands squeezing my breast weakly.

What the fuck? Damn, how is he drunk already? He only had that one beer. I pay it no mind. I push him back onto the bed, tugging my skirt up to my waist and mounting his hips, feeling the hard bulge of his groin rub against my panties.

"Fuuuuuck, baby," he moans. His voice is sluggish. "I love how aggressive youuuu are . . ."

"Shh, baby," I tell him, slipping my dress down and showing him my breasts, turning my dress into just a band around my waist. "You ain't seen nothin' yet."

I swear it looks like he's fighting to stay awake. But I don't need long to send him to heaven. I trail my hands down his abs and down to his happy trail. Reaching his belt, I hungrily unbutton his pants.

"Baaaby . . ." he moans, almost like he's gasping for air. I take the gasps as if he can't wait to be inside me. Fuck, I can't either.

I get his pants down and am about to pull his cock out and slide on a condom when he grabs onto my breasts with the force of Zeus. He holds tight and lets out an unearthly gasp, his eyes fluttering.

I stare down at him in shock as he takes one last breath and then seems to go unconscious.

"What the fuck?" I know I was about to give him the most glorious send-off he ever had, but did he really just pass out? "Hello?"

It takes some effort, but I'm able to disengage his death grip from my breasts. They ache, and I wonder if I'm going to have a few bruises on them tomorrow. "Hello?" I repeat, leaning in closer. "Jake?"

I shake him, and when he doesn't respond, I give him a little slap on the face. He doesn't move at all, and fear starts to clench in my belly.

Hands shaking, I place my hand on the side of his neck. I don't feel anything, and I'm getting more worried. What the fuck?

My heart pounds in my chest as I stare down at him in disbelief.

The Man of Steel is dead.

CHAPTER 4

ROXY

"What do you mean, he's dead?" Hannah yells into the phone. In the background, I can hear the bass of the club music, although it's nowhere near as fast or as powerful as what's in my chest. My heart's pounding a thousand beats a minute, and it feels like I have a jackhammer going off inside me.

"I-I-I don't know, he just—"

In panic, I pump Jake's chest furiously. When that doesn't work, I bitch slap him across the face with as much force as I can muster. "Wake up, bitch!" I yell. He doesn't stir, and I slap him again. Still no response, and I stare in disbelief at his still body. How the fuck is this even possible? Is my pussy kryptonite or something?

The first night out, I fucking kill a man. Just my luck!

"Roxy, stop it!" Hannah shouts over my panicked gibbering. "Where the hell are you?"

"I don't know," I moan, moving away from Jake and trying desperately to remember how I got here. "Somewhere in the back. We started to—and then he grabbed my boobs and . . . oh, God, oh, God, oh, God!"

"Stop babbling! You're not making sense!" Hannah snaps. She gives me a moment, then continues. "Tell me exactly what happened."

Taking a deep breath, I relay everything back to her. "I knew I shouldn't have let you out of the house!" Hannah snarls when I'm done. "The first guy you see, you go and fuck him to death!"

"Hannah!" I wail in protest, feeling tears sting my eyes. That one stung. I didn't mean to kill this fine specimen! I was being sarcastic before!

A lump forms in my throat. She's definitely not making this any better. "I don't know why or how this happened, but please—"

"Never mind that," Hannah says, hearing my pain. "Listen, I'm sure you're overreacting. He's probably passed out drunk. You said he started slurring, right?"

I glance over at Jake. He still has his color, but I'm afraid to go back over there. "Doesn't look dead. But I didn't feel a pulse."

"Just go check, God damn it!" Hannah roars.

"All right, all right, geez. If I ever have a heart attack, you'll be the last person I call." Sucking in a deep breath, I go back over to the bed. I force myself to stare at him. Just when I'm about to give up, I see . . .

"Oh, God!" I cry out. "He still has a hard-on!"

"He has angel lust!" Hannah gasps before laughing. "Damn, girl, you weren't messing around."

My face pinches into a frown. This isn't the time for bullshit. "What the hell is angel lust?"

"When dead guys have a hard-on," Hannah says. "A lot better than calling it zombie cock, in my opinion."

I almost gag. Just great, not only did I kill a guy, but I left him with a big, hard, raging boner. I can just see the news now—*Horny office drone kills handsome eligible bachelor and leaves him with a big, hard dick. Film at eleven!*

I take a deep breath and grab his wrist. I move my fingers around frantically, trying to find a pulse. Suddenly, I feel it!

"He has a pulse!" I nearly scream, sweat breaking out on my forehead as I'm overcome with joy. "He's alive! Alive!" I don't mean to, but I sound like a Frankenstein movie.

Now that I'm more coherent, I can see his chest rise and fall in shallow breaths, so faint that I can see why I missed it before.

"Jesus, Rox! Don't do that ever again!" Hannah yells before laughing. "You got me all worked up over here! Oh, and you owe me a night out. I was about to get my own itch scratched. Don't have time for that now!"

"How do you think I feel?" I start to feel worry all over again. "It was strange how he just passed out on me in the first place. One bottle of beer shouldn't have done something like that, even if he was drinking before. I mean, he went from rock solid to staggering in like three minutes."

"Who is he, anyway?" Hannah wonders. "Grab his wallet."

"His name is Jake, that's all I know. I don't know if I should do that . . ."

"Hey!" the short guy yells. "Get your ass back here!"

I grit my teeth and find my way back into the club and make a beeline outside, fearing every second that one of the club security is going to grab me. Those MIB-looking dudes are scary.

Hannah is waiting for me by the fountain, arms folded, a scowl on her face.

We walk to the car and get in, not saying a word until we're inside. Suddenly, Hannah bursts out laughing. "This is just so damn crazy. You were saying that you were gonna unleash the Rox, but damn . . ."

"I dunno, Han." I laugh. "It was weird! I almost shit a brick! I'm not going to want to go out for another ten months."

"Was he at least cute?"

"Oh, gawd," I say, relaxing as Hannah pulls out of the parking lot. A ripple of remembered heat and unquenched desire flushes my cheeks. "He was hot as fuck. And I bet you could crack walnuts with his ass cheeks."

We talk as Hannah drives, and she fills me in on the guy she danced with. I'll admit, I feel a little bad about ruining her night. "So, are you going to call the guy?" I ask, shifting around to try and make my ass more comfortable. "I mean, you sound like you liked him."

Hannah thinks, then nods. "Yeah, I probably will. What about Jake? You get his number?"

"I didn't exactly think about getting his number," I say sarcastically. I reach for my purse and open it, looking for my phone. When I do, I'm shocked by the thick black leather object inside.

My memory flashes back, and I remember taking it out of his pocket and laying it next to my things. "Oh, shit."

"What?" Hannah asks, pulling into our parking lot. When I don't answer, she parks and shuts off the engine. "Rox, what's going on?"

I pull out Jake's wallet and show it to her. "I accidentally took his wallet in my rush to get out of there."

CHAPTER 5

JAKE

"*J*ake!" I faintly hear a muffled voice urgently yell from what seems a million miles away. Something hits me in the face, and I mumble something. The voice speaks up again, this time closer. "Jake, wake up."

I let out a groan, my head pounding like that time I decided to do keg stands in college and lost my balance, hitting my head on the way down. I feel someone shaking me violently, but it's a chore to open my eyes.

"Jake, what happened?" the voice says, and I can finally identify who it is. That Bronx accent is pretty much unmistakable.

Still, even if I recognize Nathan's voice, it's a struggle to open my eyes. I finally force them open, but when I do, all I see is a blur.

"Fuck," I groan. "You get the number on that truck?"

"Jake, you're fucking smashed, man," Nathan says, and I swallow thickly, my mouth feeling both swollen and somehow dry at the same time. "Damn, I haven't seen you like this before."

I feel like my chest has been cast in concrete and like my limbs are weighed down by stone. I blink my eyes rapidly, trying to focus, but it takes several moments for me to see Nathan clearly. He's standing over me, staring at me with disbelief, concern, and yeah, a little amusement.

"Where is she?" I mumble, my words sounding like a jumbled mess. I'm trying to get my bearings, remember what's going on. Some things are a little hazy, but her . . . I can't forget her. Her lush body in my hands, those sweet lips . . . fuck.

Nathan frowns. "Huh? I don't understand you."

I realize I'm not going to get anywhere for at least several minutes with the brain fog that is filling my mind. "Water," I rasp, trying to imitate drinking motions. "Get me some water."

Nathan looks like he's about to make a wiseass comment but instead goes to the corner of the room and grabs a water out of the small refrigerator, bringing it over to me. I'm barely able to take it from his hands, but he plucks it out of my weakened fingers and opens it for me. Taking it, I chug some, the water churning in my stomach, but at least I've got something to focus on besides the jackhammer between my ears.

"Damn, dude," Nathan continues, "What the hell is going on? You disappear and now I find you back here passed out, looking fucked up as all hell. How much did you drink?"

"Not drunk," I say slowly, focusing on every syllable to make sure I'm understood. I remember throwing back that one beer, my second drink for the night. The champagne was the other, and it was a half glass.

"Not drunk?" Nathan demands, his face twisted in confusion. "Jake, you know damn well we can't be having drugs in . . ."

"Drugged," I say, not knowing if I'm thinking clearly enough. That had to be it. The beer. It had to be. It just doesn't make sense any other way.

Nathan looks shocked. "What?"

"I was drugged," I manage in a froglike croak. "I don't know how or why, but someone spiked my drink."

"It was that fucking tramp I ran into on the way here!" Nathan half yells, jumping to his own conclusion. "I knew there was something fishy about that broad being back here!"

"Roxy?" I ask, remembering her flirty dimple-filled smile. I don't consider myself naive, but I don't think my angel is responsible.

"That's her name?" Nathan snarls, turning away. "I'm gonna go out there, find her, and call the cops . . ."

I hold out my hand and tried to stand, but I collapse back onto the bed, my head pounding. "Wait!"

Nathan turns back, scowling.

I shake my head weakly. "Don't call," I rasp. "Seriously."

"Why the fuck not? If we let this type of shit happen, we're going to be finished."

"You're usually more levelheaded than this. Think about it. I'm the one fucked up and I'm thinking more clearly. If you call the cops, that's all everyone's going to be talking about. We don't need the negative press. Let's just look at the security tapes and figure out what to do."

The rage flees his face and his shoulders relax. "Shit, you're right. I wasn't thinking."

I nod. "And there's no need to call the ambulance. I just need a little time and some fluids. I can already feel the effects wearing off a little bit."

Nathan runs his fingers through his hair. "What were you thinking, bringing her back here . . ." His voice trails off as if he suddenly seems to notice that I'm sitting on the bed. "Shit, did you at least hit it?"

I shake my head. "Was about to."

"Man, what the fuck? All your talk about being on the straight and narrow, but you're bringing sluts to the back room on our grand opening night—"

"She's not a slut," I cut in.

"Really? Then what the fuck is she?" Nathan asks.

Nathan shakes his head when I can't answer. "She probably robbed your ass blind."

I pat my pockets and realize my wallet is missing. "Fuck me!"

Nathan is staring at me incredulously. "See? What did I tell you? Why else would she drug you if not to rob your ass!"

Anger tightens my stomach. Fuck, how could I be so stupid? "I'll call and cancel all my cards. She won't be able to get shit off them. Listen, my head can't take much more of this shit right now. Leave me be for a bit and go check the tapes."

I'm glad when Nathan leaves without an argument, and I can't help but see Roxy in my mind. That sweet, angelic smile and her

irresistible laugh.

But no matter how hard I try to reason things, the fact of the matter is that my wallet is gone. Which leaves me with only one explanation.

My little angel is a thief.

※

"ROLL THE FOOTAGE," NATHAN ORDERS ANDRE, OUR HEAD SECURITY guy.

I'd sat in the bedroom for twenty minutes, trying to gather myself before Nathan came back and helped me through the back to the security room. I can stand on my own, but the world's still spinning a little, and I know I probably sound drunk as hell. Still, I've got my wits about me, more or less.

"That's her!" I half-slur, pointing as I get up. I grab the edge of the desk as a wave of dizziness washes over me. On the video, Roxy is approached by some guy, and I recognize him. He was there when I approached her. He orders her a beer, and she never touches it, but when she looks away, you can see as clear as day that he slips something in the bottle.

"Son of a bitch," Nathan breathes. "That bastard slipped something in her drink!"

I grab the edge of the security desk in a white-knuckled grip, my lip curling as I stare at the image on the screen, searing the man's face into my memory. If I ever see him again, he's going to get a beating. "Find him."

Andre clears his throat. "I'll get on the radio to the floor guys, and

I'll keep checking footage here. Trust me, if that asshole shows up again, he's gonna catch a beatdown."

"Okay, maybe I was wrong about the girl," Nathan admits as we leave. I'm angry and would love nothing more than to go track this guy down, but the drug's effect is too strong for me. "But it still doesn't explain the wallet."

"I'm going to go with it was an accident." It's the only alternative to *she stole it* and the one I want to believe most. Even an angel makes mistakes.

"Either way, we got a huge problem on our hands if this motherfucker is going around doin' this shit. We have to catch him. I just don't know if we should call the police now or after we catch him," Nathan says while I recover. "This type of shit is bad for business."

"No cops for now," I half growl, pissed off. "I want to teach this guy a lesson first."

CHAPTER 6

ROXY

"You can't be serious! You're not going back there!" Hannah says, pacing the floor of our apartment. Moonlight is shining in from the floor-to-ceiling windows, and even in this state, I have to admit that the view is the thing I like most about the place. Hannah is wearing Barney pajamas, of all things, and has put her hair into pigtails. I swear she looks like a big-eyed Angelica from the kids' cartoon *Rugrats*.

Our grumpy looking cat, Mr. Felix, an orange and white Persian who adopted us when we were seniors in college, lazily watches her pace the room from his perch on the couch. I'm sure to him, his only concern about all of this is whether he's going to have to get strict when it comes time for his humans to put out his food in the morning.

"Why not?" I demand. "I have his wallet. He's gonna think I stole it."

Hannah stops to scowl at me. "Honey, by now, he already thinks you stole it! Because, well, you did."

"I did not!" I protest. "I just didn't realize I'd stuffed it in my purse in my panic to leave."

Her words sink in, and I feel a feeling of despair creep through me. "There must be something I can do. I can't keep his wallet. The longer I have it, the guiltier I'll look."

Hannah nods. "There is. Just go by Monday and turn it in to the club. Or better yet, mail it to the guy. You have his address, assuming his driver's license is up to date."

"Wait," I say. "Let me look him up." I don't know why I didn't think of it before. Taking out his wallet, I pull out his license and see that it's out of state, which makes me worry. But I have his full name, and I type it into Google on my phone.

The first headline makes my eyes go wide, and I jump so hard I nearly drop the phone. *Corporate Executive And Stock Wizard Opens Club Jasmine*. I click the link and see that most of it is a PR piece that was published just yesterday. My heart hammers in my chest as I read about how the two friends came together to open up Club Jasmine and how they wanted to make a new type of night-club for the city. But the photo catches my attention more. It's the same face, the same piercing eyes that captured me earlier tonight. He's standing in the picture with the same guy who accosted me in the hallway.

"Oh, my God, he owns the club with his friend. That's the same guy I saw in the hallway."

"Let me see." Hannah grabs the phone. "Shit, you weren't lying. Mr. Jake Stone is sexy as hell. He's got those looks and money. Life ain't fair."

plished nearly everything that a woman could ask for. She's cute as a button, and if she's anything like her mother or her aunt, Mindy's going to have her hands full.

"How's my favorite little niece doing?" I ask. "Still wrapping every man she meets around her little finger?"

"Of course. She's starting to talk more, and I'm trying to take her out so she can make friends with other kids her age," Mindy says. "It's crazy keeping up with them."

"That's wonderful. I wish I could see her." That's one of the things I regret about living far away from family. I have missed out on the important moments.

"I wish so too," Mindy says wistfully. "You know, Oliver asks about you all the time. I think he thinks of you as our good luck charm, or maybe the sister he never had."

I hold my tongue because she's right. I feel like I somehow, in a weird, fucked up way, had a hand in getting them together. And some of my favorite memories of the past few years have been with Mindy and Oli. "How's work?" Mindy asks.

"Stressful," I admit. "I work an insane number of hours, but I'm still learning and it's getting easier. I'm getting a promotion, though."

"You are? That's wonderful!" Mindy says earnestly. "I knew you could do it. Are you excited?"

"I am," I say halfheartedly. "I start Monday."

Mindy's quiet for a moment, and when she speaks again, her voice is soft, worried. "Is everything all right, Roxy?"

"I'm fine," I say. "Just tired."

"I did not!" I protest. "I just didn't realize I'd stuffed it in my purse in my panic to leave."

Her words sink in, and I feel a feeling of despair creep through me. "There must be something I can do. I can't keep his wallet. The longer I have it, the guiltier I'll look."

Hannah nods. "There is. Just go by Monday and turn it in to the club. Or better yet, mail it to the guy. You have his address, assuming his driver's license is up to date."

"Wait," I say. "Let me look him up." I don't know why I didn't think of it before. Taking out his wallet, I pull out his license and see that it's out of state, which makes me worry. But I have his full name, and I type it into Google on my phone.

The first headline makes my eyes go wide, and I jump so hard I nearly drop the phone. *Corporate Executive And Stock Wizard Opens Club Jasmine.* I click the link and see that most of it is a PR piece that was published just yesterday. My heart hammers in my chest as I read about how the two friends came together to open up Club Jasmine and how they wanted to make a new type of night-club for the city. But the photo catches my attention more. It's the same face, the same piercing eyes that captured me earlier tonight. He's standing in the picture with the same guy who accosted me in the hallway.

"Oh, my God, he owns the club with his friend. That's the same guy I saw in the hallway."

"Let me see." Hannah grabs the phone. "Shit, you weren't lying. Mr. Jake Stone is sexy as hell. He's got those looks and money. Life ain't fair."

"Yeah, not fair that he passed out before I could ride him to heaven and back," I complain.

Hannah stares at the article for a little more, then hands my phone back to me. "That pretty much seals it. You're not going back there. There's no way they'd believe your story. You'll just be some gold digger in their eyes."

"Hey!" I protest, hurt. "I'm not a gold digging skank!" She's right, though, and I feel horrible. I wish there were something I could do. But now I'm too afraid.

Not to mention my body is all sorts of mixed up with my hormones going in so many different directions that I can't focus at all. I'm horny, scared, angry, and even a little bit hungry. "I can't believe I was about to sleep with the owner of the club," I say to myself. "Why did he pretend like he wasn't some big shot?"

"Who knows? Don't worry, chica," Hannah says, coming over to wrap an arm around me in a sweet embrace. "Everything's going to be all right."

Right then, my phone buzzes and I glance down. Tears come to my eyes as I feel a tug in my heart. "It's Mindy," I say. "Not sure why she's calling this late."

"My cue to go to bed then," Hannah says, delivering a kiss to my forehead before getting up. "Answer it and tell her all about the night. Considering how crazy you both are, I bet she has a story to one-up you. Just save some of the Cherry Garcia for me. I know how you get when you start talking with your sister."

Hannah goes to leave, but before she can totally leave, I call out. "Hannah?"

She turns around, her hand on the door jamb to her bedroom. "Yeah?"

"Thank you for being here for me. I don't know what I'd do without you."

"Probably actually end up killing guys to get your needs met," Hannah says. "And you'd probably have the freezer stocked with those dick-shaped popsicles that have sweet cream filling."

I scowl, my lip curling. "That's disgusting."

"Just joking!" Hannah says, trying to smirk before sticking out her tongue. When that doesn't work, she sighs melodramatically. "Enjoy your talk with Mindy. Goodnight."

Hannah disappears into her bedroom area, and for a split second I debate on answering the phone. But when I think about how long it's been since I last talked to her, I press the button.

"Hi, Mindy!" I answer as I would any other time.

"Hey, Roxy! How's it going?" My sister's voice comes through the phone cheery and upbeat.

I don't want to rain on her parade, and I don't want to get her worried. "Great. How's things for you and the fam?"

"Really? That's good. I didn't know if you'd still be up. I know you're wondering why I'm calling this late, but I finally got some downtime from handling Leah and thought I'd call you and leave you a voicemail."

I smile, thinking about Leah. The spitting image of Mindy if you shrank her down and made her chubbier and cute, she's the darling of everyone in the family. And with a new generation of women in the family, Grandma finally feels like she's accomplished nearly everything that a woman could ask for. She's cute as a button, and if she's anything like her mother or her aunt, Mindy's going to have her hands full.

"How's my favorite little niece doing?" I ask. "Still wrapping every man she meets around her little finger?"

"Of course. She's starting to talk more, and I'm trying to take her out so she can make friends with other kids her age," Mindy says. "It's crazy keeping up with them."

"That's wonderful. I wish I could see her." That's one of the things I regret about living far away from family. I have missed out on the important moments.

"I wish so too," Mindy says wistfully. "You know, Oliver asks about you all the time. I think he thinks of you as our good luck charm, or maybe the sister he never had."

I hold my tongue because she's right. I feel like I somehow, in a weird, fucked up way, had a hand in getting them together. And some of my favorite memories of the past few years have been with Mindy and Oli. "How's work?" Mindy asks.

"Stressful," I admit. "I work an insane number of hours, but I'm still learning and it's getting easier. I'm getting a promotion, though."

"You are? That's wonderful!" Mindy says earnestly. "I knew you could do it. Are you excited?"

"I am," I say halfheartedly. "I start Monday."

Mindy's quiet for a moment, and when she speaks again, her voice is soft, worried. "Is everything all right, Roxy?"

"I'm fine," I say. "Just tired."

"Don't lie to me. I can hear it in your voice," Mindy says. "Spill it."

For a moment, I debate on telling her the truth. It's not that I think she'd judge me, but maybe it's just a little too soon.

"Come on, Roxy," Mindy presses. "I'm not going to give up until you tell me. If I have to, I'll fly Oliver out there to start poking around, and you know how he is!"

I let out a sigh. "Fine. As long as you promise not to laugh. I'm sure I'll think it's funny later on, but it scared me shitless."

"Deal. I'd pinky swear, but this is the phone."

Smiling at the old joke a little, I tell her everything about the creep and Mr. Heartstopper.

"Holy shit, that's crazy!" Mindy says when I'm done. "I bet that creeper tried to spike your drink!"

"He . . . holy shit, you're right!" I say, impressed that Mindy thought of it. I should have thought of it too, honestly. "Still, I feel like hell. I shouldn't have even gone, but gawd, babe, it's been so hard. I haven't had a lot of time for myself, and I just wanted this one night to relax, release, and have fun." A lump forms in my throat as the words leave my lips. "I miss being the Roxy who sang her ass off for you."

Sympathy flows in Mindy's voice. "Oh, baby, don't be so hard on yourself. I know how you feel. I went through the same thing working at Beangal's. God, I was so burned out, and that was a place that was literally bought just for me to run. So I totally understand. There was nothing wrong with your going out to relax."

The tears threaten to flow from my eyes. "Mindy . . ."

"You know what? I think it's time for a visit," Mindy adds. "You got a bestie, I know that, but nobody can get you back to normal like me."

"I don't know . . ." I begin, but Mindy laughs.

"I mean for *us* to come visit you. We might have some sister time to remind you who the real baddest bitch in the family is, but this would be for the whole family. I want to see how you're living, you can have some baby time, and hell, I'll even let your roomie drool all over Oliver for a few."

It would be nice to see my family again. I need to see my new niece and nephew. "When would that be?"

"Not sure with the business and all," Mindy says with a smirk in her voice. "And I think I'll let it be a surprise anyway."

"After tonight, I don't think I can deal with too many surprises," I admit, and Mindy chuckles. "I'm serious, Min."

"I know, babe, I know. I was just yanking your leg. Listen, let me check the schedule and I'll get back with you. We'll probably be there within a month. How's that sound?"

"Good," I admit. "I can hang on until then."

There's a silence, and Mindy speaks again. "What about singing, Roxy? I mean, you always felt better when you had a mic in your hand and were belting out something."

"I guess . . . it's hard, Min. I mean, what's the point? I wasted a lot of my time on that as it is."

"I didn't say make it a career," Mindy says gently. "I said sing. Sing for you, sing for your heart. Hell, just go to some karaoke bar and sing for the crowd there."

"Maybe," I admit, thinking about it. She has a point. Maybe I just need to do it for fun. "We'll see."

"Yeah, well . . ." Mindy says, sighing. "You be safe, okay? And I'm calling you Monday. You can tell me about your new job. I love you, Roxy."

"Love you too, Mindy. Bye."

After Mindy hangs up, I let out a deep sigh. It was nice talking to my sister, but damn, I've got a lot on my plate. Having a new boss coming in is stressing me a little. I was finally getting used to things. But now, I'm going to have this Jake Stone nightmare in the back of my mind.

I pick up Jake's driver's license from the table and stare at it before I set it down on the table and sigh, getting up. "He's handsome, isn't he, Mr. Felix?" I ask.

Mr. Felix does nothing, practically glaring at me. He probably wants the darkness, and I'm keeping him from his beauty sleep.

I chuckle, walking over to the light switch to get ready for bed. Tonight may have been a nightmare, but something tells me my dreams are gonna be anything but. Just as I flick the switch, I see his ID on the table again and blow it a little kiss. "Goodnight. See you in my dreams."

CHAPTER 7

JAKE

*W*alking down the hallway from the elevator to the front door of my new penthouse, I lean against the wall, blinking and taking deep breaths. Whatever was in that beer, not only did it come on hard, but it's hanging around like a monkey on my back. Nathan wanted to follow me up and help me, but I'm too damn prideful for that.

I finally get inside and collapse into my living room chair, groaning and sitting back. At least now that I'm sitting, I can think a little easier. Besides being drugged and robbed blind, the grand opening of Club Jasmine was an overwhelming success. Everyone had a blast. I don't know any exact numbers, but we had to bring in well over six figures. Of course, that's not profit, but it was a good opening night.

"You look like shit," says a familiar voice, and with effort, I turn my four hundred-pound head with the nails stuck in it to see my sister, Sophie, standing against the kitchen counter with her arms crossed, eyeing me critically. The penthouse is a large open room, with floor-to-ceiling windows that span the entire length of the main room, giving a breathtaking view of the skyline. Honestly, I'm still getting used to it and slowly breaking in the furniture, but I like it.

"Why are you still up?" I ask, deflecting. I can't argue with her. I do look like shit. My shirt is rumpled and ripped from where Roxy tore it off, and my eyes are probably bloodshot red. "You were supposed to be in bed hours ago."

"Are you kidding me?" she asks, her luminous brown eyes gazing at me incredulously. "It's the weekend. If anything, I should have been out at Club Jasmine jamming with my friends."

"No, you shouldn't. We talked about this already. You and your friends are too young," I half groan, not wanting to go into this right now.

"So? I'm sure you got into clubs when you were sixteen."

"But you're not me and that was a mistake. I'm going to make sure you don't make the same ones," I remind her for what has to be the thousandth time. I'll give this to my sister—she's about as stubborn as I was at her age.

Sophie rolls her eyes at me. "Whatever. You could've at least brought me back one of the signature drinks as a gift. That Little Mermaid drink on the menu looks so delicious."

I hide a grin. The Little Mermaid, a sea blue drink with tropical notes, also contains a huge shot of triple sec and rum and could probably put Sophie on her ass with one glass. I came up with the name as pun for Nathan, who likes it. I think about Sophie's request for a second, then shake my head slowly. "No can do. I don't want you to turn into a full-blown alcoholic because the drinks are just that good. If you're good, I might let you have a sip for your next birthday. That means grades as well as behavior, by the way."

Sophie sticks her tongue out at me. "Thanks, Dad," she says sarcastically.

Instead of pushing the point, surprisingly, Sophie changes the subject. "I saw you guys on the news," she says.

"Did you?" I heave myself out of the chair and walk over to her, shrugging off my suit jacket and setting it down on the kitchen barstool.

She nods. "The club looked totally ah-mazing. There were A-listers everywhere, including some delicious man candy. Nathan looked hella fine." A dreamy expression comes over her face, and I feel like I have to nip this in the bud. I like Nathan—he's my boy—but there's no fucking way in hell I'm letting him near Sophie.

"Nathan is too old for you," I remind her, "and he has a new girl-friend every other week. He found a new one tonight."

Sophie makes a face. She's not listening again. "Yeah. Because he's hot."

"I'll let others be the judge of that, but if you ask me, it's because he has money. If you have a million bucks in the bank, you can buy yourself a ten. Nathan knows that better than anyone. Some people think money can buy you almost anything."

Except happiness, I think inwardly.

"Besides, the dude is like the same size as you. Do you want a man that you have to tuck into bed every night?"

Sophie flushes. "Um, no. Of course not."

"Okay then. If you're gonna go for a guy, make sure he's at least a foot taller than you." I really don't care or think it matters, the height of a man, but I just want her to stop with this Nathan shit.

"Well, I wouldn't mind having a man buy me things. You're right about that," says Sophie, forgetting about Nathan. "I want a boyfriend with money. All the guys at my school will never have anything."

"That's a horrible quality to look for in a guy," I tell her, trying not to get angry. I remind myself that she's a teenager, and that's basically another word for ignorantly immature sometimes. "Money isn't everything."

"You just said that money can buy you almost anything and now you're telling me it isn't everything. Which one is it?"

"I said *some* people think that. I didn't say it was right. Sophie, it's what's in a guy's heart that counts," I tell her. "You can find a man who will buy you the world. But it doesn't mean a damn thing if he doesn't really care about you."

Sophie's expression softens. "That sounds sweet and all. But if a dude bought me a hot red Ferrari, I think I'd be pretty damn happy."

I chuckle, heading into the kitchen. I can't really argue with that, especially with a sixteen year old. I fill a glass from the tap and drain it. It has to help in flushing this drug out of my system. "You really don't need to be thinking about boys right now, though," I say.

This silences Sophie, and I have to wonder if that means she's already got a boyfriend. I don't want to smother her, so I'm just going to forget about it for now. I'm her big brother, and while I take raising her very seriously, I'm not Dad.

I walk over to the couch and almost stumble, having to grab ahold of it to prevent myself from falling flat on my face.

Sophie is at my side in an instant. "Are you all right?" Concern laces her words. It's the one thing I have to give Sophie. I might annoy her and piss her off with my rules, but she doesn't want to see me hurt. She even tries to pamper me some. I've come home from a late night at work to find her curled up on the couch, a homemade dinner sitting on the stove, and a note for me propped on top.

"I'm fine," I say gently, brushing her aside. "Just tired."

Sophie walks over in front of me and crosses her arms, staring at me suspiciously. "Something happened tonight, didn't it? I've seen you be out later and come home looking a lot better than this. You look like something the cat dragged in."

I nod. "The grand opening was a major success. Nathan and I are both pleased."

Sophie scowls. "No, don't even try it." She gestures at me. "Look at you. Your shirt looks like you got into a fight with Wolverine." She shakes her head. "I've never seen you come home like this before."

I think about denying more, then change my mind. "Something was in one of the drinks I had. It messed me up pretty good. Nathan's double-checking the video with the security guys to see if it was intentional," I tell her. It's enough of the truth to satisfy her, but she doesn't need to know all the details.

"Jesus, Jake, are you okay?" Sophie asks, sitting down next to me. "Should you go get checked out at the hospital?"

"No, I'm fine," I reassure her. "Just a little sluggish. I'll be as good as new in the morning, trust me."

"Still . . ." Sophie says, going quiet. She curls up against me, putting her head on my chest, and I adjust, sliding an arm around her shoulders and squeezing. Maybe it's the club, maybe it's the drug in my drink, but I don't mind it right now. I can use a little bit of reassurance that I'm doing the right thing by her.

"I know," I whisper quietly. "I miss them too."

"I miss them so much," Sophie says, her voice thick, and if I could turn my head again, I know she'd be crying softly. Instead, I hug her and kiss the top of her head.

"Sophie, I know I'll never replace Dad, but bear with me. I'm kinda learning this parenting shit on the fly, you know? But that's why I was so harsh earlier. I don't care about money, and I don't want you to either. You want that red Ferrari? You graduate college and I'll get you one. I'd rather you actually fall in love with the man, not with his bank account. You can marry the garbage man for all I care."

Sophie hugs me tighter. "There's nobody better than my big brother."

"Yeah, well, I love you too," I reassure her.

We sit there like that for a few moments before my phone buzzes and I fish it out of my pocket. "It's Nathan."

Sophie grumbles but gets up. "I'll let you guys talk then," she says. "I'll see you in the morning."

I give her a smile and a nod. "Yo, Nathan," I answer the phone. "You realize what time it is?"

"Hey, man, this night was crazy!" Nathan says, still buzzing off adrenalin. "I can't believe what happened. We'll keep an eye out for both, but that dude is done if he comes back."

"Thanks," I reassure him. "Is that all?"

"Nah, man. Other than your deal, the club opening was as good as we could've imagined. We're going to make millions by next year, just wait and see. I already have three more bands lined up."

I stare at my phone, still wondering why the hell Nathan's calling. "Nathan, couldn't this wait until morning?"

"Yeah, I guess. I'm just excited." Nathan says, slightly chagrined. "Yo, man, about the girl . . . we kinda lost her. She walked out with a friend, but we're gonna keep working on it."

I nod to myself. Roxy . . . if only I could talk to her again to clear this up. "Don't worry about her. I'm sure it's all a misunderstanding. The guy is more of a concern. If he did that at our club, you can guarantee he's doing it elsewhere too."

"Okay, man, just . . . get some sleep. I just want you to know, this club . . . it's our rocket to the moon, baby. Rest easy."

"You too. Goodnight," I say, hanging up on him and lying back. I'm pretty sure I'm asleep before I even hit the couch cushion.

CHAPTER 8

ROXY

J'm a ball of nerves when I arrive at work Monday. It took me until nearly midnight last night to relax. Every time I heard a car outside on the street, I swore it was the cops ready to drag me off to jail. Eventually, Hannah got me to relax, but I still had to give myself some serious self-love to be able to get to sleep.

I've done pretty good with it so far since I got to work. I was even able to eat some breakfast after Hannah gave me a pep talk. I just need to focus on today. I don't want to look like an idiot the first day I meet my new boss.

But still, as I check on the second floor for interoffice mail, I can't stop thinking about him. How his lips felt against me. His hard body pressed into mine. The feeling of grinding on him, even if he was still inside his pants. It was . . . heartstopping.

I brush my desires and troublesome thoughts away as I take a deep breath and step off the elevator with a stack of papers in my hand, adjusting my black skirt with my right hand before making my way across the floor to my work area. Our office is at the top of a high-rise building downtown and has been around for decades. The floor plan isn't my favorite, an open floor with cubicles that make me feel like either I'm constantly running a maze or that the agents are going to show up to arrest me for talking to Morpheus.

The board room is down the hall, past the coffee room and bathrooms, while along three of the walls are several glass offices for the higher-ups. Along the far back wall are three mostly unused meeting rooms, what a lot of us 'cubey cats' call the firing room, since the executives never fire someone in their own offices and they don't like giving out pink slips in public.

"Here are the papers Byron wanted," I say, bending over to place the stack on my co-worker, Matt Brown's, desk. I don't want to. I know he's getting a decent view down my blouse, but I have to or else I'm going to lose the rest of my stuff all over the place.

Matt glances up from his laptop, raising his eyebrows, his widow's peak going back on his head, making him look like the old young version of Eddie Munster. He's tall and skinny, with pale reddish hair and brown eyes.

I expect him to at least give me a thank you. You know, tell me how grateful he is about having me run down to the mail room to get his shit for him. Instead, he sighs. "Damn, Rox, took you long enough." He looks at me critically, up and down. "You get some decent makeup yet?"

He's subtly insinuating that I'm starting to sag and look older, which makes me want to laugh. I might have a stress wrinkle or two, but it's nowhere near what his baggy hound dog eyes have hanging under them. I grit my teeth but I don't snap back. He's always picking at me, trying to get under my skin, so I'm not taking the bait. Besides, I know I look good. I'm a fabulous bitch. Or I'd better be, given how long I spent in the mirror this morning. Matt's probably jealous he can't pull off the skirt, blouse, and heels I'm wearing.

I laugh, not letting him know he gets on my last nerve. He's really the only one here whom I dislike. "Let's not, Matthew. I'm trying to be nice today." *I'm not gonna tell you about how I want to take that tie and choke you with it,* I think inwardly. *Maybe hang you from the window as a warning to all those who try to fuck with me—run away as fast as you can.*

"Let's not what?" he asks, hiding his smirk. "I was just asking you a question. How was your weekend?"

He knows damn well what he meant, but I'm not going to entertain him. "It was good. Stopped a few hearts, broke a few necks, and stomped a few balls. Ya know, the usual."

He leans back in his chair, chuckling. "You know what, Roxy? I like you. Maybe we should hang out sometime. Have a few drinks after work?"

No way in hell. I'd rather take the Devil out for drinks. He'd only want me around to get drunk and then have the freedom to make me the punchline of his jokes.

"Sorry, got plans," I say politely. I can't resist getting a little twist in, though, and add cheerfully, "Although I have a friend named Brad who you'd absolutely fall in love with."

Matt arches an eyebrow. "Brad?"

I nod. "Mmmhmm. He's tall, blond, blue-eyed, and he can drop his ass to the floor like you've never seen, then work it back up nice and slowly until you're throbbing in your pants."

Matt laughs nervously. "Hey, what are you trying to say?"

Before I can reply, Byron Smith, one of the top level executives, walks over. His tie is loose around his neck, and his combed-over greying hair gives him sort of a cloudy appearance. He's tall, and despite his skinny neck, he's got a big potbelly that's almost cartoonish over his chicken legs. I have no idea why he hangs around Matt. There's a huge gap in age, and Byron's duties have nothing to do with me or Matt. But when the two get together, it's like two grade schoolers. I swear they've swapped fart jokes sometime over the past year.

"Hey, Matt," Byron says, grinning foolishly. "Have you heard about the new computer password system?"

"No, what about it?" Matt asks, and I roll my eyes. I've heard this one before.

"Well, we have to put in new passwords," Byron says. "Tom down the hall went in and decided that his new password would be *Tomspenis*. He puts it in, and you won't believe what the computer told him."

"What?" Matt asks, grinning.

"It said *Try again. Tomspenis is not long enough.*"

I try not to roll my eyes or to turn it around on them. Instead, I just gather up my stuff. "That's my cue to get back to work," I say. "Talk to you later."

I leave the two to continue their weird bromance. Their relationship just confounds me.

I walk through the maze and around the corner to my cubicle, glad to have my own little space that I've personalized a little. My heels are muted against the tough industrial-grade carpet, and more than once, I've considered ditching them for flats, except that the company does have visitors who expect them. I open my computer and login to my desktop, getting ready for the day. Franklin Consolidated was one of the first companies to build this city, and despite being bought in a corporate takeover, it still has prestige. We're in some of the top floors of our high-rise, and the view out the windows in the break room are breathtaking. Overall, despite it being corporate drudgery, I could be doing a lot worse. Besides dealing with Matt's bullshit, this place isn't that bad.

I'm not gonna let that dickhead get me down. I figure I'll get another promotion soon and move out of this cube-farm and into the outer ring offices, and then I won't have to deal with him. Really, I'm just nervous about this new Regional President. It's been hush-hush about who he is, the corporation that bought Franklin Consolidated keeping things quiet. It's like they want it to be some sort of national security top secret or something. That, combined with knowing I still have Jake's wallet, is making me a big ball of butterflies.

There's a commotion going around the room, and as my email loads, I see why. The new boss is going to be in soon and everybody is excited. Or maybe nervous is probably the better word.

"Hey, Roxy, you excited?" Hannah asks. She's dressed to kill today, with a knee-length pencil skirt that shows off her toned legs and a blouse that is just a little tighter than normal. I guess she's playing it up some, but she's certainly got the right to.

"I think I'm holding up well," I say, flashing an anxious smile. "Just hoping he's not a huge pain in the ass," I whisper.

Hannah shakes her head. "I'd be nervous too if I were tabbed to be his assistant. Well, that and worried that the cops could kick down the door any minute. Say, how do you think you'd look in an orange jumpsuit? I hear orange is the new black."

I hold my scowl for all of two seconds before I can't help but laugh. "I can't be pissed with you," I say, leaning back. Her jokes actually make me feel less anxious. I'd do the same if she were in my position. "By the way, if I'm going to jail, you're going to jail too as an accomplice. Preferably to be cellies with some six-foot-tall girl named Missy who's hungry for blondes."

Hannah laughs. "Come on, that's why we're friends. We're each other's spirit animal. And I know if I get Missy as my cellie, you and I can alternate days on being her bitch."

"We are, I agree. Except you're more of a beast than an animal, and I'm not muff diving for you no matter who it is."

Hannah laughs. "Glad to see you back to normal."

"I have Jake's wallet," I say after a moment, sobering again. "It's here in my purse."

"I'll go with you after work and we can turn it in at the club," Hannah says. "I'll be your backup just in case."

"Thank you."

Right then, we hear talking, so Hannah and I stand up to see Tom Powers, the CEO of Franklin Consolidated, at the head of the room. He's a tall, distinguished man with white hair, dressed as always in his dark double-breasted suit. He's totally old school, but in a grandfatherly sort of way. I heard that he's taking retirement with the corporate takeover, and if so, I'm going to miss him around.

"Hello, everyone, if I can have your attention, please?" he says. "Come on up if you'd like, or if you can see just fine, your cubicles are okay. Anyway, I'd like to take a few minutes to thank you all. I know that the rumor mill has been running overtime for the past few months, and . . ."

I tune Tom out a little, thinking about the day. After this, I need to finish checking my emails, then there's the report from the agribusiness division that I'll need to get together for my new boss . . . I wonder if he's nice? I wonder if he's a he, or maybe a she?

I know who I'd like to be working under. The dirty part of my mind fills with a picture of Jake in his suit. He was so powerful, so decisive, but at the same time a gentleman. The way he commanded everything and everyone without being a braggart or a loudmouth oozed confidence and masculinity. And yeah, the way he kissed me . . .

"Shit," I mutter to myself as I shake my head. I've missed most of what Tom's said already. *Focus, Roxy, focus!*

"For over seventy years, Franklin Consolidated has stood as a pillar of this community, and while our corporate headquarters is obviously changing, I can assure you that we will continue to serve this city and its people . . ."

"Oh, my God," Hannah whispers next to me. She jostles my elbow, and I glance at her just as Tom wraps up.

"My Franklin family, it's with great regret to confirm that yes, after this month, I will be retiring. However, I am confident in the hands that I'm leaving Franklin in. Without further ado, I'd like to introduce the new Regional President . . . Jake Stone."

"Is that . . .?" Hannah whispers as Jake steps up next to Tom. I turn white as a sheet and drop down quickly before he can see me, Hannah squatting down next to me. "Roxy?"

"I'm dead . . . I'm fucking dead," I whisper, looking at Hannah, terrified. "What the hell am I supposed to do now? I almost slept with and killed my new boss!"

CHAPTER 9

JAKE

I stand before the window in my new office, looking out with my hands clasped behind my back. It's just after lunch, and the whole city lies before me, sparkling in the sunlight. This is a far better view than what I had at my old office. I can see the entire city and even the mountains in the distance.

I feel powerful. Like the world is at my fingertips, and while I haven't climbed the mountain yet, I'm getting there.

Even my office is better, a large, classical executive room with a polished oak desk and a large leather tufted chair. The shelves are lined with bookcases, and I've found it's more than just the standard assortment of old law books or regulatory books, but there are all sorts of things. I've found leather-bound classics of fiction, biographies of great leaders, and more. This could rival a lot of small school libraries.

Franklin Consolidated really wanted my talents. I found out that they requested me specifically, so they rolled out the red carpet for me. My arrival has been well-received so far, but I've already noticed one problem.

I saw who was standing in the crowd. It was just a moment. I barely caught sight of that angelic face. I swear, I blinked and it was gone, and later on, I couldn't find her when I walked the cubicle maze. But I know what I saw. She might be in my dreams, but I'm not imagining things.

I turn slightly when I hear the door open behind me, bringing me back to the tasks I have at hand. "Is there anything I can get you, Mr. Stone?" says Elena May, my new interim secretary, an elderly woman dressed in a crisp pantsuit. She used to work for Tom, and I gratefully accepted her services from him. "You told me to check in right after lunch."

"Yes, Elena," I say. "I need the report from the property management division, and the Jefferson agreement. Also, if you could get me a hot cup of coffee and something to snack on. I skipped lunch. I need something to get through the afternoon."

Elena bows her head respectively. "Right away, sir."

She turns away, ready to leave, and I know it's now or never. I tense and call out, "And Elena?"

"Yes?"

"Please send in Miss Price."

She pauses for a moment, a question in her eyes. But she doesn't question me. "Right away, sir."

She disappears, and I turn back to the window. I wasn't going to call her in. I can't even be sure I have the right person. It could be another Roxy. But I can't resist and I have to know.

It's a miracle from the highest heaven or a curse from the depths of hell if it is her. I guess it's lucky for her that it's me and not Nathan. He would have started kicking ass at nine in the morning.

Five minutes after Elena leaves, there's a quiet knock at my door, and it opens behind me.

I don't turn around immediately, drawing out the moment as I hear muted footsteps on the thick carpet of my office. Instead, I stand, staring out the window, feeling the sun warm my face.

"You called for me?" Roxy's soft voice asks, and I momentarily close my eyes. There is a hint of nervousness and anxiety in it, but her sweet, soft voice is still like music to my ears. I know I should be mad. I should be raging and demanding answers, but in those four words . . . I swear I'm hearing an angel again.

"It's a beautiful day today, isn't it?" I ask. "The sun is out. The view from this office beats the one at my old one."

"It is," she says, and I can hear the fear, the quaver in her voice, but also a note of something else, so soft that I don't even think she knows it.

I turn to see her and the breath catches in my throat. In a tight skirt and blouse, her hands clasped respectfully in front of her, she reaches out and grabs my thoughts, a jolt going through me as I take in the vision in front of me. My God, she's fucking beautiful. She's still got that sweet angelic face, that gorgeous curvy body. Maybe I should've learned my lesson, but the things I want to do to her . . .

She gazes at me with anxiousness in her eyes. I know what she's thinking, but she needn't worry. One look at her, and I know.

Whatever happened Saturday night, she isn't guilty of much more than maybe being overly horny.

I grin, hiding my desire behind a boyish mask. "I bet this is the last place you expected me to show up after you left me for dead." My tone isn't harsh but playful. I'm trying to break the ice, but it seems to have the opposite effect.

Roxy frowns, crossing her arms over her chest. "I didn't leave you for dead—"

"I checked the footage. I saw that sick bastard putting a roofie in your drink," I interrupt. "I know you had nothing to do with it."

Surprise shoots across her face. "You did?"

I nod. "We've set the bouncers and other staff to be on the look-out. But it still doesn't explain why you left like you did. And why you took my wallet and never came back with it."

Roxy looks worried at first, then she cocks her head, smirking at me. "Well first of all, I thought I sent you straight to heaven," Roxy says with spunk showing up in her voice. "I've gotta say, I've met a few guys who couldn't hang with me, but never one who finished before we even got started. I didn't peg you as one of *those*."

I chuckle. "Is that right?"

"Oh, yeah. Had Mr. Creepy Bastard not gotten in the way, I would've showed you what paradise truly looks like."

I have to laugh. It feels good to talk to her. I can't believe my luck that I ended up where she works. "But seriously," I say. "What happened?"

Roxy's expression turns serious, and she walks over to the chair in front of my desk, sitting down when I give her a nod. "To be honest, when you started acting all Weekend at Bernie's, I freaked out. I actually thought you keeled over for a second there."

I'm caught up quickly as Roxy starts with her story, telling me everything that happened in painstaking detail. "So when I heard your friend coming, who has a foul mouth, by the way, I panicked and ran out. It was only after we got back home that I realized I still had your wallet."

I stand there, silently taking in her story. It's not really that hard to believe. Especially when it's basically the scenario that I told myself happened over and over. I'm relieved to find out I was right. Because for some reason, I hate to think that the angelic vision in front of me is a thief. "So why didn't you come back?"

She bites her lower lip. "It was all so crazy. I thought no one would believe me. I still have your wallet with me, actually. It's at my desk in my purse. I can go get it—"

I shake my head. We've already wasted enough of my new work time. And I know it already looks weird that I've brought her into my office. I need to start getting work done. "You can give it to me later, after work," I say. "Did you touch anything in there?"

She shakes her head. "Everything's there. I'll drop it off here—"

"No," I interrupt her. "Bring it by the club."

She pauses, confusion coming over her face. "Club Jasmine? Why would I do that when I can give it to you here?"

I nod. "I've got two reasons I'd rather you bring it to the club. First, because Nathan owes you an apology, and that needs to be delivered face to face. Second, I'd like to start back where we left off."

I love how it knocks her a little off balance. Seeing the flush that comes to her cheeks, I'm reminded of how she looked in the club. Her lips part as she nervously licks them. "But It's a work night and—"

"It's fine. I'll make sure you're back home by ten." I give her a little wink.

I can tell she wants to. She's warring with herself. She probably can't believe I still want to be with her. "I don't know, Jake. Maybe it's better if we stay apart."

"Oh, come on. We work in the same office, and you're going to be reporting to me frequently," I point out. "Consider this a business meeting where we can get to know a little more about each other."

I don't know why I'm pushing this issue. The dynamics have changed considerably. I'm her boss now, and maintaining a respectful relationship will be a challenge. But I've always been one to take a challenge and conquer it. Looking at Roxy, I want to conquer her, but probably not in the way that I should be thinking.

Roxy gives me an evaluating look, then nods. "Fine. What time?"

"Meet me there at eight. Bring your friend if you want."

Roxy nods, then gets up. "Okay. Uhm, Jake . . . this is weird."

I nod, grinning. "I know. But I'll see you at eight."

Roxy goes to the door and opens it. "Oh, and Miss Price?" I call out, slipping into more formal talk now that Elena might overhear.

"Yes, sir?"

"Don't forget the wallet."

Roxy smirks and walks out of the office.

CHAPTER 10

ROXY

"So, how do I look?" I ask, turning away from my bedroom mirror to face Hannah. Instead of the bright red, tonight, I'm opting for something darker. I don't want to admit that I'm dressing up for Jake again, but as soon as I got home from work, I couldn't imagine going back to Club Jasmine wearing what I wore for work.

So I found this, and I'll admit it feels even more like coming back to who I am. Dark makeup and a dark dress help slim my frame, while I've got on four-inch open-toe heels that make my legs and ass look good. "I can't believe I'm going back there," I admit to Hannah, who's sitting on my bed and giving me an critiquing look. "I mean, after what happened, I figured Club Jasmine would be one step from the seventh circle of hell in terms of places I didn't want to visit."

"So why are you doing it again?" Hannah asks, and I turn, adjusting the gold chain belt that I have around my waist.

"I feel guilty for leaving him there," I lie. Well, I do, sort of, but I'm also obviously attracted to him. "So how do I look?"

"Like a five-hundred-per-hour hooker," Hannah jokes. "Maybe a thousand if you do something about that damn hair."

I scowl. "Not funny."

Ignoring Hannah, I turn to address the only furry critic in the room. "You think I look good, don't you, Mr. Felix?"

Felix, perched on the chair next to my makeup table, stares as if he gives zero fucks with his grumpy face. *"Rowr."*

I stick my tongue out at him. "Fine, forget you. I'll remember that come feeding time."

Mr. Felix still doesn't give a fuck, giving a yawn and resuming his mean face.

"Really, you look beautiful," Hannah says, dropping her humor. But she pauses, a serious expression coming over face. "Still, though, I wonder . . ."

I turn to appraise her. "Wonder what?"

She swings her leg over the side of my bed and gets up, shaking her head slowly. "Do you think you should be seeing him outside of work?"

"What do you mean?" I ask.

"It was all fun and games before, and if it were anyone else, I still would tell you to go for it. But Jake is your boss now. And considering how you tried to screw his brains out on your first meeting, I'd say y'all aren't starting on the right foot professionally." She takes a deep breath. "I just don't think this is a good look."

I place my hands on my hips, trying to think of every damn

excuse I can to justify going. "Just because he's now my boss doesn't mean I can't go meet with him. Which he guilt tripped me into doing, I might add. Plus, I still have to give him his wallet."

"Yeah, I know that but—" Hannah starts, but I hold up a hand.

"And who's saying I'm going to sleep with him?"

At least not tonight.

Hannah opens her mouth to speak and then sees the look on my face. I've seen it before. It's one I've inherited from my mother and my sister, the one that says *Proceed with caution. Your ass is on thin ice.* She takes another deep breath and lowers her voice. "Look, all I'm trying to say is that it's different when you work with someone. Especially someone who's your boss. If this is going to be friendly cordial, keep it friendly cordial. I just don't think you should let it go beyond that, even if that's how this all started. You don't want people saying shit around the office."

I want to deny Hannah's words, but I have to admit that the same thoughts occurred to me as soon as Jake asked. But I've tried to ignore them. I just want an ending to our first night, dammit! I'm hungry for it. I want to know what lies behind those gorgeous eyes and that sun-bright smile. And yeah, part of me feels guilty and wants to make it up to him for leaving him like that in the club. That was a dick move on my part.

"I'll keep it in mind," I finally say. "You're right. It won't be good if this turns into something else. So I'll keep it all business. Strictly professional." I almost sound like I've convinced myself. "I'll go there, give him his wallet back, let him know I'm truly sorry for everything, and leave it at that."

Hannah lets out a sigh of relief. "Thank you. Don't be mad at me. I just want what's best for you."

"I know," I say. "Come here." I hold my arms out to her and we embrace. "You're not Mindy, but you make a decent placeholder."

Hannah laughs. "Oh, shut up."

Mr. Felix just *rawrs.*

❄

ON THE WAY OVER TO THE CLUB, HANNAH AND I TALK VERY LITTLE. My mind is filled with what I'm going to say to Jake. The first night I met him, my mind was overrun with hormones and I couldn't even focus on what he was saying. All I could see were those eyes that could command me to do anything. But now . . .

We pull up to the club. Surprisingly, there's a lot of cars for a Monday night. This is a nightclub, not a sports bar showing *Monday Night Football.*

"Remember," Hannah says as I get out, "keep it business."

"Right. All business," I say as we hug briefly. "I'll be back by ten. Jake said he'll give me a ride home, but I'll be home by eleven at the latest, okay?"

"Okay," Hannah says, giving me a look in the eyes. "Ten would be better."

"Okay, Mom," I half tease, patting her on the cheek. "You know he said you could come too."

"Yeah, I'm sure he would like that," Hannah teases, giving me a wiseass grin.

The line isn't out the door like it was Saturday night, but still, the place is fairly busy as I go inside. The music is good, more low-key than it was over the weekend. Thankfully, Jake is expecting me. I doubt I'd get in right now otherwise. "Hi," I tell the doorman. "Mr. Stone is expecting me. Roxy Price?"

The doorman, still one of the MIB crew, checks his tablet before nodding. "Just a moment, Miss Price."

He turns and talks quietly into his earpiece before nodding. "Is there a problem?"

"Not at all," the doorman says as another of the MIB come over. "John, here, will take you to see Mr. Stone."

"Right this way," John, who looks like he should be in the Secret Service instead of working nightclub security, says with a slight bow of his head. As we make our way through the club, I see that my first impression was wrong. This place is nearly packed.

I think the difference is the clientele. Over the weekend, most of the clubbers were younger, twenty- and thirty-somethings. This group is at least a decade older, and the music reflects it. I'm hearing some stuff that hasn't been in heavy rotation since the turn of the millennium. Then again, Will Smith is pretty smooth on *Switch*.

As John walks with me past the bar, I feel a moment of rising anxiety as I look around for the creepy bastard who tried to drug me, but I don't see him. John notices and gives me a reassuring smile. "All clear tonight, Miss Price. Come, Mr. Stone is waiting for you upstairs."

I look up and see Jake leaning on the railing of the VIP section, giving me a little wave. I wave back, and John leads me up, giving me the same little nod before he peels off to watch the steps to the VIP level. I'm surprised when I see that Jake's alone up here. We have the whole level to ourselves.

"You're looking dapper," I comment as he comes over. He's changed from the suit he wore to work into a slightly tighter fitting, brighter gray suit that just barely gleams in the club lights. "How many suits do you own, anyway?"

"Enough," he says easily, and as he steps closer, I'm just staggered again by his magnetism. He has this confident ease about him that isn't cocky. It's more like he's saying *Yes, I have the looks, but I'm more than that.* "Come on, I have a booth for us."

He leads me over to a nice booth, all done in black velvet with a low ebony table in the middle. "Let me get you a drink," he says, signaling the waitress. "A Little Mermaid," he says, "and a Highlander."

I give him a raised eyebrow, and he chuckles. "You'll like it, relax. You look amazing, by the way. Love what you did with your eyes. It totally changes your expression from work."

His eyes roam over my face, causing my skin to feel like I've got a low grade sunburn. I feel sexy, and when I do a switch on my legs, crossing my right over my left, his eyes watch every movement. I love the way he makes me feel. It's like we never left off. "Are you saying I looked bad at work?" I ask playfully. "Less feminine?"

Jake licks his lips and laughs. "Hardly. But you looked scared out of your mind. Not like you do now. You look at home."

I shrug, reaching into my purse. "Here's your wallet. Uh, just to let you know, I robbed you blind."

He chuckles and takes it from my hand. "I doubt that."

Without even opening it, he takes the wallet and slides it into his jacket pocket. I stare at him for a moment, shocked. "You're not going to count the money?"

"I trust you," he says confidently. "You look more like an angel than a thief."

I blush, then I laugh. "Okay, just don't get mad when you get the credit card bill for that trip to Hawaii I booked, complete with matching Louis Vuitton luggage."

Jake laughs again. "You're not the type for LV luggage."

The waitress comes back with our drinks. His Highlander looks interesting, almost like root beer, of all things. "What the hell is that?"

"Two ounces Japanese sake, two ounces of Scotch whisky, and the rest is Coke over crushed ice," he says, lifting the clear beer mug. "Basically a Duncan Macleod, but we use real Highland scotch, so we renamed it."

I nod and take a sip of mine. It's fruity, with bright highlights, and I can already tell I'm going to have to go easy on it. I've got work in the morning, and I'm not supposed to be going home with Jake. "Damn, this is good."

"Thank you. I had a hand in making it," Jake says, sipping his mug.

"Did you? And did you have a hand in the drink the first night too?" I ask, and Jake shakes his head.

"No, wish I could say I did. The name alone is nice, though, don't you think?"

I laugh as I take another sip of my drink. "It certainly makes memories. And the club?"

"Nathan and I had an architect help with the details, but we chose most of the layout. I wanted something different from the average club."

"It's one of the nicest I've ever been in," I say honestly. "Nothing like Trixie's."

Jake takes a slow sip of his Highlander and sets it down, raising an eyebrow. "Trixie's?"

I nod. "The club I used to sing at." *And shake my ass like nobody's business.* "It was my favorite place back home."

"You're a singer?" he says with some surprise. "You're just full of little talents, aren't you? What kind of music?"

"Nothing anymore," I say, feeling the pain in my chest that comes with talking about it. Those days are gone. Despite Mindy's encouragement, I haven't given much thought to singing. But looking over the railing of the VIP lounge at the stage, I feel that same longing and admit to myself that there's a void where singing used to be in my heart. I force myself to look away, feeling a lump form in my throat. "I stopped when I went back to college."

"Why?" Jake asks, leaning forward. "I can see in your eyes that you practically want to run down there right now and grab a mic."

"Yeah, well," I say softly, shaking my head, "I didn't think it was right that I wasn't really making any money doing it and instead was mooching off my mom and stepfather. I thought it was time to move on, support myself."

Jake nods, but he doesn't look convinced. "Let me ask you, which makes you happier, singing or working at Franklin?"

"Singing," I answer without even pausing for breath. "I don't care what. Rock, pop, just about anything but country. But . . . like I said, I'm done living off someone else, Jake."

Jake hums, then finishes the rest of his drink. "Mind singing something for me? Call it . . . call it your penance for accidentally stealing my wallet."

"I don't think so," I say. "I haven't sung in so long, I'm pretty sure my voice would crack. I don't want to burst your eardrums. I thought I killed you once as it is."

Jake chuckles. He looks like he wants to press the issue but doesn't. Instead, he leans back, crossing his hands over his left knee. "Point taken. For now, but I'm not giving up just yet."

I'm almost tempted to say that I could maybe sing a little tonight, but before I can, Nathan comes up the stairs, cursing and yelling into the air. "I told you to check the fucking hidden costs, didn't I? In fact, I remember specifically telling you, 'No way in hell should you sink your money in this, Titus. It's a golden turd.' Now you're calling me to bitch that you're losing money? Get the fuck outta' here!"

"You guys been friends long?" I ask as Nathan heads off to the other end of the VIP section, where I see a laptop on one of the tables there.

"Since childhood," he says. "He moved into the neighborhood when he was nine, and we've been friends ever since."

"He certainly has a way with words."

Jake chuckles. "That he does. Not always to his benefit."

I nod, smirking. "I think his first few words to me were *sleazy broad*, and I'm sure *fuck* was in the first sentence."

Jake swallows, looking embarrassed. "Was it? I'll have to talk to him."

I shake my head, waving him off. "I was running out of that back room. He had no idea who the hell I was."

Nathan comes over, his eyes twinkling in curiosity like he's waiting to be introduced.

Jake gives him a head nod. "Nathan, this is Roxy. She brought back my wallet. Not bad for a *sleazy broad*, huh?"

Nathan looks abashed, but he laughs. "You're right. Roxy, I apologize. My mouth gets the better of me sometimes. I looked at the video, and I promise you, if that asshole who tried to drug you comes in, he's gonna find out I haven't forgotten the old ways from the neighborhood."

I offer my hand, and Nathan shakes it, then kisses my knuckles. "I like this side of you a lot more than the first impression," I say.

"Of course. You know—" Nathan says when suddenly, there's a crash down below. A drunken woman decided that Club Jasmine's chairs were just perfect for her recreation of The Pussycat Dolls' *Buttons* dancing, and she's knocked a table, a waitress, and a bunch of other stuff onto the floor. "Oh, for fuck's sake. Excuse me."

Nathan heads for the stairs, talking loudly in a juicy Bronx accent that I'm sure has plenty of people quivering in fear even as I try to hold in my laughter. "You know who he reminds me of?"

"Who?" Jake asks, and I laugh again. "No, really, who?"

"Joe Pesci. Like, how he looked in *Goodfellas*. Like Nathan would totally be at ease carrying a baseball bat right now."

"Oh, don't give him any ideas," Jake says, chuckling. "Nathan's a genius when it comes to making money, but there's a reason he's not working for a firm. He tried working for Goldman Sachs right out of college and ended up getting fired."

"Why?" I ask, and Jake laughs.

"One of the Vice Presidents had a proposal, and Nathan told him in his typical manner that he disagreed with it. When the VP decided to defend himself by saying that one of the Seven Dwarves shouldn't be worrying about what real men said, Nathan decided to get even. By the time Nathan was done, the VP was crying. I still don't know how he didn't get arrested for that one."

"Damn, and you're business partners with him?"

Jake laughs. "Don't let his foul mouth fool you. He's sharp as a blade when it comes to running a business."

I nod, intrigued. "Well, maybe I underestimated him then."

"So, how long have you been working at Franklin Consolidated?" he asks me, changing subjects. "I decided not to pry."

"For almost a year. I recently got a promotion, so I'm moving up some," I say with a touch of pride. "Apparently, I'm decent at something, too."

"That's nice," Jake says. "But no offense, you just don't strike me as the corporate monkey type."

"I didn't think I was either. Before going back to school, I was . . . I was more free-spirited."

Jake hums in appreciation. "You know, I think I saw a hint of that the other night. Unless you're in a habit of being that . . . free-spirited."

At the mention of my behavior on Saturday, I feel myself blush all the way to the roots of my hair, and I scratch at my chin. "Yeah . . . about that. I'm embarrassed about that. I'm normally not that hard up," I say bluntly, feeling my confidence rising. "I'm usually a straight shooter, but I'm not *that* forward." I take a deep breath and blurt it out brutally. "It's been a while—let's just leave it at that."

He watches me intently, like he's studying me. "I believe you."

I'm tempted by the look in his eyes. He's so handsome, so confident and assured, that I almost want to slide across the seat and kiss him. I want him to take me in the back and to finish what we started Saturday night, but Hannah's right. *All business, all business*, I think to myself. In desperation, I try to think of something else to say. "So . . . how'd you get to where you are at your age? I mean, you're not that much older than I am, are you?"

"Probably not," Jake agrees. "I had a fire lit under my ass after I become caretaker for my sister."

"Your sister?" I ask, surprised. "I didn't know you had a sister."

"Yes, she lives with me. Has ever since our parents passed," Jake says. He leans forward, and looking at him, I feel like I'm seeing a side of him that few people do, and it's a side that I want even more than what I saw on Saturday. "I had to grow up quickly."

"I'm sorry for your loss," I say honestly, reaching out and patting his hand. "You must care for her very much."

The conversation flows, the two of us growing closer as we find so much in common. Besides the surface things like similar tastes in music, we both see the world as a place to stand on your own, to make your own mark somehow. I order another Mermaid, but Jake stops me after my second, and it's with a shock that I realize it's near midnight. "Oh, wow," I say, not slurring very much. "I guess it's time to go home."

"Come on, I'll drive you like I said," Jake says, helping me to my feet. He's so close, I can't help it as I press myself against him, looking in his eyes, and his hand falls to my lower back. He lowers his lips, kissing me softly, and I kiss him back, not with the fiery passion of Saturday night but with something truer.

"Jake . . ." I whisper when I step back, biting my lip in torn desire. "This is the hardest thing I've ever said in my life because I want you so fucking badly right now, but I need you to call me a cab. You're my boss, and we can't finish what this starts. We need to keep this strictly business."

Jake swallows, and I feel his hand pull me even tighter, but he stops and lets me go. With a shuddering breath, he nods. "Okay. I'll have the staff call you a cab."

I nod and reach down, grabbing my purse. "Thank you. Jake . . . this is like the best club I've ever seen, but I don't think I should come back here. I think you know why."

Jake swallows and nods. "I do."

He calls John the security guy over, giving him instructions. John nods, and Jake turns back to me. "You're all set. I'll see you tomorrow?"

"I am, and yes," I say, giving Jake a smile. "Goodnight."

John escorts me downstairs and out to the already waiting cab, closing the door for me. Just as the cab gets ready to pull away, I see the door to Club Jasmine open again, and Jake steps out, giving me a wave. As the cab pulls away and I give him a wave back, there's something inside me that says this is just the beginning.

CHAPTER 11

JAKE

*S*trictly business.

Roxy's words run through my mind as I button up the cuff links of my dress shirt, the early morning sunset peeking in a fiery orange through the window behind me. I finish my shirt and turn around, keeping my eyes directly from the sun but looking out over the city. It's peaceful, certainly not as bustling as New York or one of those other cities that never seems to sleep.

It shouldn't really be a problem. Being Roxy's boss definitely changes things. I can't even lie about how I'm new in town or that she doesn't report directly to me. It'd be a problem eventually if we kept seeing each other. But I can't divorce myself from the way she felt underneath my hands. The images flash in my mind, making my dick swell in my custom-tailored Italian slacks, and I unconsciously reach down to adjust myself as I turn away from the window.

But more than her body, I can't get over what she told me.

I run my hand over my freshly shaven cheeks, checking for any missed spots as I think about our conversation yesterday. I just can't get over the look in her eyes when she told me she'd given up her dream to work in the soul-sucking corporate world. It crushed me, and her tiny attempt at salvaging her pride by saying she got a promotion just made it worse. It made me feel for her, not as a woman I'd like to fuck, but as a person I'd like to help.

Here I am, living part of my dream by being able to start my own business, which by every measure is going to be hugely successful, and she has to work a job she isn't happy with. I could see the spark she has for life is dimmed by it all. And being around her makes me want to reignite it. I just don't know how.

Saturday night, if I'd heard her story, it would have been easy. Foolish, most likely, but easy. Now, we're bound by rules. There's corporate protocol we have to follow. And I fucking hate rules. I've played by my own as much as I can for my whole life. It's the main reason I always want to be the one in charge. I know that eventually, my penchant for doing it my own way is going to make enemies if I'm not the one making the decisions. One misstep will have my ass flapping in the wind.

I finish up my grooming, grabbing my suit coat off the bed. The bed is an absolute mess, but my maid will be in here to clean it up. I throw my coat over my shoulder and leave my bedroom. I'll save the coat for later when I'm getting ready to go to the office.

I walk down the hall and knock on Sophie's door. She's been a sleepyhead recently, and I'm not going to let her skip school because I trusted her to get up on her own.

"Get up, Sophie," I say. "Rise and shine."

I hear a groan in the room and a creaking bed. Great, she hasn't even woken up yet. When she doesn't reply, I open the door and peek in. All I see is a spray of hair sticking out from under the sheet and what looks like her left foot hanging out below.

"Sophie, get up," I say, tapping on the door. "You've got twenty minutes."

Sophie's reply is a low, grumbling moan. "Ugh, I'm trying to sleep."

With no warning, I grab the blanket and sheet near her ankle and yank the covers.

"Ohmygawd! It's cold, you ass!" Sophie yells, trying to grab the blanket, but I pull it the rest of the way off. Her disheveled hair gives her a stringy, mop-top appearance as she looks up at me with red eyes. She must've been up late last night, and I only hope it's because she was cracking her history books.

"Get up. You have that test, remember?"

"Can't you just give me a note and call in sick?" Sophie says, reaching for the little decorative blanket over her headboard, but before she can, I snatch it up and throw it out the door. "I fucking hate that class!"

"Doesn't matter," I reply, knowing the feeling. "Get up unless you want me to get the Super Soaker."

I'm not one to be physical with a woman, but I've found the squirt gun a great way to get a teenage girl out of bed quickly. "Jerk," she mutters. She grumbles and gets out of bed. "You're the world's biggest asshole."

"An asshole who wants what's best for you," I say, holding back my grin. I know she doesn't mean anything by it. "And be careful. I don't want you to fall and crack that big head of yours."

I leave her room and go in the kitchen, indulging in one of my personal hobbies. Setting my coat across the back of a chair, I grab the cast-iron skillet and start making breakfast. Six minutes later, I have scrambled eggs, toast, marmalade, and a glass of orange juice sitting at the table. Sophie comes out, and while her eyes are still red, she's at least brushed her hair out and looks cute, in a sort of teenage high school *fuck the world, I wanna be in bed* sort of way.

"You stay up all night?" I ask. "You seemed to be sleeping when I came home."

Sophie nods. "I tried, but I woke up. I was on my phone."

Alarm bells go off in my head. "With whom?"

"Jax," she says flippantly, as if texting with someone that late is normal.

My stomach tightens. "Who's he?"

"Just a boy from my math class," she says. "We talk sometimes."

I bite my tongue. That's something I don't really want to touch unless I absolutely have to. "Cool," I say, trying to be nonchalant. "Bring him by sometime so I can meet him."

She's mortified. "Seriously? You're cool and all, but I don't want to scare him away."

Exactly, I think inwardly.

We finish breakfast and go out and get in my ride, a ten-year-old Maserati that I keep in tip-top shape. I could let the horses loose on her and smoke just about anything on the streets if I wanted. But it's not my thing anymore. Like I told Roxy, I had to grow up fast. I usually drive Sophie to school instead of having a driver take her unless it's unavoidable. I work so much that I don't see enough of her as it is.

The early morning traffic is just starting to get brutal on the way to Sophie's high school, but we talk about things on the way. Most importantly to me, this Jax. She tries to be as secretive as possible. I'm not liking it, but I'm not going to make a deal of it.

Sophie looks over at me as we pull to a stop light. "You look handsome today," she says, changing the subject.

"All right," I reply with a laugh. "What do you want this time?"

"No, seriously. You have an extra pep in your step or something today," says Sophie. "Something just seems different. I'm not trying to be weird or say you don't dress well usually. All my girlfriends seem to notice."

"Good for them," I say. "But I'm too old and definitely not the Prince Charming they think I am."

Sophie laughs. "Just trying to poke and see if there's something going on I don't know about. It'd be nice to see you focus on yourself for once. You've done enough for me."

I'm silenced, and I'm glad we've reached her school. It's not really something I want to talk about right now. I pull up out front, seeing the crowded student parking lot. I've considered getting her a car for her next birthday, but as crowded as that parking lot is, I'm not sure it'd do any good.

Sophie opens her door and grabs her bag, starting to get out before she stops and sits back down, giving me a half-pouting look. "For real, Jake. Chill out some. Go have some damn fun."

"I'll think about it."

She grins and jumps out. "Thanks. You're still a jerk for threatening the Super Soaker, but I'll keep you around."

"You'd better ace that test!" I call after her as she closes the passenger door.

I pull away and turn left at the first light, catching the main boulevard to head into the office. As I park and take the elevator up to Franklin Consolidated, I watch the city rise through the glass outside the elevator. It's beautiful, and I'm looking forward to the day, maybe even more than a normal Tuesday. I glance down at my Rolex as the doors open. "Just on time."

It's a bustle of activity as I walk onto the main floor. People are calling clients, and I can hear the hum, the lifeblood of business flowing through the cubicle maze. I see people hustling, and I wonder if just my presence here after one day is making the changes that I want to see.

My eyes scan the room as I walk through on the way to my office, but I'm really only looking for one person in particular. Finally, I see Roxy, my stomach going tight as I take in her dark skirt and blue blouse. She looks up, almost as if she felt my eyes on her, and our eyes meet. She tears her gaze away, but not before I see the slight flush of pink on her neck. The corner of my lips lifts into a grin, and I turn away, heading to my office.

I get in and set my briefcase aside. Pulling my laptop to me, I fire it up and get to work. There's a report request from corporate about my first impressions on the managers and who I might see being potential 'trimmings', but it's too early for that. I send back a message saying that I need the rest of the week for evaluations, but I'll get them my initial ideas by Friday.

Elena sticks her head in ten minutes after I finish, a folder in her hands. "Here's the building inventory report Tom wanted to give you," she says, setting it down on my desk.

I glance at it, knowing I'll need to read it over but not wanting to. It's just not that important to me. "Thank you."

"Is there anything I can get for you, sir?"

"Get me the Hendricks report and the projections for next quarter. I'd like to review those before lunch."

"Right away," she says, walking briskly to the door.

My next words fly from my lips before I can stop them. "Oh, and Elena? Send Miss Price in, if you would."

Once again, she looks at me with confusion in her eyes. Roxy is supposed to be an assistant but not my secretary. She's not even high enough up the ladder to be talking with me at all. I can see Elena wonders what the hell I'm doing. But she doesn't question me. "Of course, sir."

When she leaves, I sit back in my chair, inwardly shaking my head at myself.

Was there any reason for that? I don't need anything from her right now. But I can't help myself. I just want to see her, hear her.

Several minutes later, there's a knock at the door, and I set down the pen that I've been spinning across my knuckles. I quickly adjust my tie and turn to my laptop, trying to look like I've been working and not daydreaming. "Come in."

The door opens, and Roxy walks in. I have a hard time keeping my jaw from dropping as she closes the door. She's so beautiful dressed in her tight skirt and blue blouse, her curvaceous figure seeming to taunt me with the promise of paradise. Under my desk, my blood warms my crotch as I think of the things that I want to do to her. That I almost had.

"You wanted me, sir?" she asks softly.

Sir. All business now. None of that playful spark I've noticed since first meeting her. I see how it is. She's trying to put a barrier between us by being professional. I don't like it. I want her spread out on my desk, her legs wrapped around my hips as I fill her with my cock.

"Sir?" she repeats when I don't reply, breaking me out of my reverie. My cock is twitching in my pants, and I take a deep breath before replying.

"Yeah. How're things going?" Damn, I sound like a moron.

"They're going fine, sir." She continues to hold her facade. But beneath, I can tell it's hard for her too. "Elena told me I had to get some projections ready, and I've already pulled the data. It's printing now."

"That's good," I reply, still feeling like an idiot.

"Is there anything else you need from me, sir?"

Yeah, I need you in my lap with your tits in my face as you ride me in that skirt. It's almost criminal the thoughts she invokes in me.

I part my lips to tell her that I want to see her again. That the night before, she awakened a need in me that I haven't felt for a long time. But then I think twice. "No, thank you. That is all."

She nods respectfully to me and turns away.

"Roxy," I call.

She stops and turns, one graceful hand on the door handle, and the words dry up in my throat again.

Tell me you want it, I think to myself. *Tell me you want me to take you, bend you over my desk and fuck you like you've never been fucked before.* Her lips are parted, and I imagine her saying yes if I just say the words. "Enjoy your day."

Something flashes in her eyes, so fast that I can barely register it. "You too, sir."

Then she's gone, the door closing softly behind her. I drop my head to the desk, thunking softly on my blotter, feeling a cauldron of emotions swirling in my gut. I know I shouldn't be doing this. Maybe I should have her transferred to another floor so this doesn't get out of hand. But when I think about actually doing it, I know I can't. Looking up as my email dings softly with another request from corporate, I realize one thing.

"I've got to get myself under control," I mutter.

❆

OVER THE NEXT SEVERAL DAYS, I DO MY BEST TO JUGGLE WORK, overseeing the night club, and basically being both Mom and Dad for Sophie. During the work day, I spend my time concentrating on staying busy and settling into my new role of playing house-cleaner for the company, keeping thoughts of Roxy from my mind. I even use my lunch hours to use the in-building fitness center, hoping to bury my desire under a giant pile of sweaty tank tops and a couple of thousand pounds of iron.

After work, I drop by the nightclub to check in with Nathan. So far, Mr. Creepy Bastard hasn't popped back up, and Andre is itching to get his hands on him. Nathan, too, and I'm not sure which of them would be preferable.

Even with all I've got going on, my thoughts constantly return to Roxy. I can't help but wonder what she's doing, if she's thinking about me, and how I can spend more time with her. She's a sweet distraction. Throughout the morning, I find myself looking at her through the big window of my office whenever she's moving around the room.

She's bedeviling, that's all there is to it. The sway of her hips as she walks, the way she parts those sweet, luscious lips . . . it's maddening. My cock is begging to have them wrapped around it, sucking and licking till I explode down her throat.

"Will that be all, sir?" Elena says, pulling me from my reverie. She's just finished giving me the files I asked for earlier, and I realize that it's nearly lunch time.

Thank God the weekend is finally here. I'm ready to relax and release some tension. I need something besides the constant distraction of Roxy.

"That's all. Any weekend plans, Elena?"

She beams at me, backing up. "Nothing much, sir. I can say it's been a good week with you here. I won't have to drink half the amount I thought I'd have to."

I laugh, and this time, I don't tell her to come back and call Roxy. I haven't seen her all morning. But I've been trying to stay away, avoiding looking out my window on purpose. The sexual tension has grown so much between us you could cut it with a knife. People are going to notice if I keep it up.

I go back to my laptop, looking at what I was supposed to be doing for the past hour, which is the damn manager evaluation report. It's nothing formal. Corporate will grind through this for weeks before they do anything, but I still need to get my recommendations right. I start pounding away at my keyboard, knowing exactly who I want to get rid of, and just as I hit *Send* on the email, my cellphone buzzes. It's Nathan. "What's up, Nathan?"

"Remember when I said we should have theme nights?" Nathan asks immediately, no 'hi' or 'what's up'. "Well, you know the bartender, Sarah? She thought it was a good idea to start a karaoke night. And I thought tonight would be a good time to do a sort of short test run. It's Friday, and a lot of people will be here to test the reception. Hell, I might even get up there and make some bitches' ears bleed."

I think, shaking my head. I'm really not sure about karaoke. But then it hits me . . . Roxy. I know I shouldn't be thinking about seeing her, but a part of me knows that she needs this. "Let's do it. Book it, Nathan. In fact, later tonight, let's talk. Maybe we can do an open mic night or maybe a singing contest, find some local talent that'll kick some ass."

"My fuckin' man! I like the way you think," Nathan says. "All right, I'll book it and see if we can get some social media marketing going on. See you later."

I get up from my seat, putting my phone away. It's near lunch time, and I see my workout bag sitting on my spare chair, ready for me, but first . . . I look through the glass into the main room. I don't see her at her cubicle, which until now, I thought was cursed since I could see directly inside.

I grab my bag and walk out into the main room, looking around.

Finally, just as I'm about to give up and head downstairs, I see Hannah, her close friend, coming out of the bathroom.

"Hello, boss," Hannah says, all business when I walk up, though I see the mischievous spark in her eyes. I can see why she and Roxy are good friends. There's a lot of smarts in that wiseass look.

"Have you seen Roxy?" I ask, trying my best to keep my voice neutral.

Her eyes furtively flit back, and she looks me up and down but doesn't push it. I wonder what secrets she's hiding. I know they have probably talked about me. "She went down to the mail room to get something for Matt."

"Matt?"

"Yeah, you know . . ." she says before pointing. "The guy that works over there."

I look over, seeing whom she's talking about. I've seen him around. He's got a smug countenance that puts me off. "And does Roxy report to him?"

"No, just—"

"Then that's going to have to stop. Matt can get his own stuff, don't you think?" I ask, glancing back at Hannah.

Hannah nods, smiling a little. "That's what I always say, but he tries to use his seniority to get her."

'What's his position?" I ask. "I don't know the full chain around here just yet."

"I honestly have no idea. He's Byron's buddy, that's all I know," Hannah says.

I'm going to have a talk with Matt, I think inwardly while shrugging. "Thanks. You have yourself a good weekend," I say, holding back my grin. If things go right, I'll probably be seeing her tonight if I can convince Roxy to come to the club.

"You too, Mr. Stone."

I leave and take the elevator to the second floor, where I see the signs for the mail room. I don't see her when I go in, and I wonder for a moment if Hannah's lied to me. But then I see her, down the hall with a stack of papers in hand. I pick up my speed and catch her just before the elevator doors close.

I stick my foot in the doors before it can close completely and step inside. Roxy's lips part in surprise when she sees me, and she practically stumbles back against the wall. "Mr. Stone," she breathes. "What . . .?"

I grin as I press the *Close* button, then the button for the fitness center. As soon as the doors meet, I turn and advance toward her, caging her in with one hand on either side of her. She shrinks further against the wall as nerves pulse from her in waves.

Her perfume wafts to my nostrils. I love the fragrance, a serious yet still light tone. She even has sultry makeup to go with it. I can't help it—being this close to her and looking into her beautiful eyes, my cock grows in my pants.

"You've been avoiding me," I say. "Why?"

She ducks her head. "We agreed that we'd be professional."

"I didn't agree to anything," I counter. "*You* said we should be professional." I know I shouldn't be doing this. I'm her boss and I am dangerously over the line on sexual harassment if she wants to nail my ass. But I don't think I can abide by the rules. "I *don't* agree."

She's panicked, her eyes darting back and forth as I move in closer, pressing my hard body against her, letting her feel me. All of me. "But, sir . . ."

"Stop calling me sir," I growl, staring into her eyes. "You're too innocent for that . . . unless you want me to give you a reason to call me sir."

I tug on a wisp of her hair, moving my lips down to her neck, tasting her sweet skin again, my body throbbing with need. Usually, I can't wait for the elevator to make it down to the gym, but this time, I reach over blindly, hitting the *Stop* button with my free hand, not caring about the dinging noise. "Oh, gawd," Roxy groans, nearly melting into me as my lips trail her flesh. I can feel her heart pounding so hard in tandem with the blood pumping through my dick. "Yes . . ."

My whole body screams for me to take her. Right here and now, to hell with the consequences. If we got caught, the whole world be damned. It'd be worth it. She's worth it.

I reach down, grabbing her ass and pulling her skirt up, squeezing her ass with my right hand as I nibble and suck on her lips, feeling her submit to my insane desire. And it is insane. Seeing an employee is one thing. But fucking her in the elevator is a good way to find myself fired.

Still, I slide my knee between hers and spread her legs. She moans, grabbing my head and kissing me fiercely, gasping as the bulge of my cock in my pants rubs against the satiny slickness of her panty-covered pussy. "We can't . . ."

"We are," I growl, staring in her eyes. "You wanted me . . . you got me, Angel."

I grind my cock against her, staring into Roxy's eyes as her hips start taking over, riding the bulge of my cock. Even through the cloth, her pussy is white hot, and I thrust against her, dry humping her. Grinding against her, I can feel my cock throb, and I don't care. I'm tempted to pull back, undo my pants, and bury myself inside her. Our tongues twist and taste each other as I pin her against the elevator wall, our bodies needing it.

I can feel her start to tremble, shaking as I push her harder and faster, and I thrust harder, staring in her eyes as she digs her fingers into the back of my neck, moaning thickly. "Jake . . ."

"Come for me, Angel," I growl, grinding into her. It's all she needs, and she bites her bottom lip, shaking and whining softly as she comes. "My turn."

I let her down to turn her around, pushing her lush body up against the wall of the elevator so I can free my cock. It's throbbing, and I can feel the precum soaking my boxers. I need her so badly. "Bend over."

She does, and I realize I don't have a condom, but I'm so fucking hard that I don't care. I'm going to fuck her anyway. I almost do, but she's saved by the phone ringing. Fucking cockblocking Building Security. I pick up the phone. "Is everything okay?" a voice asks.

I step away from her, straightening my tie and fighting down my desire. My cock is raging hard in my pants, and I know that my underpants are ruined. Fuck it, I'm going to the gym anyway, and right now, I've got some extra motivation for my workout. "Yes, just a bit of nausea, thank you," I say, hanging up the phone and starting the elevator again. I turn to Roxy, who's still gasping. "Tonight is a special night at the club." I omit telling her it's karaoke night. "I expect you to be there. And wear something flashy."

Her eyes seem to scream, *But what about our agreement?* despite the fact that we almost just fucked in an elevator. The car reaches the gym level, and with a ding, the doors open. Finally, Roxy speaks up. "What time?"

With one last look, I step out, grinning victoriously. "Make it eight thirty. I'll see you then."

The doors start to close, and just before they do, she flashes me a bit of her saucy grin. "Yes, sir."

Oh, she's gonna get it.

CHAPTER 12

ROXY

"hat happened to strictly business?" Hannah scolds me as we walk into our apartment after work and I toss my jacket on the couch. Squatting, I pull off my work heels and toss them onto the floor before I sag into the couch, exhausted by the half hour of bickering.

"And I have been!" I argue. "But I can't help that he cornered me and ordered me to go."

"Ordered you?" Hannah says, pulling off her heels and throwing them across the room and nearly hitting Mr. Felix, who goes scrambling away with a feline yowl of outrage. "What is he, your daddy?"

"No, but he's my boss!" I groan, laying my head back on the cushion, hoping to keep the headache that's threatening to break out behind my eyeballs from turning into a migraine.

"Yeah, but this isn't something you had to say yes to!"

"He didn't give me time to say no," I half lie. "He walked off before

I could say anything."

Besides, the truth is, the way he made me come left me breathless. I still haven't gotten over how good it felt to feel that big, hard cock rubbing up against my . . .

"You just want to go," she accuses with a smirk on her face, pulling me out of my lustful thoughts. "Admit it."

It's true. I can't even work up the energy to disagree. All week, I've been avoiding him, trying my best to do what needs to be done. But after that move he pulled in the elevator . . . shit. I have to go. He dropped in on me and tempted me. Now I'm like a bee that's going after her honey.

"Anyway, I'm going to get ready," I say ending the conversation without admitting anything, but my eyes give it away. She's right and she knows it. "Tonight, yes, I'm going," I say when I'm not facing her. I laugh. "Don't worry! I won't overdo it."

Hannah yells, "You lowdown, dirty tramp!"

I laugh, going into my bedroom. *Wear something flashy.* Jake's words come back to me. Flashy? Oh, I know flashy. In fact, I'm pretty sure I've still got some of my club wear somewhere in here. I never throw anything out. I go plunging into my closet, reminding myself that someday, I have to clean and organize all this shit, when I see it. *My* dress. It was a gift from some of the guys at Trixie's when I was getting scouted for a record deal. Thigh-length and sparkly, it's flowy and flirty but still clings to my curves, molding itself against my breasts and making me look hot. Quickly stripping, I wish the dress had space for a bra, but there isn't. I'm just going to have to go all-natural. It makes me feel sexy, my nipples hardening in anticipation before I go hunting for my naughtiest silver and white thong and let the dress pour over my shoulders and down.

I find the matching heels for this thing and slide them on, checking myself in my mirror. A quick tousle of my hair, and I look at myself again, stunned. "Damn," I murmur, grinning. Here is what I've been missing. Here's the Roxy who used to make people scream my name, and not just the few lucky men in bed. I do a quick little touchup of my makeup around my eyes and walk out, twirling as I do, showing off with a spunk I haven't felt in a long time. "All right girl, whatcha think? Will I blow up the club or what?"

"Okay. Fuck this shit!" Hannah, who's sitting on the couch, yells when she sees me. Without another word, she disappears into her room. I can hear her mumbling that I'm making a huge mistake and should listen to her, and I can tell she's getting dressed. In minutes, she comes back in a similar sparkly getup and heels. "Take that, bitch!"

She struts in front of me, popping a hip in my direction. "As you can see, you're not the only one with an ass around here."

I laugh. At least she's given up on lecturing me. "So you're going?" I ask incredulously. "And where the hell did you get that?"

"Just from that thrift store downtown, and you're damn right. Someone's gotta keep you out of trouble and show you how to do it. And someone's got to protect the men from Roxy's Raging Hormones!"

I laugh. "You could've at least worn something different. Copycat."

Hannah scowls at me. "Copycat? Girl, please. I look good. Better than you! Don't I, Mr. Felix?"

Mr. Felix, who is perched on the coffee table, jumps off it and crawls under the couch to the point where only his eyes are peeking out. I laugh hard. "I guess that answers your question. He knows the difference between class and ass."

"You little bastard!" Hannah rages, pointing at Felix as she goes for her keys. "I'm serious, nothing but dry food from the dollar store for you, the cheapest I can find!"

I laugh uproariously as we leave our apartment.

We get into Hannah's car, and on the way over to the club, she resumes her preaching. Thankfully, for my head, to a lesser extent.

"Remember, whatever happens," she says as we park, "keep it cute or put it on mute. Just don't go home with him. Let's have our fun or whatever."

I roll my eyes, closing the door. At least this time, we're in the main parking lot, even though it's still pretty packed. "Yes, yes . . . I've heard this all before! Please shut up, Mother!"

We climb the steps to the door, where I see John from my last visit on door duty. He gives me a respectful nod again and a slight smile. "Miss Price, it's good to see you again. Mr. Stone left instructions that he'd be waiting in the VIP section. Is this Hannah?"

Jake must've known I'd bring her. Hannah bites her lip, and I can see she's into John a little bit. I get it. He's handsome and charming in that mysterious kind of way, and anyone who could work security at a place like this has to know how to handle themselves. "Hi."

John chuckles and opens the door. "Hi. Enjoy yourself."

We go inside, and I'm immediately struck by how packed the club seems. There's a trickle of energy threading its way through the crowd, and I feel more beautiful than even the first night I was here. There's joy in the air, joy and excitement, and while I don't know why, I can't help but be infected by it.

"Come on," Hannah says, smiling too as she tugs me toward the stairs to the upper level. "Hey, you know the doorman?"

"His name's John, and that's all I know." I laugh, following her up the stairs. We reach the VIP section, and my heart stops when I see Jake. He's sitting in a huge semicircular couch, Nathan relaxing next to him. The glass table in front of them has wine bottles and glasses and ice. Jake looks like a vision dressed in black pants and a red dress shirt, a hint of his muscular chest visible. Hot desire shoots through my blood as I look at him, barely noticing Nathan, who is grinning deviously.

"Who's that?" Hannah asks, bringing me back to reality. "The other guy."

"That's his friend I told you about. The money man?"

"He's too short for me," she whispers. "Don't care about the money."

"But he has a big personality and maybe . . ." I start.

Hannah rolls her eyes. "Oh, please. Gimme some credit, I'm not *that* shallow."

"Ladies, ladies," Nathan says in greeting. "Or should I say angels? Wow, I have never been more wrong about my first impression of someone."

I laugh, shaking hands with Nathan while Jake gets up, coming over and shaking hands with Hannah before putting a hand on my lower back. "Nathan's right, you both look stunning," he says before whispering in my ear. "And you truly look amazing," he says, his voice dripping with desire. "My Angel."

Being called Jake's angel makes my knees quiver, and I'm glad when he leads me over to sit down, the boys in the middle while Hannah and I take the outsides. I'm aware more than ever of Jake as his leg presses against my thigh, and I'm glad when Nathan leans forward and pours everyone a glass of champagne. "To a second successful week of Club Jasmine, and to wrong first impressions."

"Not all first impressions are wrong," Hannah says, toasting with us. "The place still looks just as awesome as it did last Saturday."

"Well, of course. I'm still here," Nathan says with a laugh, sipping his champagne. "And with you and Roxy here, it has class, too."

I half choke on my champagne, laughing at the similarity to the joke Hannah and I had earlier, coughing a little before setting my glass down. "Sorry . . . don't mean to make an ass of myself."

Hannah must be remembering the same thing, because she starts laughing, thankfully without a mouthful of champagne to choke back, and she leans against the couch. "So, Nathan, Roxy tells me you're the brains behind the place?"

"Hey!" I protest, but Nathan chuckles.

"No, it's a team effort. He's got the show, and I've got more than enough go."

Jake shakes his head, leaning back. He teases, "Put a pretty lady on his arm in public, and he's Mr. Confidence. Just be careful,

Hannah. Get him alone and you might find yourself disappointed."

We talk back and forth, relaxing and having fun, and while I can see Hannah likes Nathan, there's not really sparks there. We finish our glasses of champagne when suddenly, Nathan gets up. "Excuse me guys, I've gotta do my announcement."

Without pausing, Nathan hurries to the stairs, leaving me confused.

"What's that about?" Hannah asks, thinking the same thing I am.

Jake bends over and whispers something in Hannah's ears. She looks at me, lit up like a light bulb, grinning a secret smile.

"Hey what was that all about?" I ask, wondering what the hell Jake and Nathan have cooked up.

Jake's smile is all mystery. "You'll see."

Just as I'm about to open my mouth, I hear Nathan's Bronx accent amplified on a microphone, and I turn, seeing him on stage. "What's up, Club Jasmine?"

There's a cheer from the crowd, and Nathan grins. He's got enough personality to look seven feet tall on stage. "It's been a hell of a week, guys. And today, my partner and I were trying to think of what we could do to say 'Thank you' to everyone who's been coming to Club Jasmine. And we came up with an idea we think you'll like. A way to give a little back to you."

I sit forward, intrigued. Nathan continues. "So tonight, we're holding an impromptu karaoke contest. For the next half hour, you can sign up at the bar. And while this is supposed to just be fun, the winner tonight gets a thousand dollars."

The buzz is huge, and less than a minute later, some guy's up on stage, belting out Bon Jovi. While he's got energy and is having the time of his life, I think, he can't sing for shit. "Jesus, my ears are bleeding!" Hannah yells, covering her ears. "Make it stop!"

Jake laughs. "I've heard worse. You should hear Nathan!"

The first guy finishes, and next up on stage is a girl. She's just as terrible, although she can shake her ass like it's nobody's business, so she gets plenty of applause as she caterwauls her way through *Break Free*.

Still, even though almost nobody can really sing, they're having a great time. I'm feeling it, the itch in my toes and the thrum in my chest as each tone deaf contestant gets up there. Yeah, none of them are singers and they know it. But they're up there, they're performing and having a ball . . .

Nathan gets back on stage. "Jasmine, thank you. You guys are bringing it! Now, I have somethin' special. She hasn't signed up, but I think up next is my new friend over here."

Suddenly, the spotlight shines up on us, and I'm blinded. It still hadn't clicked until that moment, and I turn to stare at Jake in horror. "You did this!"

Jake shrugs. "Worked, didn't it?"

I cross my arms over my chest. "No way, I'm not going!"

"Get your ass up there," Hannah says. "You know you want to!"

Hannah's right, the stage is calling to me. I can feel it pulling me. But I don't move, setting my face. Hannah gets up and runs down to the stage. I don't think she's been in on this, but you could've fooled me. It damn sure seems it. The crowd roars as she snatches the mic from Nathan and starts shoving him off stage. "Go on, they've seen enough of your ass!"

The crowd laughs, and Hannah holds up a hand. "Guys, I wish I were the singer Nathan here was talking about, but I'm just the eye candy."

There's a few whistles about that, and Hannah grins. "Yeah, thought so. Listen, the person who is supposed to be down here is my best friend and roommate. She used to be a professional, so I think it'd be unfair to let her win the money. This is just for the love of singing. Now, I never actually saw her perform, but I've heard her sing around the apartment, and this bitch can sing!"

I blush, and Jake leans over. "Just one song. For me, Angel?"

I turn to him as Hannah continues. "So what I need from you guys, we need to give her some motivation. Roxy . . . Roxy . . . Roxy . . ."

The crowd picks up the chant, and Jake leans in again. "Okay, not for me. Do it for yourself."

Jake's closeness and the crowd's chants leave me tingling, and finally, blushing furiously, I nod. "Fine!"

I get up, and I feel Jake behind me, escorting me down the stairs, his hand light on my lower back again. In my heels and outfit, I feel sexy. But most importantly, I feel special. The crowd goes nuts as I reach the steps, and Jake leans in again. "You can do this. Go knock 'em dead."

He gives me a kiss on the cheek, and I get on stage, waving. "What's up, Club Jasmine?"

I see the teleprompter, and I start thinking of some of the songs I know by heart, when suddenly, Hannah goes over to the DJ, whispering in his ear. *Oh, shit. What the hell is she going to put on?*

The music starts, and I panic, recognizing the raunchy classic *Milkshake* almost immediately. She *would* do that. One fucking time singing it half drunk for Mr. Felix, and this is what I get? Oh, my God, Hannah. I'm gonna kill you.

The crowd's into it, though, and I feel forced to perform, moving my body to the sexy high-energy beat.

I move on stage, singing my ass off, and I feel it. The buzz inside me grows into a fire as I see the crowd's reaction. At first, the audience sits there, surprised. People start looking at each other as if shocked I can actually perform, then they start getting into it, singing with me.

I get into it even more and start shaking my ass, my confidence building as I work the stage. It feels like old times again, and the crowd roars as I switch voices, a talent I picked up because I love so many group numbers, going from a low contralto to a high pitch and back as I play the various parts.

The crowd is jamming, getting into the song and loving it. I even see a few couples start dancing together, grinding, and one small group working it. They're good. They could totally be dancers on stage.

As the last notes fade, I'm covered in sweat, but the crowd roars their approval, and I raise my hands, thanking them. "Would y'all like to hear some more?"

The crowd screams. "Roxy! Roxy! Roxy!"

I grin and go over to the DJ, taking a minute to write down four songs and swig some water before coming back on stage. The next song starts, and I grin at Jake as I start with the popular club jam, Rihanna's *This Is What You Came For*. It might be more electronic than what I normally sing, but the crowd loves it, and some are even singing along before I take it even more naughty, Britney Spears' *Toxic*, and then one totally non-sexy but fun song, *Uptown Funk*.

I'm covered in sweat as the crowd roars again, and I feel my breath rushing in and out of my lungs. "Wow, thank you, guys. Now, I'd like to wrap up the same way I always did at Trixie's with something a little slower. So if you don't mind . . ."

The DJ starts the song again, the sultry, sexy tones coming through, and I'm glad that it calls for breathy singing, because right now, *Dangerous Woman* is about all I've got the lungs for. Still, I launch into it, and as I hit the end bits, the crowd's loving it, hands in the air, and even the people at the bar are on their feet.

When I'm done, I have to almost stagger off stage, where Jake catches me coming down the steps. I'm literally slick with sweat, but he doesn't care, pulling me close and kissing me hard on the lips. His arms are so strong as I kiss him back, letting him almost carry me to a waiting chair.

"I'm out of shape for this. How'd I do?" I ask. It's the first question I always ask coming offstage.

Jakes eyes burn with desire, but he grabs a bottle of water, handing it and a towel to me. "You were absolutely incredible."

❄

"KARAOKE NIGHT WAS A HIT!" NATHAN CROWS. HE LOOKS AT ME. I've recovered enough that I've rejoined everyone upstairs in the

VIP lounge as the club closes. "Jesus, Roxy . . . if you can sing like that, what are you doing working in the same shithole as Jake? You should be on a stage selling out stadiums!"

"Trust me, I tried," I say, feeling the pang of regret that comes with his words. "But when it's not paying the bills . . ."

"Fuck that noise," Nathan says as I shrug. "If I had a voice like yours, I'd crash a record exec's office and say you only need ten seconds before you'll wanna sign me."

If only it were that easy, I think inwardly. "What can I say? A&Rs are assholes."

Hannah, who's had a few too many Little Mermaids, giggles. "Hey, can I get another? I'm not ready to give up!"

I shake my head, knowing I'm going to have to take Hannah home. Besides, her last comment sort of stings, even though I know she wasn't talking about me. I didn't want to give up either. But in an industry where if you haven't made it by twenty as a woman, you're almost never going to make it, I just couldn't face it anymore. Hell, some of the songs I sang tonight are damn near golden oldies, and the girl at the top of the charts this week wasn't even born when *Toxic* came out.

"Yeah, well . . . listen, can we leave Hannah's car here overnight? I don't think she's good to drive."

Jake, who's been smiling with Nathan, looks over. "Sure, but what's wrong?"

"Nothing," I lie, feeling a wave of depression start to creep in. "I'm just exhausted. I haven't done that in a long time."

Jake seems to understand. "Would you like to go home, then?

"I'd appreciate it," I say honestly. "But Hannah . . ."

"Babe, I'm fine," Hannah says, and I can see she's 'happy drunk' but not 'stupid drunk'. "You sure you're okay, though?"

I make sure my voice is convincing. "I'm okay, just tired."

"Okay then, go on, get out of here and get some rest. I'll be along in a little bit."

"But I can't just leave you here. How are you getting home?" I ask, but Hannah waves it off.

"Honey, don't worry about me!" Hannah assures me. "I'll get a cab if I need to. But what I do need right now is another Mermaid!"

Nathan laughs. "One more and then I'm cutting you off. After that, black coffee. Owner's orders," he teases. "Don't worry, Roxy. I'll call her a cab or take her home myself if she wants."

"Thank you, Nathan," Jake says. He stands up and takes me by the hand. "Come on, Angel. I'll make sure you get home safely."

CHAPTER 13

JAKE

"You were amazing on stage," I tell Roxy, turning left. I'm driving her back to her place, glad that I only had a few drinks. Roxy did too, but she's exhausted. The set on stage gave her a huge high that's now crashing on her. She's been quiet since leaving the club.

Thinking about Roxy, I'm still blown away. Her voice was pure heaven. She worked the stage like a pro. Every time I thought she couldn't do more, she did. Watching her sway her hips to the beat heated my blood. Three times, I had to pick my jaw up off the floor when she dropped it down on some of the songs, never missing a note as she did moves I don't think are legal in some states.

Even more than how hot she was, watching her on stage ignited a crazy desire inside me. I want to help her. I mean, it wasn't like I thought she was lying about the other club. I was sure she could hold a tune. But watching her tonight . . . she really has talent.

"Roxy?"

"Thank you," she says quietly. Something is on her mind. I saw it in her eyes, the disappointment when Nathan was complimenting her. It was like it only made her more depressed.

"What's wrong? The crowd loved you."

I loved you, I think inwardly, remembering how she looked so in her element. But those three words are too close to something else, and I don't want to have any confusion.

Roxy sighs, leaning her head against the window, looking out at the lights. "It just brought up memories, that's all. Reminded me of everything I went through."

My heart breaks for her. Her desire is one of those that sits right next to her soul, maybe even *in* her soul. Not having it is making her sick. I wish I could do something. I don't know anything about the world of music, but I'd learn just for her. "You did so well out there."

"I'll admit it was fun and all. And the crowd gave me life. But after the adrenaline wore off, it kind of hit home. I'm not angry at you, Jake, but maybe I should've never done it."

I'm speechless. It hurts to hear her say these words. I thought the exact opposite would happen. I was hoping that by showing her how good she is, she'd feel a jolt of energy again.

Roxy turns to look at me. "I'm not like you, knocking everything I try out of the park. I tried my hardest. Oh, my God, the number of hours I worked on my voice, doing lessons and sticking to diets to make sure I wasn't just overlooked because of that alone. And you know what I've got for it?"

"No," I reply, stopping at a red light.

"I've got a stack of demo CDs fifteen inches high. They'll never be heard."

I cringe inside, hating the defeat in her voice. "Did something happen to make you question your confidence in yourself?"

Roxy nods, looking in her lap. "Well, I've never told anyone this. But I did get an interview with this record exec while I was finishing my degree. He said he worked for a subsidiary of one of the major labels. He wanted to hear my voice, said he listened to my demo CD. I borrowed my stepfather's car and drove five hundred miles to this guy's office. I thought maybe he'd want to listen to me sing with a band, or maybe in person, so I took the time to work up my best piece in three different genres. I could do fast pop, a ballad, or one of those tearjerker songs."

"Sounds like you took it seriously," I admit. "What happened?"

"I didn't even get to sit down before the guy said he'd get me a deal . . . if I gave him head. He said I'd get a Grammy inside of two years if I fucked him."

"Son of a bitch!" I half growl, clenching the steering wheel angrily. "I've always heard the rumors of shit like that."

"So yeah. I told him the only way his dick was getting off was by being jammed in his own ass. I'm pretty sure he spread rumors about my being difficult to work with after that, but I don't know that for sure. I just know all interest whatsoever dried up after that. I ended up going back to college, then applying for Franklin Consolidated. The rest is history."

Roxy falls silent as I drive the rest of the way to her apartment. I know this building. It's a great place. Not quite as good as my penthouse, but it's a good building.

"I guess this is it," Roxy says, reaching for her purse. "Can you make sure Hannah gets here safely?"

"I will," I say. I was gonna go back to the club, but now . . .

"Goodnight," she says, getting out. Earlier, she was ready to take me right there in the club. I could see it, but now she's down and I can't help but feel responsible.

"Wait," I say, getting out of my car. "Roxy, wait!"

Roxy turns, looking at me suspiciously as I approach, and I know she's distrustful of me right now. After that story about the record exec, I'm sure she sees me like I'm a snake.

"Let me walk you up at least?" I ask. I can't let her leave like this. She needs something to unleash all that emotion on.

"I don't know," she says, but I ignore her, taking her hand.

I hit my remote on my car, glad I parked in a visitor's slot. Then again, Roxy's worth a ticket and a tow.

She grips my hand back, and I tug her gently to come on. "I mean, the place is a mess," she finally says.

"I'm not worried about your dirty socks," I reassure her.

"And then there's Mr. Felix . . ." she says, giving me a half smile and a sigh. "My cat."

We get to the elevator, and I'm reassured when Roxy hits the button for her floor. She doesn't let go of my hand when the door opens, and instead, we walk down the short hallway, Roxy fishing her keys out and unlocking the door.

"Welcome," she says, and I'm immediately greeted by the yowling of a big orange cat that goes streaking away from me at first sight.

"That's Mr. Felix."

"I see he doesn't like me," I joke, closing the door behind me.

"Don't worry, he doesn't bite. He does scratch, though, so make sure you're on your best behavior."

I laugh, and Roxy smiles. She lets go of my hand to hang her purse on the coat hook near the door, giving me a look before walking over near the couch, which has a great view of the floor-to-ceiling window and the skyline around us. I walk over, admiring the view. "This is a nice place."

"Hannah and I make ends meet, but not much more."

"You said your stepfather's got money," I note, turning around. "He doesn't help out?"

"He would in a heartbeat, but I don't need it," she declares. "It's nice to know I have a backup if something ever happened, but I'd rather handle things myself."

I don't respond. Instead, I lean in, kissing her on impulse. It's deep and soft, not the hot passion of that first night or the seductive intensity of the elevator moment we dangerously shared at work. I'm kissing her because it feels so right, and Roxy kisses me back, her tongue touching mine, feather light.

"Jake . . ." she whispers, putting her hands on my chest. "You're my boss. You need to leave. We can't keep this up."

I look into her eyes again, my hands tightening on her waist as I pull her closer. "I know I should . . . but I don't want to. You're driving me crazy. You're all I think about. I don't know if I care about shoulds and should-nots."

Roxy looks like she's about to protest when suddenly, she melts into my arms, her arms coming up around my neck to kiss me hard. This time, the passion, the need is immediate, and I push her against the window, my hand running under the hem of her dress to cup and squeeze her ass as I trail kisses over her lips and down her neck.

"Oh, God, this is . . ." Roxy moans as she runs her fingers through my hair.

"This is right," I whisper as I tug at her ear with my teeth, pulling her closer. "I need you."

"What if Hannah comes back?" Roxy moans, running her fingernails over my neck, pushing my shirt back a little as I squeeze her ass and move back to kissing her lips. "What if she walks in?"

"We just got here. She's not going to be home anytime soon," I growl, pulling her away from the window. "But we can still go to your bedroom . . . or the sofa, if that's too damn far."

I pick Roxy up. She feels like she weighs nothing in my arms as I carry her across to the couch. I set her down, and she lifts her dress for me. I'm stunned to my knees as her beautiful body is exposed to me.

I lean forward, pulling her into me as I kiss down her neck to her breasts, finding her right nipple and nibbling on it, the light bites making her gasp and moan. "Jake . . . oh, fuck."

I let my tongue tease the stiff nub of her nipple. It's perfect, tender and responsive. My cock throbs and my heart pounds as Roxy moans to every touch of my tongue, and when I start sucking on her nipple, she's shuddering, her hips bucking in the nearly see-through white panties she's still wearing.

"Oh, fuck, Jake . . . don't stop."

I reach down, sliding my hand inside her panties while I suck harder. Roxy throws her head back, gasping as I trace the wet outline of her pussy until I find her clit, lightly rubbing my thumb over it until she cries out. I look up at Roxy as her breasts quiver at the power of her orgasm. "Holy shit."

"Just getting started. I need to see you, taste you," I growl, tugging her panties down. She's glistening, soaked in the light of the overhead lamp, and before she can even take another breath, I devour her, sucking and licking her pussy. I run my tongue deep inside her, savoring her wetness until I'm moaning even more, ravenous for her.

"Jake . . . fuckfuckfuck," Roxy moans incoherently, tugging on my hair as she grinds her pussy into my hungry lips. "That's it, baby, that's how I like it."

"Mmm, your milkshake *is* bringing me to the yard," I half tease as I pull my tongue out to lick her clit. It's perfect, and at the first flicker of my tongue over the tip, she lifts her hips, letting me slide my hands underneath her ass cheeks and not allowing her any respite.

There's something about Roxy that drives me to new levels of passion and hunger. Growling, I suck and nibble at the tender button, my ears ringing with her cries as I push her, squeezing her ass even as my tongue flutters over her clit, circling it and driving her higher and higher.

My cock throbs in my pants, and I'm glad that I've already given her one orgasm, because the way I feel, I don't know how long I'm going to last once I get inside her. Suddenly, Roxy pulls my head back, almost as if she senses my worry. "Fuck me! Pull your cock out and fuck me!"

I grin as I hurriedly undo my belt and yank my pants down, my cock standing thick and proud. I pull again, buttons flying as I tear my shirt off.

I don't care. All I see is Roxy as she holds her long, perfect legs open for me, her pussy calling to me as I line myself up. I stop, just before taking her, realizing I don't have a condom. I hadn't thought of it. "Roxy . . ."

"In my bedroom nightstand," she says, knowing what I'm thinking. "It's the room on the right. And hurry. If you don't fuck me now, you're never getting another chance," Roxy growls.

I practically run, grabbing a condom and getting back to her as fast as I can. Who am I to deny a lady what she needs? She's writhing on the couch, moaning for me to hurry. With a deep growl, I slide it on in one smooth motion. I take a deep breath, then thrust forward, filling her in one long stroke that leaves us both wide-eyed. Her pussy is perfect, gripping me and massaging my shaft as I stay deep inside her, grinding my hips against her as I claim her. Never have I felt anything like it, and I pull back, pausing for a moment before I sink into her again, relishing the sensation. I moan deeply as Roxy wraps her legs around me, both of us lost in a haze as our bodies fall into rhythm.

I thrust hard and deep, each stroke of my cock making Roxy's body shake as I pound her into the couch. Reaching up, I grip the back of her head as my lips find hers and we kiss hungrily. My hips stroke over and over into her, slapping against her legs and ass as I abandon myself. She's perfect, squeezing and clenching around my cock so tightly that it feels like my balls are going to explode.

With each hard, driving stroke, Roxy's eyes darken and her mouth drops open, her body overwhelmed by the feeling of what I'm doing to her. There's no breath for words, just the harsh pants and grunts of two people meeting in deep, intense, passionate sex. My fingers clutch the back of her couch as I give her everything I have, my muscles rippling and the sweat running down our bodies as we hurtle together toward what I know is going to be an earthshaking orgasm.

"Almost there," I grunt harshly with the last of my control, my cock throbbing and steely hard within her.

"Come for me, Jake!" Roxy moans, and I'm pushed over. I thrust deep into her, crying out as I come. She's right with me, and her body shakes as she comes around my cock. I kiss her, holding her close as I tremble, staying deep within her as I catch my breath.

I pull back and rip off the condom when we can finally breathe again, looking at her, and she realizes I'm looking for a trash can. "Over there." She points. As soon as I toss it in, I realize this may have been a mistake. We're not going to be the same at work after this.

Who gives a shit? The little voice inside me whispers as I pick up her exhausted body and carry her toward her bedroom. I didn't even notice before, but looking around, I can see the music posters adorning the walls. And next to her bed sits the pile of demo CDs she told me about earlier. *You want her. She's worth breaking the rules for.*

"I'm going to have to go," I whisper quietly as I stroke her angelic face. Roxy nods and gives me a hopeful smile. "I don't think Mr. Felix is happy with me as it is."

She smiles, looking at me with those same deep eyes. "Jake . . ."

"I know," I whisper, kissing her softly. I'm so tempted to stay, but I have to go. It just isn't the right time yet, and Sophie will probably wonder what the hell happened if I'm not there in the morning. "I'll see you Monday?"

"Monday," she murmurs, dozing off. I watch her fall asleep, and I slowly make my way out to the living room, where I grab my shirt off the floor and shrug it back on. I let myself out quietly, a new thought coming to my mind.

Fuck any rules. I don't care about any of that. All I'm thinking is that she's got the talent, and she needs to rediscover her heart for it.

CHAPTER 14

ROXY

I come awake with a gasp, my heart hammering in my chest. For an instant, I don't know where I am. I reach for Jake, but I moan in disappointment when I realize he's not here.

"It was just a dream," I mutter. A dream in which Jake stayed the night, then served me breakfast in bed. Followed by the hottest morning cuddlefuck a girl could dream of.

"What's the saying?" I yawn, stretching out my arms above my head and hearing my bones pop. "If it's too good to be true then . . ." An ache runs down my side, bringing my mind back to last night.

I don't know how long it was before Hannah came back in. She'd woken me up, but I dropped off again quickly.

I've never felt anything like what Jake and I did last night. It was amazing, the way his lips danced on my skin, the way electricity crackled from every touch. He was powerful, tender, demanding, and giving, all at the same time. I've never been driven so wild to demand that a guy fuck me. I blush as I remember telling him to fuck me.

"Those eyes," I say to myself, lying back and putting my forearm over my eyes. "The way he touched me, the way he looked at me . . . he almost stopped my heart."

There's that nickname of his again, and as soon as the words come out of my mouth, I feel something I haven't felt in a long time. Words and a tune start flowing through my head like a river.

> I can't stand this creep, where is my Superman?
> He's late, but I don't give a damn.
> One glance in his eyes, and I know what I need.
> Gimme mouth to mouth, because he's a total
>   Heartstopper.

I jump out of bed and grab a pen and notepad from my night-stand, scribbling down some lyrics as I hum the tune that's running around in my head. It's been a long time since I had the urge to write a song. I've always been more of a performer than a creator. But being with Jake seems to have inspired me.

"What are you doing?"

The words pierce my consciousness, and I let out a cry, my pen clattering to the table as I jump and look in the doorway. Hannah is staring at me, clearly hungover, with her hair in a disheveled blonde halo, looking like a crazy cave woman. "Jesus, Hannah, you scared the shit out of me. Ever heard of knocking?"

"Sorry, I didn't expect you to be working with Mr. Rabbit," she half jokes. She comes over and flops on my bed, throwing her arm over her eyes and groaning melodramatically. "Shoot me, would you? I have the worst headache."

"So much for being the responsible one," I tease, closing my notebook after picking up my pen. "Talking shit about me, and you look like you got fucking wasted."

Hannah's mouth pinches as she keeps her eyes covered. "I'm a grown ass woman. I can do what I want. But it won't happen again . . ."

The door creaks open, and we both jump and let out bloodcurdling screams. Mr. Felix stops and peers curiously back and forth between us, padding into the room before hopping up on the bed, looking at us both like he'd like to give us a long lecture on duties to the boss . . . namely, him.

"Jesus." We both laugh. "Can we get any jumpier?"

Hannah lies back on the bed, still shading her eyes. "So how did you get home last night?"

She knows damn well how I got home. That's not what she's asking. "Jake drove me home, remember?"

Hannah lifts her arm, peering at me suspiciously. "And that's all that happened?"

I do my best to keep a straight face. "Yes, what did you think might happen?"

Hannah grins painfully. "I don't know, maybe you screwed him and actually killed him this time with that hungry pussy of yours? Is his body in the closet?" She gets up off my bed and goes over, yanking the door open and taking a look. "Yoo-hoo! Jake? You in here?" she calls. "If you're alive, tap your foot. I'll rescue you!"

"Oh, stop it!" I laugh. "He's not here." I grin, deciding to turn the tables on Hannah. "Speaking of getting hot and heavy, did you get down with Nathan?"

Hannah closes my closet, turning to look at me like I'm crazy. "You must be out of your damn mind. He's cute and all, but he's not my type."

"Mmmhmm," I say, unconvinced. "I don't know, you were giving him a few looks like you were more than ready to ride his pony."

Hannah growls. "I'm gonna kill you." She starts toward the bed, then stops, nodding at my notebook. "What were you doing, anyway?"

"Writing a song."

Hannah gawks in surprise. "A song? Now I know something's *really* going on. It's Jake, isn't it? He's got you seeing stars."

"No," I reply, even as I blush. I'm a terrible liar when it comes to Hannah.

"Come on, spill it. No teasing, no bullshit."

I look at Hannah, who's got her arms crossed, then roll my eyes. "Okay, maybe he is the reason, but singing at the club last night awakened something in me that I didn't think was there anymore. Something I buried, and I want to find it again."

I expect Hannah to laugh at me, to call me silly or something. Instead, she bites her lip then gives me a sad smile. "Okay, babe. If you need it, then I've got your back. Just . . ."

"What?"

Hannah sighs. "Don't fall in love with Jake, okay? I could see it in your eyes, in the way you performed. You weren't there for the crowd. You were cock teasing him and loving it. But more than that . . . I saw the way you looked at him. Just, be careful."

"I am," I reply, and Hannah sighs again. "What?"

"Nothing. I've got your back."

I bite my lip. "I know."

✳

AT WORK THE FOLLOWING MONDAY, I TRY TO AVOID JAKE whenever I can. I don't know why I'm doing it. I want to see him. I want to talk to him. I want to be with him.

Even though I try not to, I find myself stealing glances at him when he's in his office. As he talks, as he gestures, everything he does, he's sexy. He commands the room like he owns it. His confidence is pure arousal, and I can't help but rub my thighs together as I try to get work done.

Also, I can't get the song out of my head, and I find myself scribbling lyrics whenever Jake is around. Not all of them fit in this song, but there are some that do.

"Keeping a diary over there?" Matt asks out of the blue while I'm in the midst of trying to write the song instead of working.

"What's it to you?" I growl, snapping the notebook closed.

"You keep looking off into space lately, scribbling in that book. Got someone on your mind?" He raises his eyebrows toward Jake's office, and it unsettles me. I'm sure he's just fishing. How the hell could he know anything?

"Why don't you mind your own damn business?"

Matt walks away, grumbling under his breath about moody bitches, and I'm pissed off. But more importantly, I'm wondering if he's actually picked up on something. If he has, other people probably have also.

After lunch, I get up and go knock on Jake's door. Elena's still out at lunch, but Jake just came back from downstairs, and if I'm going to have any private moments with him, this is the time.

"Come in!"

I step inside, closing the door quietly behind me. "Hey."

"Hey," he says back, giving me a smile that makes the warmth between my legs rise to a deep burn. I do my best to reserve myself, but it's hard. He looks so handsome with his tie loosened and his hair ruffled from a fresh shower. He just finished his lunchtime workout. Watching his biceps flex as he fixes his shirt and tie, I remember how his lips and hands felt all over my body. The tension is so thick, I want to run and jump into his arms, sweep the stuff off his desk, and have him take me right here on top of his blotter.

I blink, clearing my mind. I'm about to tell him that what happened in the elevator and later when we got down and dirty was a fluke, that it can't happen again. Suddenly, he grins, holding up a hand. "Wait, I can see what's in your eyes, and I'll let you tell me, but first . . . I have a proposition for you."

"What?" I ask, hoping and also not hoping it's for me to get on my knees under his desk. Because I just might do it if he asks.

"Nathan's been going gaga all weekend, and I have too. We want to put you as a drawing act. One night on the weekends. You said you love to sing. The pay would be good. Not better than here, but it's only one night a week."

I stand in shock. I hadn't expected something like this. Sexual? Sure. But to sing . . . "Oh, my God."

"The people loved you. Nathan and I were shocked by how many people requested for you to come back. Seriously, you should see the club's Facebook page. There's over three hundred likes to someone requesting that you sing some more. They want you."

His eyes gleam, seeming to say, *And I want you too.*

I breathe, still stunned. The tune of the song I've begun writing for him hums in my head. Staring at his face, I realize I can't say no to him. I'm weak in the knees. But I also don't know if I should say yes.

"Well?" he says, taking his seat behind his desk and giving me that same smile. "I know you want this."

I stand there, leaning against his office door, uncertain. The fact is, music to me is like an addiction. It was so hard to walk away from it last time. I spent weeks unable to sleep on Fridays and Saturdays because those were my performance nights. I still wake up sometimes with a little voice inside me wondering where the stage is, where the crowds are.

If I do this, I don't want that to happen again. Jake doesn't know what he's asking for. I'll have to train again. Vocal exercises, getting my body back in shape to maintain the high energy performances that I have to do . . . wardrobe, practicing lyrics, all of it. How's it going to affect my work?

I tried the club scene before, and it went nowhere but having one club love me. This can't be much different. Sure, I'm excited right at this moment, and yeah, Club Jasmine loved me Friday night, but once people got used to me, it would die down. I'd be right back to being a local act and that's it.

Still, maybe it's enough. The idea of singing, of being on stage . . . even if it's not my name selling out big shows, it feeds a piece of my heart. When I sing, I put my soul out there, vulnerable and excited to see if the audience will respond with cheers. And I can see Jake genuinely wants me to do it. Damn me, there's a part of me that wants to please him, too. Finally, I take a deep breath and look into his expectant eyes.

"I'll think about it."

CHAPTER 15

JAKE

I hate the smell of cigar smoke. Sure, it's got the whole alpha male mystique attached to it, but damn if most cigars don't smell like burning dirty undershirts.

Tell that to Nathan, though. "We're looking at recouping our investment and turning a working profit within six months," Nathan says over a haze of his cigar smoke. Thank God we're up here where nobody except security is allowed and the air conditioners can deal with his disgusting habit.

"Show me the money," I say, sitting back and rubbing my hands in relief that this is going well. I was half-expecting for us to fall flat on our faces. I knew the market. So many clubs fail. But everything is turning out better than I dreamed.

"We're killing it, Jake!" Nathan says, grinning while sipping on some champagne, "And with karaoke night being a success, I think we should adopt it regularly. By the way, did your girl say yes about doing weekends?"

My girl. The thought is strange, but I like the sound of it. After I tasted her, after I filled her up and carried her to bed, I know that Nathan's right. Even now, I can't stop thinking about her.

"She said she would think about it." I don't point out that she isn't my girl. She will be soon enough.

"Think about it?" Nathan asks, surprised. "Didn't you say she was crazy about singing? What gives?"

I think back to what she told me and what I saw in her room. "She has some hang-ups. She's been burned before. But I think she'll come through."

Nathan shakes his head and puffs some more cigar smoke toward the ceiling. "Shit, I hope so. Those people were in fucking love with her! She rocked that stage like nobody's business. Shit, Beyoncé who? Selena what? Fuck that skank bitch Miley Cyrus. I'm telling you, man, Roxy should be a household name! One name too. She's gonna be so big if you say Roxy, the whole fuckin' world knows who we're talkin' about."

I sit back, sipping my own champagne and chuckling to myself. It's funny how Nathan went from calling her a sleazy broad to this. But I don't blame him. Part of that is Nathan. He's always been one to do a lot of shit talking until he really likes you. Most of it is Roxy, though. Her taking this gig will end up doing big things for her. I can just feel it.

I chuckle. "Brother, I totally agree. She is pretty amazing, isn't she?"

Andre's voice crackles over the small walkie Nathan carries. "Hey, I think that creepy dude is back at his shit."

My heart jumps in my chest as we both leap to our feet, Nathan just a fraction of an inch faster in snatching the radio up. "Where?" Nathan almost yells.

Andre's voice crackles back. "At the bar. Near the bathrooms. He's wearing a fucking purple blazer. Can't miss him."

We both take off, Nathan running ahead of me, pumping his shorter legs as fast as they will allow. I'm behind him simply because I don't want to send him tumbling down the stairs. It's early still, and the club isn't quite packed since it's just a Thursday night. We reach the foot of the stairs and I reach out, grabbing Nathan's shoulder. "Wait!"

"What?" he asks, turning. "Let's go bust this motherfucker!"

"No doubt," I reply, "but we need to make sure we don't freak everyone out. Go chill, okay?"

Nathan takes a big breath but nods. "Fine, I'm chill. Now where is he so I can go unchill?"

We look, and I see him first at the bar, that loud blazer making him stand out. He's pressuring some girl who's saying no in heavily-accented English.

The game is up, though, when the girl's eyes flicker over to Nathan and me in desperation and the guy turns. Seeing us, he takes off. Nathan flies through the crowd while I cut at an angle. He's so busy looking behind him for Nathan that I barely have to do anything to grab his arm and spin him around, locking him in an armlock with my other hand grabbing the back of his horrendous jacket. "Shouldn't have come back," I say in a threatening tone.

"Let me go, man!" the guy whines, squirming in my grasp. "I didn't do nothing!"

"You're full of shit, you . . ." Nathan yells before he lowers his voice, getting up close to the guy as I start pulling him toward the door. "You're fucking scum of the earth," Nathan rasps.

Nathan leads the way to the side door as we drag the guy outside. I see John, one of the security guys, covering our back, which I'm glad for. The former Delta Force operative can make sure we don't take things too far.

"Is this your thing, going around and drugging women in clubs?" Nathan demands as I hold onto the guy. "How many?"

The guy sputters, trying to play it innocent. "I didn't drug nobody. I don't know what you're talking about."

"You're lying, asshole," I rasp in his ear, jerking him around. "I drank one of your little spiked beers. So Nathan, what do we do to him?"

"You already know my answer. I say eye for a fuckin' eye," Nathan growls, cracking his knuckles. "He wants to drug and fuck women? I say we make him a bitch."

Nathan's threat makes the man struggle wildly, and he jerks his head back, catching me on the lip. I feel my lip split, and I grunt in pain as I pull my head back, loosening my grip just enough that the guy breaks free.

He takes off, trying to make a run for it, but Nathan's quick for his size and tackles him around the knees, taking him down to the ground. Before Nathan can move, though, the guy kicks Nathan in the shoulder and tries to get up before my flying bodyweight drives him onto his back on the concrete.

I pop him once in the face, his head rocking back and hitting the concrete. I rear back again, but Nathan grabs me, pulling me off.

"He's done, man!" he says. "His head went down pretty hard. You keep going and you'll be talking with the cops."

He's right. Adrenaline just kind of took over. "John, call the cops," I say.

"Just a second," Nathan says, turning and punting the guy as hard as he can in the ass. He howls in pain, and I gotta believe that a size eight pointy wing tip up your ass has to hurt. "Get this fucking piece of shit outta here!"

After the cops come by, we go back in the club, where we're both treated to a standing ovation and cheer from the patrons—the story's spread that fast. "See, brother?" Nathan says, patting me on the back. "Take out the trash, and the people love you!"

It's just after midnight when I walk into my apartment. I know I look like hell. I'm wearing another torn shirt, and I've got a bruised hand to go with my busted lip. Icing it helped some, but I'm going to look strange in the office tomorrow.

As I step into the living room, I surprise Sophie, who quickly flips her tablet face down on the sofa. "Jake," she says, jumping up, her eyes looking furtive and nervous. "I didn't know you'd be back so early."

I'm sure I just caught her doing something, but my brain is too overloaded to consider what it could have been. "It's after midnight, Soph. What were you doing?"

Sophie's guilty look makes me more curious as she shifts from side to side. "I was just watching this gross video. You know, girl stuff, disgusting, really. You wouldn't wanna see it."

I can tell she's lying, but I'm too exhausted and emotionally drained to push the issue. Instead, I remind myself to keep a closer eye on her. "Well, you've got school tomorrow."

Sophie squints her eyes, peering at me. "Jake, your lip . . . what the hell happened to you?"

I shrug, not wanting to go into it. "Just some club business. Roughed up some douche."

"What the fuck?" Sophie asks, shocked. "Jake, you got into a fight?"

I shake my head. "Remember when I said I got drugged? Same asshole came in tonight, trying the same angle on some girl."

Sophie grins, going into the kitchen to return with a popsicle, which she hands to me. "Glad you got him."

I take the frozen treat gratefully. "I am, too. We already called the police, and the girl he'd been stalking tonight gave a statement. His ass is going down for a while."

I put the popsicle against my lip, sitting down on the couch. I pat the spot beside me, saying nothing when Sophie moves her tablet out of the way. She sits, curling her leg underneath her, and I give her a lopsided smile. "So what's been going on with you?"

"Oh, you know, just school work, the usual," Sophie says. "Oh, I got a B on that test you were hyping me on."

"Did you? That's great," I reply, feeling a little bit bad. I haven't been able to spend as much time with Sophie as I'd like. I've been so busy with the club, and when I have been home, I've been distracted so often by thoughts of Roxy. "And you're getting along well?"

"It's okay, really. I mean, I've been thinking of joining the track team, so I've been able to get along, make some new friends."

Track, huh? That is new for Sophie. "Well, I want you to know that I love you and as soon as I get a hole in my schedule, we're gonna do something special."

That makes Sophie grin, and she gives me a hug. "Oh, thank you, Jake! You know, I was really hoping you could take me to—"

Before she can answer, there's a buzz on my phone. "One sec," I say, holding up finger. I pull out my phone to see a text from Roxy."

Fuck it. I'm in. Next week?

"What's that?" Sophie asks curiously.

I shake my head. I knew she couldn't resist. I'll get that spark to ignite in her if that's the last thing I do. I quickly hit reply.

I knew you'd pull thru. Incidentally, we caught that creep. He won't be spiking anymore drinks. Talk details tomorrow at the club, nine thirty.

Buzz.

Thank God. I owe u 1. 9:30 OK.

"Jake?"

"Just some club business," I half-lie to Sophie, sitting back and relaxing on the couch with a satisfied sigh. I wrap my arm around her shoulder. "Now, where were you saying you wanted to go? I'm thinking Sunday would be a great time for some 'us' time."

CHAPTER 16

ROXY

" *L*alalala . . . la la lah lah-la," I sing, doing my vocal exercises to open my throat. Standing in front of the mirror in my room, I know I look stupid, but it's what I have to do. Ever since agreeing to perform, I've been getting my voice in shape, torturing Hannah and Mr. Felix with my late night and early morning exercises.

I'm going to have to change into my outfit soon. It's my first night where I perform my own set, and I'm feeling the nerves. "Mimim-imimi . . . eeeeoooahhhchchch—" I cough and start choking a little. I pushed that last low note a little lower than I really needed to. "Fuck."

"Damn, girl, sounds like you're gargling a mouthful of cock," jokes Hannah. "Keep that up and Mr. Felix might decide to attack. He's about to lose it in here. He's rolling around and giving me faces."

Going to the door, I look over to see Mr. Felix mean mugging me, looking like he wants to scratch my face off. I've already learned to avoid making the 'ssss' sound with my vocal exercises if he's around. The last time I did it, he hissed back and nearly clawed my leg to pieces. This time, though, it helps. I place my hands on my hips and throw my head back and laugh. "Oh, I so needed that, thank you. I can't believe I'm so nervous!"

Hannah chuckles. "If it helps, I am too. Still can't believe you agreed to do this, but at the same time, I'm happy for you."

I'm excited. I still can't believe I'm getting to do it again. I'd given up on it. And I know I shouldn't have accepted Jake's offer because of everything it entailed, but being up there on stage brought me back to life. That place in my spirit I thought I'd lost forever is back.

"Thank you, Hannah. And thank you for being there tonight."

"Don't thank me, just please don't sound like this on stage? The free drinks can only go so far."

I laugh and go get ready. I already know exactly what outfit I want to wear. It was the same one I wore for my best performance ever at Trixie's. With a frilly, lightweight skirt that'll flare some when I spin and a sparkly red top that hugs my curves, I feel sexy. I pull up the thigh-high sheer stockings and boots that complete the outfit, giving myself a once-over in the mirror. "Oh, yeah," I tease, shaking my hair side to side. "I'm gonna have them in the palm of my hand!"

You know what you want in the palm of your hand . . . and in your mouth, my inner voice says, and I blush, thinking about it. *Kinda shaped like a microphone too, with a long, hard shaft and a flared head that you want to . . .*

I curse myself to focus on the task at hand. Just as I finish lacing up my left boot, my phone rings. Checking, I see it's Mindy. "Hey, babe!"

"Ooh, someone sounds excited. What's going on?" Mindy asks. I bite my lip. I haven't told anyone about this, but Mindy's always been supportive of me.

"Well, I'm getting ready for an event," I answer.

"Oh? Who're you going to see? I'm glad you're going out to have some fun."

"Uh, it's for me," I say nervously, holding my breath while I wait for her to reply. "Min?"

"Roxy, I'm so happy for you!" Mindy exclaims, and I feel relief rush over me. "I always thought your totally giving up singing was too much. So tell me, what's the gig?"

"Nothing big, just a local nightclub," I reply. "It's a bigger place than Trixie's, but really, it's just a once a week little gig. About an hour total."

"Just a little gig," Mindy mocks me, laughing. "So you're going to tear up the stage and break hearts for an hour. Remember, I've heard you. You're gonna have everyone eating out of the palm of your hand."

"Yeah, I guess so."

Mindy laughs. "Come on, don't be nervous. Just go out there, Rox the place out, and tell me all about it tomorrow, okay?"

"Okay. I promise, we'll Skype tomorrow or something."

From out in the other room, Hannah yells. "Move your fat ass! You're gonna be late!"

Mindy laughs. "Yeah, you two match up. Okay, Roxy, love you. Talk to you later."

"Love you too. Bye."

❄

Club Jasmine is packed, with cars stretching all the way down the street from the overflow lot. The line out the front is enormous, and I'm so thankful that Jake arranged for Hannah and me to be brought around the back.

"Nice to see you again, Miss Price," John the security guy says. "And you too, Miss Fowler."

"John, I'm beginning to feel like you're my personal bodyguard around here," I joke, trying to allay my nerves. It's not working. I can feel my chest get tight and I'm starting to pant.

"Hey, Rox?" Hannah says, patting me on the shoulder. "Just relax. Get it together. You got this shit."

"It's harder than I thought it would be," I say. "It's been so long since I did a real show."

"If it helps, I think you have an amazing voice," John says as he passes Hannah's keys to the valet. "You'll do just as well tonight as you did before."

"Yeah, what James Bond said," Hannah jokes. "You performed great last time. There's nothing to be scared about."

I gulp, taking deep breaths as John leads Hannah and me through the back of the club. He leads us to a dressing room, opening the door. Jake's inside, and he gets up, looking so fucking handsome in his black suit, emerald green shirt, and blood red tie. "You look amazing," Jake says, even though I'm wearing a trench coat. "But what's wrong?"

"Can you please tell Miss Heart Attack here that she is beautiful and she can sing the face off any diva?" Hannah says. "She's been gargling cock all afternoon she's so nervous."

Jake looks at me with concern. "Should I be jealous? Do I need to beat someone up?"

I smile, and he pulls me into him, wrapping his arms around me and kissing me gently. His lips pressed against mine cut off my worries in an instant, and I feel myself melt into him. He pulls back, looking me in the eyes, his voice low and comforting. "Go out there and kick ass. I'm rooting for you. I know you're going to be great."

Looking into his eyes, all I see is sincerity. He truly means it. His words and his touch and presence calm me down and my heart rate steadies. I feel safe in his arms. "I'll do my best."

"Oh, so that's all it takes?" Hannah mock complains. "Fuck, next time, I'll lay a kiss on you back at the apartment. It'll save me some stress!"

I chuckle, looking up at Jake. "I don't think so, Hannah."

Jake smirks and lets me go. "Come on, Hannah. I reserved a spot in the VIP section for us to watch from. Let's get up there and get ready."

Jake and Hannah leave, John giving me a nod as he closes the door. I take off my coat and get ready, checking my makeup and sipping some water. Just as I finish stretching out, I can hear Nathan in the front of the house, getting everyone hyped.

There's a knock on my door. It's John. "Miss Price? You ready?"

I grin. For the first time, I see his face change expressions when he sees me in my stage outfit. "Let's Rox."

I go to the wings, swallowing my nerves as Nathan turns toward me. "And now, Club Jasmine, by popular demand . . . she's baaack. Roxy!"

Swallowing my nerves, I go out on stage, waving to the lights. I can't see shit. The lights are dazzling, and the crowd goes silent.

The crowd stares at me expectantly, and sweat beads my brow. Oh, my fucking God, I've never had stage fright in my life. I even worked the stage like it was nothing on karaoke night, but now I'm standing here like a petrified tree.

I clear my throat. I can see Jake and Hannah seated up above, Hannah giving me *come on* motions with her hands. I feel like I'm about to pass out when Jake gets up, strides to the railing, and calls out, "You got this, Roxy!"

There's something in that voice, and I don't know what I'm doing when I bring my mic up. "Okay, boys . . . hit it!"

The first song hits, and I feel lifted by the notes and by Jake's eyes as I start with my first number, a club remix of the Tom Petty classic *American Girl*. The song's fast. Even with a dance bridge where I shake my ass, it's only four minutes, but it breaks the ice, and when the last notes hit, I feel it.

I've got the crowd.

"Okay, guys, thanks for the patience," I joke, and they cheer as I grin out at them. "Now, I've been racking my head, thinking of good songs for you guys. I started thinking about my roomie. So this one's for the *second* baddest bitch in the building, Hannah!"

It's not as well-known as most of my set, but the pulsing bass and lyrics of the RnB classic *Freak Like Me* gives me plenty of chances to do my thing, and the crowd is digging it. It's a little dirty, sure, but damn if they're not singing along until the very end.

The crowd dances as I move through my set. About halfway through, I gesture to Jake and Hannah, waving them down to the stage.

Jake's grinning ear to ear when I spring the little surprise that's been buzzing in my head. I whisper in Hannah's ear, and she grins, nodding as she runs to the side of the stage, pushing Nathan and Jake. Nathan's grinning, and Hannah comes back with two chairs, plopping them down.

"Now, I want to dedicate this next song to the guys who bring us this wonderful club."

The music starts, and the crowd cheers as Rhianna's *Rude Boy* starts playing. It's a little slower than some of the stuff I've done, but I pour myself totally into the performance, ignoring everything but Jake as I circle him, grabbing his tie and pulling his head between my breasts before practically giving him a lap dance as I sing.

He brings his hands up on instinct, but I wink and move away, teasing him and making the crowd cheer more as I catch Hannah giving Nathan almost as dirty a dance. He's got to be ready to have a coronary as hard as she's grinding on him. I get through the chorus again before I work my way back over to Jake, reaching down and pulling his shirt open, allowing the whole club to feast their eyes on his pecs as I go back to grinding on his lap.

Oh, my God, he's so hard. I can feel him pressed against my ass as I sing, and he's got me so turned on, if I'm not careful, I'm going to be giving Club Jasmine another kind of performance very quickly.

Love me, love me!

I reluctantly climb out of his lap and drop it low to the floor, letting him see my hips sway side to side as the last notes fade away, and the crowd goes apeshit. I glance back at Jake, whose face is beaded with sweat, but at least he's not as pink as Nathan, who looks like he might have come in his suit pants as he grabs both chairs and hurries off stage. Hannah gives me a smirk and a wink as I thank the guys over the mic for being good sports. Jake gives me a look too, one that leaves my throat dry for an instant before I remember . . . I've got one last song.

"Okay, Club Jasmine, now I've got a habit," I tell them, looking out at the happy crowd. "I'm such a big sappy romantic at heart, I have to end on a ballad. So . . . enjoy."

The first notes are almost soft and plaintive as they ring out over the club, but as I start the lyrics, everything goes quiet . . . I have them enthralled.

Maybe Celine Dion's made a whole career off power ballads, and sure, it might not be her most famous, but *Power of Love* is amazing to me, honest and poetic. I sing my guts out, and as I hit the high notes, the whole club erupts into cheers and applause so thunderous it almost drowns me out as I wrap up the song.

It's like a dream when I finish. The crowd is calling my name, wanting my attention. Suddenly, Jake is at my side, raising my hand and leading the applause. Getting off the stage, I'm almost swamped by people, Jake protectively next to me the whole time. People are coming up to me, giving me hugs, some even asking for my autograph. I'm barely aware, still wrapped in euphoria from my performance. Before I know it, Jake is taking me by the hand toward the back of the club. Luckily, I see Hannah is preoccupied and doesn't notice, because by the way Jake's moving, he has an idea in mind. The same fucking one I do.

Jake looks back at me, and the look he gives me is filled with need. I swallow, nodding as he leads me to the back, the same place where we were that first night. There's something magical about coming back here, almost like we're fulfilling an interrupted destiny.

I turn to Jake, who's looking at me with so much intensity that my knees weaken, and I sit down, unable to look away from him as he shrugs off his jacket and undoes his tie.

"Now . . . now you can send me all the way to heaven," he says, pulling his shirt off. He climbs onto the bed, urging me down, and I'm unable to resist, not wanting to either. His lips find my neck and I nearly melt into his arms. Should this be happening? I said it wouldn't, but as his tongue flickers along my jawline, all resistance is futile.

"Oh fuck," I moan, laying my head back as Jake runs his hand up my top and under my bra, his fingers finding my right nipple. His lips mash against mine again as we kiss hard, my hands pulling him down as he rubs his thumb over my nipple. I'm left moaning, my pussy throbbing as he holds me down on the bed, his greedy hands roaming over me and setting my skin aflame.

Suddenly, Jake rolls, pulling me on top of him. I blink, half-stunned, and look down at him. "What are you doing?"

"You said you could take me to heaven," Jake teases, lifting my top. I raise my arms, shrugging out of it and my bra, leaving me topless but everything else on from the waist down. "I hope you weren't lying to me."

I grin, leaning down and brushing my nipples against his chest as I tease his lips with the tip of my tongue. "I never lie about that. Just be warned—once you've been to heaven with me, it's all that will be on your mind."

He smiles. "I have no doubt about that."

I grind on top of him, feeling the bulge of his cock inside his pants as I roll my hips against him, nibbling on his neck. He brings his hands to my ass, squeezing and massaging my cheeks and making me moan. He pulls me up higher until my nipples are even with his lips, and I'm left breathless as he sucks and pulls on them with his teeth.

His right hand slips over my ass to tug my panties aside, and suddenly, he's rubbing my pussy, lightning shooting from his fingers through the rest of my body and jolting up my spine. He rubs deeper, the edge of his hand parting my ass cheeks and his thumb brushing over my asshole as he slides two fingers into my pussy.

I'm caught between two unbelievable tortuous pleasures, Jake's mouth as he switches between my breasts and his fingers pumping in and out of me as I ride him. "Oh, God . . . oh, Jake . . ."

"I've got you," Jake says, wiggling his two fingers and sending me into spasms of pleasure. "I've always got you. You're *mine*."

His words release something in me, and I plunge back onto his fingers, feeling his thumb press against my ass but not go in as I kiss him hungrily. Am I his? I don't know, but I want to be, and as

Jake's fingers and my hips roll together, he kisses me again hungrily.

I can't take it any longer. My pussy clenches, and suddenly, I'm coming, and I moan deeply into his mouth. Jake holds me close as my body trembles, shaking over him as I ride out the waves of my orgasm, finally collapsing against his chiseled chest, gasping. "Holy fuck."

Jake pulls his fingers out of me, bringing them up to his lips, licking and sucking them clean. He growls, pushing me down until my pussy rubs over the bulge in his pants, and a fresh wave of heat fills my body. "Get on your knees, Angel."

"Fuck me, Jake," I beg. "Please, fill me. I need it so fucking badly."

I slide off him, getting on my hands and knees as he slides off the bed. I hear the soft sound of his pants zipper sliding down and he steps out of them, pulling me to the edge of the bed. I hear the crinkle of Jake tearing open a condom and sliding it on, filling me with anticipation. My panties are soaked, and he pulls them to the side again, lifting my skirt and rubbing the head of his cock between my pussy lips, the huge, steely hard tool leaving me breathless.

"We're going to heaven together, Angel," Jake growls, smacking my left ass cheek with his hand as he slides his cock into me. I can't hold back my cry of joy and pleasure as his cock stretches me open, my pussy clenching around him with every glorious inch that disappears inside me.

Jake growls as his hips meet my ass, and I gasp as he smacks my ass again. Without giving me any chance to adjust, he pulls back and thrusts again. His hips slam into me, and I'm left breathless as he starts fucking me harder, his throbbing cock plunging in and out of me as he takes me. There's no pause, no mercy in his body as he fucks me with everything he's got.

I'm overloaded, my brain exploding in pleasure as Jake sends jolts up my body. I can't make any noise. I'm left a raw, sex-crazed animal as he hammers my pussy, my body shaking with every intense, long stroke of his cock in and out of me. I've never experienced something like this before, and I love it. I thought last time was good, but this . . . oh, fuck, I can't live without this anymore.

Jake grunts, grabbing my hair and pulling me back into him as he speeds up. "Now you know you're mine, Roxy. I'm gonna have you every fucking night if I want, and you're going to give it to me, aren't you?"

"Yes," I moan, my eyes losing focus. All I can feel is the pounding of my heart in my chest and the pounding of Jake's cock in my body. Everything else disappears, and I'm left in a world of pleasure. I squeeze his cock with everything I have, clawing at the bed to try and give him what he's giving me, but it's useless. I can't resist. His powerful muscles drive his perfect cock so deeply into me that I can feel him reach places I've never thought possible.

Jake pulls me up, kissing and biting my neck as his hips pound me harder and harder, his hands reaching around to squeeze my breasts, pinching my nipples. My mind goes, and I can't feel anything except the white hot pleasure of what he's giving me. I'm not even sure I'm breathing. All I can feel is what he's doing to my body.

Time loses all meaning. I'm left shaking and unable to do anything as I feel his cock drive into me deeply, again and again. I can feel him swell, his cock is throbbing hot and deep inside me, and suddenly, he's coming, driving me insane with primal fulfillment and pounding the last sparks of consciousness out of me. I'm coming too, so hard that black stars bloom in front of my eyes as our bodies, slick with sweat, hot with passion, come together, and I know that I can't be without him.

I don't know if I passed out or not. All I know is that the next thing I'm aware of, we're in bed, Jake spooned behind me, his cock still inside me but softening. His arms are wrapped around me, and I unconsciously reach up to stroke his forearm.

"That was intense," he says.

"It was perfect," I reply, sighing happily. I snuggle against him, and as he pulls me close, I realize something. It's not just the sex I need . . . I'm starting to need him too. I'm starting to care about Jake.

A lot.

❄

I BLINK, WAKING UP. JAKE'S STILL ASLEEP, AND I TURN OVER, JUST watching him. At some point, we've stripped naked, and I take a moment to admire him in the soft light in the room. He's got long, almost sensitive lashes. I know women who'd kill to have lashes like Jake's. But his face is powerful, with a strong jawline and chin that leave me with no impression of him being weak. I reach out, tracing the thick swell of his chest muscles, down to the chiseled ridges of his abs.

He's a moving, breathing, speaking human sculpture, a Michelangelo in the flesh. Best of all, I realize he's done so much for me. Tonight, I felt more alive than I have in years. The club, the crowd, it was like I woke up from a long nightmare and found out that I'm not from Kansas. I'm from Oz itself.

And then, afterward, the way he took me. We've had sex twice, and each time, my body's been left shaking with the intensity of how hard I've come. But both times have been different. The first time was mutual, almost tender in some ways. Tonight, he was powerful, conquering, taking me and making me his woman, and I loved it just as much.

But he's done all of this . . . for me. No wonder I'm getting feelings for him. He's done all of this for me simply because he believes in me. For the first time in my life, someone is reaching out, doing something for me out of a genuine desire to see me happy. He's called me his angel, but I feel like he's *my* guardian angel, descending from the heavens to pluck me out of a life I wasn't supposed to lead. He's reminded me of what I am, what I'm meant to be. He reached out and touched me, and in that touch, he's laid a finger on my heart as well. Scared? Sure, I'm scared. But I'm more scared of not having him.

As I watch him, I hear the song in my head again, the same song I've been working on, and in a moment that shakes me to the bone, it all clicks. *All* the lyrics, all of them in order, the tone that I'll use, even the notes. I think if I wanted, I could even tell you what each instrument will play, and who I want to play them.

I roll out of bed and see a pen and tablet of paper on the small bedside table. I start writing, my hand flying across the paper as I feel sweat dot my forehead again. I'm gripping the pen so hard my fingers ache, but it's as intense a pleasure as when Jake was inside me.

"What are you doing?" Jake says softly behind me. He's woken up.

I turn, blinking. God, he's so handsome. "You're scribbling like a madwoman."

"Maybe. I'm writing down how awesome you are," I reply. I don't want to tell him the song is about him. Yet. I don't know if I should reveal how much he's touched me.

"Really?" Jake asks, smiling. "Can I read it?"

I look down at the papers, and I see I'm missing just the final line. Still . . . "It's not ready yet. But I promise it will be good."

Jake sits up, grinning. "Oh, come on. Let me see."

I toss the pad aside, reaching out and grabbing Jake's hard cock. I can't believe he's so hard again already. I can feel it pulsing in my hands. Jake stops, moaning as I start stroking him, and I tug him to the edge of the bed as I get on my knees. Looking at his cock, I know I want to taste it. I want to give back to him since he's given to me.

"You'll see it when it's ready," I tease him. "Now, lean back and let your Angel see if she can get a treat out of this big cock."

CHAPTER 17

JAKE

*T*he last two weeks have proven to be a titanic struggle. My feelings for Roxy have only grown, but our relationship has been more or less confined to the club. We see each other at work, but we try to be on our best behavior. We talked about it, and we're clear on things. It's better if no one knows. She's even tried dressing a little more . . . well, I'd say modestly, but it's just not working. I swear I go home with a case of blue balls every day after work.

Thankfully, I've gotten to relieve them with her a few times after work. But an hour here or there of passion in the back room just isn't enough. I want more. I want to be able to strut through the city with her on my arm like she's my real girl. At work, as bad as it may look and sound, and at the club most of all. Rules be damned. The fact that I can't bugs the shit out of me, and it's getting harder to keep my desire under wraps.

Her last two performances for Club Jasmine have exceeded all our expectations, bringing in hungry crowds every weekend to hear the hot new voice everyone is talking about. It's to the point where I feel like we should be cutting her a bigger check for the amount of business she brings in.

My obsession hasn't taken long to start affecting my work and personal relationships, too. Some of my reports to corporate have been flawed because I've been devoting a lot of time to the club and helping get Roxy's name out there. I know Elena's probably feeling like I've lost trust in her. Even Sophie has begun to wonder what's up.

I've made a pact with myself to do better and get control over my desire, but every time I see Roxy, I can't stop the emotions. It wouldn't be so bad if we didn't have to hide it. I love seeing her happy, seeing that spark in her eyes just after she gets off stage and taking her to the back and drowning in her. It's like I'm addicted to her smile. And being with her pulls me deeper into the addiction. I find myself . . .

"Sir, your friend Nathan is on line two," Elena tells me, snapping me back to the fact that I'm at work. It's Thursday, nearly one week from Roxy's last show-stopping performance. Already, I'm counting down the minutes until I can see her again. She said that she had some new songs she wanted to introduce to keep things fresh. If they're half as sexy as most of her performances, I'm going to need to do that ice bucket challenge thing to keep myself under control.

"Thank you," I say. "And can you get me the . . . uh, the report on the . . . oh, damn it."

Elena stops, giving me a raised eyebrow. "Sir, are you okay? You seem really . . . off lately."

"I'm fine," I reply, knowing I sound like a lying asshole. "Just busy strategizing for next quarter."

She knows it's bullshit. "Well sir, sometimes a little break can help. But if you'd like, I have the quarterly projections from each of the divisions ready. Shall I get them ready for you?"

I sigh, nodding. "Thank you for that, Elena. I'd appreciate it."

"Of course, sir."

I white knuckle the desk when she's gone, cursing myself for being a fool. She hasn't said anything, but I can tell it's obvious to Elena that something is going on between me and Roxy. Roxy's been by my office too often. I thought we'd done a good job of being professional since that elevator incident, but it's definitely getting harder to keep my hands to myself when I see her. So far, only Elena seems to suspect something, or at least she's the only one I know of.

The flashing of my desk phone pulls me out of my thoughts. Shit! Nathan! "Yeah, Nathan."

"Yo!" Nathan says, his voice filled with excitement.

"What's up? You know I prefer not to talk at work."

Nathan guffaws. "Dude, you're not gonna believe this shit."

"Spit it out," I hiss irritably, wanting him to hurry up and get to the point. He might not take it seriously, but dammit, calling on my work line during work hours for something club related isn't cool!

"A music exec's assistant called me. He wants to come to Roxy's next show."

"The exec himself?" I ask, sitting forward. "Holy shit."

"No, the assistant. He's more like a talent scout. He wants to see the show first, and if he likes it, he'll pass on the word. Shit, man, this is motherfucking big time!"

My heart thumps in my chest at the good news. It's something that Roxy had given up on, and she hasn't seemed like she thinks it's a possibility anymore, even with performing at Club Jasmine. This news would excite her in ways she hasn't been in a long time. "Roxy will love to hear this," I say, glancing out the office window. I can't see her in her cubicle. She must be out doing something.

"Ya think? Dude, she's bringing in so much business. Listen," Nathan says, his voice dropping, "When you told me about karaoke night, I was like 'eh, it won't hurt, and it'll let my boy get his rocks off.' Then when I saw her, I had ideas, but I never thought this would happen. If this continues to go well, we're gonna have to start giving her more money, because she sure as fuck deserves it."

"She does," I confirm. "Okay, I'll pass it along to Roxy, but I've got to handle some business here. So I'll skip the club tonight. I'll see you tomorrow."

"Sure, man. Actually, I'll see you at the show. I've got some business of my own tomorrow. Bye."

I hang up the phone. Other than the good news, Nathan didn't say anything that I wasn't already thinking to myself. I've been thinking about this the past week and started working on a surprise that should be finished any moment now. I'll start by giving her the respect and station that she deserves. Something to show she's important.

I guess I've now got a double surprise. A smile forms on my lips as I check my tie and leave my office, going out to the floor. I check

Roxy's cubicle, but she's not at her desk again, so I go looking for Hannah. She always knows where Roxy is.

"Hello, Mr. Stone," Hannah greets me politely. In all the times I've talked with her in the past two weeks, she hasn't said anything. Roxy tells me that Hannah doesn't suspect the sexual side of our relationship and she's told her we're being professional, though I'm not sure if she's just saying that to calm my worries. I mean, I did lay a kiss on Roxy right in front of Hannah. She even joked about it.

Before I can ask where Roxy is, she smirks. "She's down in the supply room getting something for—" She doesn't get to finish her words, as a familiar and now thoroughly unwanted face walks over.

"Matt."

"Yessir," he says behind me in his slight Southern drawl.

"New policy. Get your own shit from the mail and supply rooms. Your co-workers have their own jobs to do. Thanks."

He sputters, and I walk off, giving Hannah a little wink as I do. I walk down the stairs to the supply room, where I find Roxy struggling with an armload of junk that makes me wonder what is going on in Matt's head. "Hey."

She jumps in surprise. She was so focused on trying to find what's on her list. "Mr. Stone, what—"

I reach out, taking the object from her hand, a red Swingline stapler, and put it back on the shelf. "Shh, you don't need to be doing this," I tell her. "He can get his own shit."

A smile hits her face. "If you insist. Definitely not going to argue against that."

I close the door, smiling. "I do."

I approach her, her perfume filling my nostrils and making my head spin in that oh, so familiar and needed way. It's been at least two days since I got in this close, and I can't help myself. She arches her neck as I inhale deeply. "Actually, I have a surprise for you."

"Please tell me it's as big as the one in your pants," she says huskily. "I . . . oh, God, we're not supposed to do this at the office."

"Not quite that big. But I still think you'll be impressed by its size." I take her hand and place it on my crotch, lowering my lips to kiss her. She melts into my touch, and I'm so tempted to take her here and now. But I can't. She squeezes my cock through my pants before I step away, both of us breathing heavily. "So, are you impressed?"

"Your ego is showing," she says, giving me some of that sauciness that I adore. "Careful it doesn't get bigger."

"You love it," I tease. "And you need it."

"I do," Roxy murmurs before stomping her feet like a frustrated child. "Fuck, just tell me already!"

A grin curls the corner of my lips. "After work. I'll take you out for dinner first. Think about it—we haven't had anything other than the club and the office."

"Are you sure?" Roxy asks, and I nod. It's been on my mind for a week. I want to take her out and treat her like a lady. "I mean, we probably shouldn't fuel any suspicions."

"Leave that to me. Be ready by eight, and wear something a princess might wear. I'll be by to pick you up."

She seems to melt at the promise of being wined and dined. "All right. But it had better be good."

I smile, taking her hand and kissing it. "I promise, it will be."

❄

I PULL UP OUTSIDE ROXY'S PLACE RIGHT AT EIGHT O'CLOCK. WHILE I thought about hiring a driver for the night, I decided to give tonight a personal touch and drove myself instead. I'm glad, because as Roxy walks out, I'm stunned. She's in a sparkling black gown, silver threaded through the fabric to create almost a waterfall effect. Her hair is sleek, her skin so enticing as she approaches me. She's so beautiful that I can barely think, and I get out almost a beat late, coming around to the passenger side of my car and opening the door.

"You are truly a vision of beauty tonight," I greet her, taking her satin gloved hand and helping her in. "You look like you're ready for the red carpet."

"You said dress like a princess, and when I dress up, I go all out," Roxy says. "So thank you."

I go around to my side and get in, still so drawn by her looks that she has to clear her throat and give me a raised eyebrow. "I hope you didn't mean just getting dressed up to sit in the parking lot and make out. I don't do back seats. Well, not anymore anyway."

Her joke breaks my paralysis and sends blood to my cock, and I grin. The back seat—that sounds fun. But I turn my attention back to the road. "You'll see."

The drive takes a while. When I told her not to worry, I made sure of it. She's giving me a look when we pull up and I hand my keys to the valet. "What's this place?"

"An exclusive, private members-only restaurant," I tell her, leading her through the plain, unmarked door. "We're totally safe here."

The maître d' checks my ID against the reservation list and seats us. As we make our way through the small, ten-table place, Roxy stops. "Is that . . . no way."

I glance over, seeing who she's talking about. "Kevin? Yeah, he's a member. Now, one of the rules is that everyone in here is equal, so he's just a guy."

"Okay," she says uncertainly. We sit down, and she looks around. "Wow. The decor here . . ."

"Is what gives the place class. This is one of those places where you get what the chef prepares. You just have to trust his judgment. But I checked the menu, and we're getting surf and turf with matching wines. So enjoy."

"Thank you," Roxy says, sipping her water. "So, Jake—"

"You can ask me anything you want," I say, cutting her off. "Come on, I can see it in your eyes. You've got a thousand and one questions about me. Now's the time for them."

"Well, okay," Roxy says, blushing. I understand. We've been having sex for weeks, and while I know a lot about her, she's not heard my story as much as she might like. "Well, you told me about your sister and how she came to live with you, but . . . well, you don't strike me as a rich boy."

"I'm not, if you mean whether I inherited my money," I tell her.

"My mother came from a rich family. But she met and fell in love with my dad, who was a working-class guy. They defied my grandfather to get married in Vegas, and there were a lot of hard feelings for a long time."

"Hard feelings?" Roxy asks, and I laugh.

"Well, actually, hard feelings as in a fist fight between my father and grandfather." I chuckle. "They buried the hatchet after I was born, but Dad was stubborn. He never let my grandfather shower me with gifts or anything like that. He did let Grandpa set up a college fund for me and for Sophie, and of course, his name helped open some doors."

Roxy nods. "Sounds like John, my stepfather. When he and my mom got together, I could have just mooched off him, but I had some good role models. I mean, after my biological dad died, Mom had to make it on her own for a long time. It taught me to be independent. What about you? What drives you?"

"Sophie," I say immediately. "Our parents died just after I finished college, and it pushed me. I mean, Dad always made sure I knew what a real day's work was. I did plenty of afternoons splitting logs for the fireplace, mowing lawns, stuff like that. But when I was literally a month after graduation and suddenly, I've got a little sister to take care of . . . it made me grow up a lot faster."

Roxy's eyes tear up, and I tilt my head, worried. "Are you okay?"

She nods. "Just . . . I can hear it in your voice. You miss your parents."

I stop and have to look down at the table. She's right. "There are times I don't like thinking about it. I try not to remember the hard times. I just try to remember the stuff they taught me. My dad

161

taught me how to be a man. My mom . . . well, if I'm not a total asshole, that's her doing."

"Well thank you, Mrs. Stone, then," Roxy says. "Because I think you're anything but an asshole. Most of the time."

I laugh. "Most of the time."

"Oh, yeah. You know, if you want to meet an asshole, you should see my boss. Always making demands of me in the supply room, calling me into his office . . . total asshole."

I chuckle. Our food comes, and it's as delicious as I expected. As she chews the last bite of her seared scallop, she sets her knife and fork down, looking directly at me. "Jake, thank you for letting me in more."

I reach across, taking her hand. "You're worth it. You're pretty special, you know that, right?"

She blinks. I know I touched her, and it takes her a moment before she grins. "Yeah, well, you just remember that or else I'll break a high heel off in your ass!"

I laugh. "Come on, time for dessert."

"Wait, we're not having dessert here?"

"No, the real dessert," I tell her, taking her by the hand again. We drive to Club Jasmine, where I lead her in through the back.

"Here we are."

"What's this?" she asks, eyeing the door that has a star with her name emblazoned across the center. It hasn't quite dawned on her yet.

"Open the door and you'll see."

She looks at me, looking like her heart is suddenly racing, and opens the door. The breath escapes her lungs as the door swings open. "Ooh."

We step into her new dressing room. It's equipped with a high chair, mirrors, a professional vanity for hair and makeup, and a clothing rack that is already filled with show dresses. "I checked your size and got you an entire wardrobe. Of course, you can pick and choose what you want. Roxy, you may not be a star yet, but you will be, and you're already a star in my eyes."

"Oh, Jake . . ." she says as tears fill her eyes. "How?"

"I had the crew paint and do all this during the day so I could surprise you. It only took them two days. I couldn't wait to show it to you."

"Oh, my God," she whispers. She turns and pulls me into a tight embrace. "This is so sweet of you."

"Wait, that isn't all," I tell her. "I have better news."

Roxy pulls back, staring at me. "Don't fuck with me. How can it get any better?"

I tell her about Nathan's call and the talent scout coming Saturday, and her jaw drops. "You're kidding, right?" I shake my head. "I can't believe it."

"Believe it, darling, because it's happening. You've got a shot."

She presses back up against me, a tear escaping down her cheek. "Jake, all this . . . but what I want—I want to be with you. Your girl, and none of this hiding in clubs or private dinner restaurants, even if the food was orgasm-worthy. I don't want to abide by the rules."

In this moment, I want to give her everything she wants. The whole world. I nod, pulling her close and kissing her tenderly on the lips. "You *are* my girl. But we still have to *try* to play by the rules in the office, at least for a little while longer. At least while you're working there."

Roxy looks at me with hope in her eyes. "Oh, my God, do you think it can happen?"

"I know it can. I have faith in you."

She shakes her head, tears swimming in her eyes. "I . . . I don't know how to thank you. You've done so much for me. Thank you so much." Roxy swallows, then wraps her arms around my neck.

She kisses me on the lips, and I pull her close. "You are more than welcome. Now blow their minds so I never have to see your ass around the office again."

She grins, giving my ass a squeeze. "That'll be one thing that'll suck about getting a deal. I won't be seeing your cute ass around the office either."

"Nope," I say, patting her ass back. "But you'll get to see more of it."

"Then they won't know what fucking hit 'em."

CHAPTER 18

"Your own dressing room?" Hannah asks in disbelief as we step inside. She looks around, her eyes going to the clothes rack. "Whoa. This is fucking amazing."

It's Saturday, and my nerves are frazzled. I'm trying to get ready to perform. Except this time, the stakes are higher. I couldn't believe when Jake told me about the scout. This is all happening so fast that I feel like my head's spinning.

Hannah is in shock too. "It's gorgeous!"

"Isn't it?" I say dreamily. "I still can't believe Jake had all of this done for me."

"Hmm," Hannah says, tapping her lips, her eyes flashing.

"What?" I ask.

"Nothing, I'm just not surprised at all. Have you seen the number of people who are packing in here to see you?" She turns around, checking out the rack of dresses, and I can tell that she thinks there's more to it than that. She's just giving me time to come out with it.

My phone buzzes, and I see it's Mindy. I'd texted her about my show. "Hey, it's my sister."

"I'll let you two talk. Nathan's got a great seat reserved for me. No way in hell am I dancing with you on stage tonight," Hannah jokes. "Have fun."

I give Hannah a quick hug as I pick up Mindy's call. "Stick around. Min?"

"Hey, how's my Grammy-winning sister doing?" Mindy asks. "You ready?"

"Fuck no, but hearing you helps," I admit, relief flooding through me. "Can you believe this?"

"Nope. Hey, turn on your camera."

It takes me a few seconds, but when I do, Mindy's face pops on screen. Her face has a little more weight on it than the last time I saw her, but it looks good on her. "Heeeey guuurl," I greet happily.

"Hey, mini me, what's going down?" Mindy asks. "And who's the babe next to you?"

"Mindy, this is my best friend, Hannah. Remember, I told you about her when I first moved here? She's my roommate." I put the camera on Hannah. "But you're blind. I'm the babe."

Mindy laughs. "How long do you have?"

"I don't have long," I admit. "You want to help me pick out my outfit?"

Mindy nods, and I hand my phone to Hannah as I go over, pulling out a tight black number with a cutout.

Both of them reject it, and I go through several more before we all settle on my outfit, red and silver, and I grin. Mindy's grinning too. "Okay, I'll let you get ready. Kick some ass for me!"

We hang up, and Hannah gives me a hug. "Kick some ass for me too. I'm gonna go get my seat."

She leaves, and I quickly get ready. Just as I finish my vocal warmups and stretch, there's a knock on my door. Jake sticks his head in, grinning when he sees me. "Hey, I don't want to distract you, so . . . just knock them dead. I already know you're amazing. Just show them what you show me."

"Show them my boobs? I don't think this is that kind of show," I tease, and Jake blushes. "Thank you. I'll see you afterward."

Jake leaves, and three minutes later, I go to the wings of the stage. Surprisingly, I'm not nervous at all anymore. The DJ is supposed to play my music, but I'm getting a band soon. It's a total pipedream, but I'd love to have my old one from Trixie's.

I shake my head. I can hear Nathan out there. He introduces me with his normal gusto. "And now . . . she's baaaaa-aaaaaaaaack!"

The crowd goes wild. It's like Nathan's catchphrase now. "Here she is . . . ROXY!"

❄

"I can't believe how awesome you were!"

They're the first words that Nathan says to me as I get off stage, and I can feel it. I had the whole crowd, and the place was so packed there wasn't even much room to dance.

I grin, then bite my lip nervously. I was hoping he'd say something about the exec coming to watch the show. "Think anything is going to come of this?"

Nathan grins and pats me on the shoulder. "Come on, let's go up and see Jake. He's been charming that guy's ass off."

I laugh, some of my tension relieved. "So you think he liked it?"

"The guy is fucking deaf if he didn't. You know, I don't even like pop or any of that shit, but your voice . . . it's hard not to enjoy it."

Nathan takes me upstairs, where Jake's sitting with Hannah and some guy who I assume is the talent scout. Seeing me, Jake gets up, so handsome that even with all of my nerves I'm feeling breathless watching him approach me to give me a kiss on the cheek. "You were amazing, Angel."

The scout nods, standing up and shaking my hand. "Honey, you were hot—like fire out there. My boss is totally going to be in touch!"

He heads for the stairs, and I force a smile as Jake rubs my arm and talks softly. "See, you just had to have faith."

It makes me feel better, but I'm not going to get my hopes up too much. If it happens, it happens. Hannah touches me gently on the leg, noticing I'm not quite jumping for joy. "Relax, I heard him gushing earlier. They're gonna call."

Before I can reply, there's a huge commotion down below. Jake and Nathan's heads whip around, trying to see what's going on. I see it quickly, two guys fighting over a girl. She's small, with coal black hair that to me looks like a wig.

"Hey, cut that shit out!" Nathan yells. It's useless. We're in VIP and there's too much noise down below, but security is getting to them.

Meanwhile, Jake is squinting hard at the girl. "What the fuck?"

Without warning, he takes off, dodging people as he plunges down the stairs. The look in his eyes and the way he's so in a rush fill me with worry, and I go after him. I don't know what's happening. Is the asshole who tried to drug me back?

I reach the floor of the club, gasping for breath, trying to keep up with Jake as he makes his way toward the commotion. He's grabbed ahold of one of the dudes, and the other one's disappeared off into the crowd. I'm sure security will get him.

Suddenly, Jake stops, and the other guy shakes his way free, right into John's grasp, of all people. Jake, however, looks stunned as he reaches out and grabs the girl who was in the center of the fight by the arm. "Sophie?"

"J-Jake," the girl says, pulling off her wig to reveal hair just like Jake's.

"What the hell are you doing here?"

"I . . . I came with a friend and—"

Jake looks furious, and he points at the guy John is holding. "How old are you? And don't you dare lie to me."

The guy struggles, but he sees something in Jake's eyes. "Nineteen!"

Jake's eyes go ice cold. "John, get him out of here."

"Wait!" Sophie cries as they begin dragging him away. Thankfully, they're dragging him toward the front door and not the back. She rushes off into the crowd after her brother but is stopped by another of the bouncers. I watch as she struggles violently against him. He's not hurting her. He's just not letting her pass.

"What the hell just happened?" Hannah says from behind me. I turn and see her and Nathan approaching, Nathan peeling off to talk to the security guy.

"A family squabble," I said, not really knowing much else yet. I just know Sophie's in high school and shouldn't be in here.

Jake comes back, his face as serious as I've ever seen it, staring a hole at Sophie. Jake says a few quiet things to her and Nathan, who nods and starts leading Sophie toward the back of the club.

"Jake, what's going on?" I ask when he gets close.

"I'm taking Sophie home," he says, his eyes still burning, but he manages a smile. "You did great tonight."

"Wait," I say, grabbing his arm. "Can I go with you?" I can't let him go like this. I've never seen him this mad before.

Jake looks like he's about to say no, but then he nods curtly. "Okay. Five minutes, grab your stuff. The car will be out back."

CHAPTER 19

*O*ther than the purr of his engine, it's totally silent the whole way to Jake's penthouse. This is my first time coming to his place. I would be ecstatic under normal circumstances, but this is like a dark cloud on my happy moment. In the rearview mirror, I can see Sophie fuming. Her hands are balled into fists, and they press hard into her thighs. She's probably going to have bruises there tomorrow.

I want to comfort her, to tell her everything will be okay, but I know that to her, I'm a total stranger and it's not going to mean shit. I don't even know if Jake's told her about me.

Finally, at a stop light, Sophie can't take anymore. "I can't believe you did that!" she snarls. "You didn't have to treat Jax that way!"

Jake clenches his jaw. "Can't believe I did that?" he asks in disbelief. "You snuck into the club with a nineteen-year-old boy with fake IDs. I had every right to throw him out on his ass. He's lucky I didn't call the police on him. Wait . . . Jax? *That* Jax? I thought you met him in school! What's he doing at your school if he's nineteen?"

She ignores that part. "He's only two years older. I'm turning seventeen soon. It's not that big of a deal."

Jake's grip on the steering wheel tightens but I see him take a deep breath to try and relax. "Do you realize what you did? Do you know what could've happened if you were caught with a fake ID?"

Sophie's scowl softens somewhat. "Just a fine."

"Maybe. But if they wanted to make an example of you, they could get you for a felony." Jake says. "That's not something you want on your record."

"I didn't know that," Sophie says softly.

"Not to mention that if the cops know that you're my sister, they're going to assume I let you in on purpose. The club could lose its liquor license over that."

I look into the rearview mirror, and I see her fidgeting. I think it's setting in how serious this situation is.

"You need to think about—" he starts, but I interrupt him.

"Jake," I say softly, placing a hand on his arm. "Let's talk about this at home?"

He swallows and relents. I can tell he's both upset and worried. It's obvious Sophie means a lot to him. "Okay. At home."

Sophie falls into sullen silence the rest of the ride. We reach his penthouse and go inside. I'm floored by how opulent it is. It's like everything in my apartment has had the volume turned up to eleven with a sprinkle of fairy dust thrown on top.

"This is beautiful," I begin to say, but I'm interrupted by a sharp cry. I spin around to see Jake grabbing Sophie's purse that she just put down.

"What are you doing?" she cries as he opens it and takes out her phone.

"Taking away your phone for now. There has to be some kind of consequence. I can't believe—"

"Give that back!" she yells, trying to snatch it away from him, but he yanks it back, stepping away and putting the phone in his jacket pocket.

"No. You're going to have to earn it back, and I don't want you talking to Jax. He's a bad influence on you."

"You can't do that!" she says, struggling against him. She lunges, but he holds her back with an arm. I place my hand on my throat, unnerved by how Sophie is acting. I want to do something. Anything. But I don't feel it's my place. This isn't my home, and as much as I feel for Jake, I'm not part of this family.

Jake holds his voice steely. "I can, and I will. You're my responsibility."

"Fuck you!" Sophie screams. "You're not my daddy!" she says, running to her room, crying her eyes out. Her door slams, and a sudden silence falls over the room.

Jake's shoulders slump when she's gone and he looks despondently at the floor. Tears burn my eyes, and I go over and place my hand on his shoulder. "Jake?"

"She's never told me something like that before," he says quietly, and I can hear the pain in his voice. "I've never tried to be a replacement for Dad, but . . ."

"Jake, I'm so sorry," I say. "I know you care."

"It's not your fault," he says. "I haven't been paying attention to what she's been doing. I've just been so busy with . . ."

His uncompleted sentence hangs in the air, and I fill in the gaps. He's been busy with his new job, the club, and me. "Let me go talk to her."

"It's pointless right now. Might as well let her cool down."

I shake my head softly. "I can at least try. I'm a woman, and I'm a stranger. Maybe that's exactly who she'll listen to."

He looks in my eyes for a moment before he nods. "Her room is down the hall, second door on the left."

I walk down the hall and stop in front of her bedroom door. Even if Jake hadn't told me, I would have known it was Sophie's. She's got a pink My Little Pony on the door.

My palms are sweating and I'm nervous. I'm sticking my foot in deep, and this could be a minefield. I take a deep breath and knock on the door.

"Leave me alone! I don't wanna talk to you!" a harsh voice calls from inside.

"It's not Jake. It's his girlfriend, Roxy," I say quietly before I pause. It feels weird to say that, but wonderful too. His girlfriend. I like the sound of it. "Will you please let me in?"

Silence greets me, and my nervousness increases. I stand there for what feels like forever, shifting from side to side as my feet start to ache like they always do after a concert. I'm just about to give up when I hear a small, "Come in."

I open the door and go inside. Sophie is perched on the bed, her eyes red. Moonlight streams through the window, and there's only a soft bedside lamp on as I sit down and the bed creaks. Sophie stares at me for a moment, and I reach out, stroking her hair. "You're so pretty," I tell her softly. "Don't take this the wrong way, but you and your brother are both beautiful people. You share a lot in common."

She looks over at me and sniffs. "Thank you."

Her voice is so small, like she's disappearing. She reminds me of me when I was younger. "Your brother really loves you."

She's quiet, but she nods her head slowly.

"He's not trying to be an asshole by taking your phone. He just wants to protect and look out for you."

"But Jax isn't a bad guy. I mean, he really likes me."

I shelve that comment. I think Jake's right. If he's got her using a fake ID, what's next? "That might be true, but he's a few years older than you," I say instead.

"So? Age ain't nothing but a number," Sophie says defensively. "I've heard it plenty of times."

Did I sound this idiotic when I was sixteen? I was probably worse. "That's true, but sometimes, numbers do count. I know a little over two years doesn't seem like a lot, but you're at that age where you do a lot of growing up fast. Besides, you guys were in a place you shouldn't be. If Jax were really concerned about you, he wouldn't have brought you there."

"We just wanted to have fun," Sophie says, and I can see her struggle with tears again. "Is that so bad?"

"Nope," I agree, forcing a smile. "Honestly, I did a lot of stupid shit back when I was a teenager. I'm surprised my big sister didn't kill me a few times. I'll tell you something that I was reminded of tonight. The Bobby Gardner Rule."

"The what rule?" Sophie asks, and I laugh quietly.

"Bobby Gardner. He was this big stud jock when I was a freshman in high school. He was a senior when I was a freshman, and my sister kept telling me not to get with him. She said he was bad news. Our age gap is just right so she knew him when she was in school too. Of course, I didn't listen to her. So when Bobby asked me out, I accepted."

"What happened?" Sophie asks, and I chuckle.

"He picked me up in a stinky as hell beat-up Camaro, we go to the winter formal, and during the second slow dance, he tries to cop a feel. I busted him in the nose with an elbow, and he cried in front of the whole school."

"I don't get it. What's the Bobby Gardner Rule?" Sophie asks.

"Elbow in the nose trumps hand on ass," I say, and Sophie laughs. It's a good sign. "There you go. Feeling a bit better?"

Sophie nods. "A little. Um . . . girlfriend?"

I nod. "It's my first time saying that, but yes. Listen, Jake feels like shit, too. He thinks he's been ignoring you because he's been spending so much time with the club and with me."

"I guess Jake deserves it," Sophie admits, but I don't know if she's just saying that.

"Don't worry, you guys will work it out. Men are stubborn pains in the ass most of the time," I say, trying to loosen her up. If I were Jake, I'd be worked up too.

Sophie smiles. "Can't argue with that. I don't have anyone but Jake, though."

"I'll come around more if you'd like," I say. "I'd like to get to know you. Jake talks about you a lot, actually. He's proud of you."

"Okay . . . if you can teach me how to shake your ass like that?" she says, referring to what I was doing on stage.

I laugh. "I'm pretty sure your brother would kill me if I did that. Listen, you get some sleep, and try to talk to Jake about this, okay?"

"I'll try." Sophie nods. "I'm kind of tired anyway."

I give her a hug and go back out to the living room, where Jake's sitting on the couch, wringing his hands. The worried look on his face tells me everything I need to know, and I feel my heart swell as I sit down.

"How'd it go?" Jake asks.

"She'll live," I say. "At least she's not wanting to take your head off. Anymore."

"Good," he says, relief flooding his body and making him collapse back into the couch, leaning his head back as he closes his eyes. "Thank you."

"You're more than welcome," I reply, putting a hand on his knee.

"Was I too hard on her?" Jake asks, opening his eyes and looking at me. "You must think I'm terrible."

I shake my head. "Not at all. I understand that you're trying to protect her. Just give her time, and no, I don't think you're terrible. She'll come around. She's got a good head on her shoulders."

He sighs, putting his hand over mine. "I've never had to deal with anything like this. We've always been close and she told me everything. She's been perfect."

I can understand his concern, and it touches me how much he cares for his sister. In a way, it turns me on to see a man who is so caring and kind. It sets my ovaries ablaze, talking to the deepest primal instincts. Here's a man who would fight for me, protect me and his children . . .

Is he the one? I ask myself. *Is he the man I've been waiting for?* They talk about them in romance novels and I've sung about them hundreds of times, but I never really thought one existed. They've always been like unicorns, nonexistent.

Watching him, I see in him a father figure, a man who will be everything I could ever hope for. God knows, if I ever have kids, they're going to need a strong father because they're sure as hell going to inherit some of the Price hell-raising DNA.

"Jake?" I murmur, reaching over and taking his hand. He turns his head, looking at me with loving eyes.

"Yes, Roxy?"

"I have something I need to give you," I whisper, my heart thudding in my chest.

"What?" Jake asks, and I shake my head.

"Not here. Take me back to the club."

CHAPTER 20

JAKE

*I*t looks different, pulling in after everything's closed up. The sun's just lightening the sky in the east, and I feel a little strange shutting down the engine on my Maserati, the silence deafening.

For the first time, I can say that Club Jasmine doesn't look like a museum or a temple, with trash littering the parking lot. There are napkins, a few cigarette butts, and I see some glass from smashed beer bottles. I comfort myself by knowing that the cleaning crew will come in a few hours, making Club Jasmine a jewel again.

I don't say anything, my head still swirling. After losing my temper a little with Sophie, and then the tension of watching Roxy somehow put a bandage over things, then now . . . what is it she wants to give me?

I turn to her, trying to figure things out. "You couldn't have given me this back at my place?"

There's something reassuring in her smile. "Nope. Plus, I didn't want your sister to hear."

I arch my eyebrow inquisitively. Now I'm really curious. "Okay, you got me. Let's go inside."

She gives me a secretive smile that only increases my intrigue, and as I lead her up the steps and unlock the door, I feel like I'm being drawn into something that will change my life forever.

Hitting the lights, I see that the club's mostly cleaned up. The early crew can get the last of the tables wiped down as they restock the bar. Roxy looks around, her eyes still wide. "It must be wonderful to have all of this," she says with a sigh. "To know that this place is yours."

"Half mine," I remind her. "We're off to a good start, but I've seen clubs do well at first and then fall flat. We can't get complacent."

"I have faith in this place," Roxy says, walking up on stage. It's dark up there. I can barely see her except the glint of sparkles from her outfit. "Where are the lights?"

"Off to the side. To your left."

Roxy disappears, and I can hear her fumbling around in the darkness. "Found it!" she yells. There's a click, and the LED floodlights come on, illuminating the stage. Roxy comes out, a pleased look on her face. "That's better. Now, can you come stand over here please?"

I see where she's pointing, and I climb up, chuckling. "What are we doing, reenacting a play? I'm telling you now, I'm horrible at remembering lines."

"No," Roxy says, going backstage again before returning with one of the microphones. "I know this isn't turned on, but I just can't do this without one."

She points to a chair that's in the middle of the dance floor, and I grab it, sitting down. "Okay, okay . . . so what's all this about?"

"I'm calling this *Heartstopper*," Roxy says as she lifts the microphone to her lips, and what comes out is . . . angelic. *"It's been too long, gotta get out, hittin up the new spot with my girl. Lookin' sexy as hell, workin' the floor, hoping to give this place a whirl . . ."*

There's no backing track, no instruments or sound system. Just the purity of Roxy's voice as she sings for me. It's slow, and I can tell that the song's supposed to be faster, but as she starts the second verse, realization sets in . . . she's singing about me.

"Your touch is electric, has been from the start. Give it to me, baby, or I'ma stop your heart . . ."

I'm grinning as Roxy finishes, smiling as she lowers the useless microphone away from her lips. "Well, now."

Roxy's face falls, and she blushes as she begins rambling. "It's crap, isn't it? I just wanted to write a song for you, and in my head, it sounds good. I just have to get everything right. I didn't know how to tell you. I didn't want to come off as a fucking cheeseball. I should have waited and prepared more. I'm sorry, every time I try and write something myself, it ends up coming out sounding like eighties shit-schlock . . ."

"I think it's amazing."

My quiet declaration cuts off her self-defeating rant before she can even get warmed up, and she looks up at me, her eyes full of hope. "You think so?"

I nod, getting out of my seat and walking up on stage. I reach out, taking her hand. "Roxy, it's not a ballad, but I heard it. I heard the beat. I can see you singing that in front of like, fifty thousand people. It's great. Two things, though."

"What?" Roxy asks, and I chuckle.

"Let's get a drink first. I feel like a good one right now."

Roxy nods, and I lead her over to the bar, going behind to start mixing. "I'm not a bartender, but I know my way around a kitchen or bar."

"I've noticed that," Roxy says, her eyes full of curiosity. "What are you making?"

"The evil version of the Little Mermaid," I say, adding in a second shot of Curacao. "When Nathan first tried it, it knocked him on his ass."

I add a splash of maraschino cherry juice, and Roxy hums. "That's not gonna be blue."

"Nope," I agree, shaking up the mix and pouring it into two martini glasses. It comes out just the right shade of purple, and I grin. "We call it *The Ursula*."

Roxy laughs and lifts the glass. "So I was so bad that you need to get me wasted to numb the pain?"

I shake my head and raise my own glass. "No, a toast. To you and to *Heartstopper*."

We clink glasses and sip, and the drink is just as strong as I remember. Roxy gasps, setting her glass down. "Shit, now I know why you only give a martini size. Whooo!"

"Yeah, I'm not trying to get you sloppy drunk," I agree, setting my glass down. I come around the bar, sitting down on the stool next to her. "So, about the song . . ."

"Yeah?" she asks, and I reach out, putting my hand on her warm, smooth thigh, my body thrilling as the feeling of having her so close sweeps over me.

I pull her closer, taking her hand and putting it over my heart. "You have to know something. You've stopped my heart, too. In fact, you've captured it."

Watching Roxy's face, I can tell when it hits her what I'm saying. "You mean . . ."

"I mean I've fallen in love with you, Roxy. You want my heart? It's yours."

I place my hand on Roxy's chest, just like in her song, and I feel the rapid thrumming of her heart. She feels as fragile as a hummingbird. Roxy steps closer, pressing her body up against me. "Jake . . . I love you too."

I stroke my hand over Roxy's breast through her top, her nipple quickly hardening as I lower my head, kissing her soft lips. There's a hint of the curacao and cherry on her breath as our tongues wrap sinuously around each other, Roxy moaning into my mouth as I stroke her nipple through her dress, her body pressing against me as our hunger rises.

"Oh, God, Jake . . . I need you," Roxy whispers, and I can hear in her tone that she means more than just for a good fucking. I lift her up. She's so light that putting her on the bar is easy. "What are you . . .?"

"Having dessert," I tease, kissing along her neck. I find the zipper on Roxy's dress, and I love the tension that builds with every click of the tiny teeth as I ease it down her back, my fingers exploring and stroking her sensitive skin. "Mmm, never done this before."

"Done what?" she half moans, sighing as I suck on the hollow at the base of her throat.

"Sex on a bar," I joke, pulling her dress down her body. As soon as her breasts are exposed to the soft light, I devour them, sucking hard on her right nipple as I pinch and tug on its twin, Roxy gasping and clutching my head to her as I feast upon her curves. "Lie back."

Roxy looks at me in wonder as she leans back, but it's not quite wide enough, so I twist her body, glad we're on a corner of the bar. Laying her back, I lift her skirt, enveloping my head in shadows as I kiss up the inside of her thighs. Roxy trembles, and I love that she can't see anything, just feel, as my tongue traces over her skin, moving higher and higher until I'm licking the edges of her panties.

She groans as I trace around them, moving closer and closer to where she wants "Jake . . ."

The first touch of my tongue to her pussy makes her jump, and I'm ravenous as I taste her, my cock throbbing in my pants as I pull the cloth to the side and slide my tongue inside her.

Her hips are shaking, thrusting against my quick tongue as I trace up and down her slit, sucking in between. I slip my tongue as deep as I can inside her, wiggling it and feeling her pussy clench around me before I pull out to flick the tip of my tongue over her clit. Roxy reaches down, grabbing my head again as she grinds her pussy against my mouth, pulling my hair. It's another thing I love about her. She's a woman who knows what she wants when it comes to sex, and she isn't going to just lie there for me.

"That's it, baby, that's how I like it," Roxy moans as I nibble and lick her clit. "Oh, Jake, oh, fuck, right there . . . oh, fuck, right there . . ."

I find the spot that she's looking for and lick faster, but with feather light strokes I devour her, my body aching as my cock presses against the fabric of my pants. I want to fuck her so badly.

Suddenly, Roxy's hips lift off the bar, her thighs clamping around my ears as she comes. I hold her close, my hands reaching up to take hers as her body shakes like a leaf in the wind.

When she comes down, she's still gasping, her face covered in sweat as I pull my head out from under her skirt and she strokes my face. "You sure do like going down on me, don't you?"

"It's a gift," I tease, pulling her closer. "Now . . ."

"Your turn," she says, glancing around. "This is way too high for you to fuck me though."

I look and realize Roxy's right. I pick her up off the bar, looking at a nearby table before she squirms and turns around, bending over one of the barstools as she grabs the thin chrome railing that goes around the whole thing. I can't help it, I grin. "You know just how to look sexier every time."

Roxy looks back, giving me a saucy grin. "Well, are you going to fuck me or compliment me?"

I growl lightly, lifting her skirt before smacking the upturned curve of her ass, Roxy gasping at the flat crack of my hand on her skin. I can just see her glistening pussy lips from behind the way she's bent over, and my cock pulses to my heartbeat as I pull my shirt off and reach into my pants pocket, taking out a condom.

"No," Roxy whispers as she sees the package. "Please, Jake. I love you. I want to feel you. All of you. No condom."

I nod and let the condom tumble from my fingers to the ground, instead running my hands over Roxy's ass. I undo my pants the rest of the way and take my cock out, letting it bob to my heartbeat as I line myself up. I take her hips in my hand as I thrust my hips slowly, letting her juices coat my cock as I slide between her lips, my cockhead rubbing over her clit as she moans.

I line up my cock with her pussy, pausing. "You sure?"

"I am," she says softly, looking over her shoulder. "Never been surer."

I nod, pushing forward. My cock stretches Roxy open, and the feeling as I thrust into her in one long, deep stroke sweeps away all thought in a wave of static. I can't think. I can only feel as I grab her by the waist and pull back, thrusting harder and deeper into her.

My body is on fire, and I stroke in and out quickly. I can't take my time. There's no way I can hold back as she drives me wild. I'm grunting, sweat dripping down my face as I spank her ass, Roxy yelping and pushing back into me, meeting my thrusts with her ass, our hips smacking together with sharp slapping sounds. I pound her body, driving deeply into her with each hard stroke of my steely hard dick. I pull her harder into me, grabbing her elbows and fucking her harder, each moan and cry from her lips pushing me faster and faster.

I feel my cock swell. I can't hold out much longer, but I don't care. I'm going to fill her up. With one more stroke, I'm pushed over the edge, and I cry out harshly, slamming my cock deep into Roxy. She cries out too, her pussy clamping tight on my cock as she comes with me, the both of us frozen as I hold her, unable to let go.

When our bodies relax again, I slide her off the barstool, gathering Roxy in my arms as she wraps her legs around me, burying her face in my neck. "I've got you, my love."

"Love . . . I never thought I'd hear a man say that to me," Roxy whispers. "Jake . . . even if it's secret, I have to have your love."

Her words hurt, and I set her on the barstool, stepping back to shake my head. "No."

"No, what?" she asks, and I hear a hint of fear in her voice.

"It's not going to be a secret. Roxy, I don't care about the rules anymore, consequences be damned. Nathan won't care. It's only the office. Well, you're more important than being Regional President of Franklin Consolidated."

Roxy beams as she looks around and finds her top, then she grins. "I guess I'm pretty special?"

"The most special," I reassure her, finding my pants and pulling them on. "Now, there is one thing we still need to do before we get out of here though."

"What's that?"

I chuckle and point behind Roxy. She turns, gasping when she sees the glint of light on the camera lens. "We were on camera?"

"Yep. Unless you want to run the risk of becoming Internet infamous, I think we should stop by the security office and delete the past hour or so of tape."

CHAPTER 21

I feel like a new man Monday morning as I get ready for work. The shackles that constrained me? I've released them. I no longer feel the need to play by the rules. I'm going to proudly have Roxy on my arm. Let the whole world see that I'm the luckiest man in all the world.

Of course, I'm still going to do my best to uphold decorum at work and keep it professional, but I'm not going to deny anything if I'm approached about it. It's my business what I do when I'm not at work, and there's no way I'm going to let anyone dictate anything to me. If Corporate wants to throw a piss party about it, let them.

I finish buttoning up my shirt, the classic blue with white collar, and tighten my tie before I get my coat and leave my room. I pause in the hallway, admitting to myself that I'm not looking forward to going to Sophie's room after the other night. We haven't talked much since. Sunday had about three words, and Sophie only came out of her room when it was time to get take-

189

out. She wouldn't even let me cook her breakfast but instead took a couple of packets of Pop Tarts into her room.

I try her doorknob, but it's locked. I lean my head forward and almost rest it against the wood. I want to bang on the door, demanding she let me in. We've been lucky. We haven't had anything like this happen before. Instead, I remember what Roxy told me, and I take a deep breath. Knocking softly, I force myself to talk normally. "Sophie? Time to get ready for school."

Her door opens so quickly that I don't even have time to lower my hand. "Already am," she says sullenly, brushing past me as I take a stunned half step back. She stalks down the hallway, and I follow her into the kitchen, watching as she half slings her backpack onto the table.

"So what would you like . . ."

"Not hungry," she says before I can set my coat aside and grab a skillet. "Already had a Pop Tart."

I can't lie, her words really sting. I've cooked her breakfast every morning that I've been home for as long as I can remember. Now, she's eating goddamn Pop Tarts, of all things. But at least she's talking.

"Okay," I say, mixing up a meal replacement smoothie of my own. It's green and tastes like I'm licking the inside of a lawnmower, but it's quick. Just as I choke down the last of the gloop, Sophie crosses her arms over her chest.

"Can we go?"

I grab my jacket, fishing out a breath mint as we go downstairs. On the way to school, she's silent, staring out the window as the city rolls by. Finally, when we're about a half mile away from school and stopped at a red light, I can't take it anymore. "Look, I'm sorry about what happened. And you're right, I'm not Dad, but I can't allow you to break the rules or the law, no matter how much that makes you hate me."

"I don't hate you," she says quietly, still looking out the window.

I snort. "Sure have been acting like it. We've always been close."

Sophie turns, looking at me, and I see the same stubbornness that I swear must run in our family. "I just didn't think it was fair. Jax is not a bad guy."

I could argue the point. "It might be true," I say, "but the fact that he's going out with a minor and thought it was okay to bring you to a club says he doesn't think."

"Jake—"

"Hang on, I'm not done," I say quietly as the light turns green. "Sophie, I'm only going to say this once, and I don't have a lot of time. First, I love you. I'm kind of learning as we go on, so I'm nowhere near perfect. But I know guys like this Jax. Maybe he does care about you. But if he does, then he should care enough not to be doing the things he did. He should respect you. Don't settle for a guy who won't."

Sophie says nothing. I pull up in front of her school and look over at her. "I'm on your side in this. I know I've been lax and haven't been paying attention to you. I promise I'll do better."

"Right," she says sarcastically. Shit, most of my talk didn't get through to her. "Have a nice day at work." She gets out and shuts the door hard, just short of slamming it.

I sigh. With all the good things going on, I guess everything in life can't be perfect.

※

"AND THAT'S HOW I'M GOING TO BRING THE FRANKLIN DIVISION back to profitability within two quarters," I say. It feels a little strange to be doing a presentation when most of the board of directors aren't even in the room. "By shifting focus toward the emerging biotech markets and out of the old markets, things are going to turn around."

"What about layoffs?" one of the members asks. They don't have the power they used to have, but they still have advisory and speaking rights in meetings like this.

"Thanks for asking," I reply. I hit the button on my laser pointer and continue. "I've spoken with the union representative for the non-salaried employees, as well with various senior management. By limiting new hires and encouraging an accelerated retirement program for workers who are reaching that age, Franklin will reach appropriate manpower levels within one fiscal year. We might need to shift some workers to different departments and trim a little fat, but our losses should be less than 1% of employees, and even with severance packages, we'll reach all of our transition goals.

"The fact is, we need a strong workforce at Franklin. While cutting the workforce with broad-scale layoffs might have the corporate shareholders happy for the next quarter, we'd be shooting ourselves in the foot if we do. We need to have happy, experienced workers in key positions. We owe it to the employees who stayed with Franklin through this transition to make sure we do everything we can to take care of them. If we do that, they'll work their asses off for us because they'll be working their asses off for each other."

I can see nods and even a few smiles as I continue, and by the end of my presentation, I've done what I thought would be the impossible a month ago—make both sides of the Franklin merger happy with the changes we're going to make. Corporate is happy that I'm turning around a non-profitable division, and the Franklin people are happy I'm not going all slash and burn around here.

There are several more speakers, but I zone them out as I go over my notes. When it's all over, I'm pulled to the side by Tom Powers as I walk out of the room.

"Jake," the white-haired man says, clasping a firm hand on my shoulder. Over the past month, we've had meetings, as he's preparing for his retirement and the handing over of Franklin to me. "I've never witnessed such fire and passion."

Falling in love will do that to you, I think to myself. I'm not ashamed to admit it now. I'm in love with Roxy. I don't think I've ever felt this way about another human being. "Thank you, Tom. I'll do my best to fill your shoes."

"I wouldn't worry about that," he says, smiling. "You've done a phenomenal job with the division since starting here. But I have to say, I was getting a little bit worried for a second. You stumbled there for a week, and I had doubts, especially with your . . . other business. But you've pulled it out remarkably."

I smile, relieved. "Thank you, sir."

He grins. "I'm leaving this place in good hands. Thank you, it's an honor."

He offers his hand, and I shake it. "It's an honor for me as well, sir. So I guess I'm still invited to your retirement party on Friday?"

Tom laughs, nodding. The party's been Elena's big project this past week other than helping me with this presentation, and she's even roped herself an assistant, Hannah. "Of course. Just don't let me see your back while I've got the knife for my cake."

I laugh and head down the hall back to my office. It's a little after quitting time, and I feel a slight pang in my chest when I don't see Roxy, but I understand. She's busy, and she's gone home. No reason for me to stay either.

I head downstairs and get in my car. It's early, but I figure I can stop by Club Jasmine on my way home and see how things are going. Nathan's really enjoyed being hands-on with it, although Andre's doing a great job as our assistant manager. And of course, Nathan will want to show me the new numbers after Roxy's most recent performance.

I don't even get in the door before Nathan's coming across, grinning ear to ear. "Yo, man, what did I tell you? The exec called. He wants to see Roxy's show live."

I stop, a stupid grin on my face. "You serious?"

Nathan nods, laughing. "Hell yeah, man! Looks like we're gonna have a star on our hands."

I shake my head and head toward the bar. "That's amazing. When's he coming?"

"Two weeks from Saturday," Nathan says. "Just think about it, Jake. Roxy performing at our club, it's so going to raise our status to have our own in-house pop star. We gotta get her signed to something ASAP. My God, the money's going to roll in!"

I'm not sure if I like Nathan's idea. I get it, he's thinking about the business, and he doesn't realize the feelings I'm having for her. If Roxy gets her big chance, I want her to be free to do what she wants. If she's content with performing on the weekends, even better. "Two weeks? That's great, man. We'll have plenty of time to promote it and Roxy will have time to rehearse. She'll be amazing."

"Hell, she always is. By the way, is everything going okay with Sophie? I know you were stressing when you two left Saturday night. I still feel like shit that it happened. John and Andre are already going through the door staff, making damn sure we don't fuck up like that again."

"She's better. She's still sort of pissed at me, but she's coming around I think. We're talking some more, and I'm gonna make sure I have some more one on one time with her."

"Yeah, well, if you need to back off here to do time with her, you do it, okay? I'll keep the Club on lock for you, Jake."

I nod, making up my mind. "You know, I think I might do just that. Email me the numbers if you want, but I'm gonna skip tonight."

CHAPTER 22

ROXY

"Jake seemed happy today," Hannah says as I use my hip to bump open the door of our apartment. I stroll in and kick off my heels, immediately stretching my toes out to their widest, unsexiest stretch and padding around in what I call "Hobbit Style."

"That's because we've decided to not hide our relationship," I announce cheerfully, walking to the kitchen, rooting around for that bottle of herbal tea I put in the fridge this morning. It always helps before I start my vocal exercises.

"What?" Hannah says, kicking off her shoes. She must have really put some oomph into her left leg, because I turn to watch as her heel lands dangerously close to Mr. Felix, but an instant later, he's safely under the couch with his tail hanging out under the end. Hannah, however, is staring at me in shock. "What the fuck?" she asks, placing her hands on hips. "You have a lot of 'splainin' to do."

I flip the cap on my tea, taking a deep swig and swirling it around my mouth before answering. "What? You had to know that I was still seeing him. After all this time, the number of times I was at the club late, all that."

Hannah rolls her eyes. "I figured. I just didn't want to argue with you over it. I hope it doesn't cause a problem at the office."

"Whatever happens, happens. It's not like we're gonna start screwing on his desk in his office during work hours," I say, though thinking about it, that would be fucking hot.

"Mmmhmmm," Hannah says, unconvinced. "I notice you added in 'during work hours.'"

"Seriously. I just mean we're not going to deny it if anyone asks. We don't care who sees us."

Hannah gives me a look. "I can smell the hormones from here. You'd better get a grip on them."

"Look, it's more than just great sex. I really care about him. He's the first guy in a long time who's made me feel this way. He's more than just a big wallet with a big dick. I give zero fucks that he's my boss."

She gives me a neutral look. "You don't have to convince me. I have your back no matter what. I'm just looking out for—" she says before she suddenly jumps up, looking panicked when her phone buzzes. "Oh, shit! I've gotta go."

I frown, confused. "Huh?"

Hannah doesn't respond, snatching up her purse and jamming her feet into the Nikes she keeps next to the front door. She yanks open the door, and I'm still confused. "Hannah!"

Before I can move, she rushes out of the apartment, slamming the door behind her. "The fuck was wrong with her?" I mutter in puzzlement. The way she looked at her phone and rushed off was bizarre. I look over at Mr. Felix, who's just starting to emerge from under the couch. "You got any ideas?"

He gives me a look. "Yeah, that's what I thought. Face it, Felix, be glad you're a cat because bitches be crazy."

I finish off my tea and rinse out the bottle. I'm just putting it in the rack when there's a pounding on the door. I wipe my hands off. It must be Hannah. She must have forgotten something.

"What did you forget, your pocket rocket?" I ask, about to grill her on her odd behavior, swinging open the door. It's not Hannah, and my breath catches in my throat. There, standing in his suit, looking hot as hell with a happy smirk on his face, is Jake.

"What are you doing here?" I rasp. Never mind the fact that I was thinking about dropping by the club to see him so we could roll around a little bit in the back. It's the first time he's come to my place unannounced. I guess I should expect more things like this since we're officially 'out', but I just wasn't expecting it after Hannah's weirdness.

"I brought this for you," he says, "Caymus Special Cabernet Sauvignon. It's a very special wine for a very special person."

I take the bottle from his hand, looking at it. I know the winery. My stepfather has some, and I'm shocked that Jake just dropped a few hundred dollars for a bottle of wine. "Thank you, but what's the occasion?"

Jake grins silently for a moment, drawing it out. Just when he's starting to really get me anxious, his handsome face breaks off into a huge grin. He steps in and grabs me in a big hug, swinging me around before setting me down. "That record executive is coming to see your show in two weeks. How's that for an occasion?"

I gawk, nearly dropping the bottle of wine between my shock and the huge hug. "You're shitting me!"

Jake shakes his head, stepping inside and closing my front door behind him. "Nope, just came from the club where Nathan told me face to face."

I manage to set the bottle down, glad that Hannah and I have a table next to our front door, before I let out a squeal of happiness and jump into Jake's arms, kissing him hungrily. "You amazing, wonderful fucking man! You did this for me!"

Jake kisses me back. His tongue is hot in my mouth as we stumble toward the couch. I can hear Mr. Felix run out. I guess he knows what's going to happen, but I don't care. Jake picks me up in his arms, and I wrap my legs around his waist.

"No, you did this all yourself," he says as his hand cups my ass and squeezes. His fingers slide lower, and I can feel the tip of his middle finger sliding lower and lower. "You have the talent and the heart. I only gave you the canvas to paint your masterpiece on."

"You're a poet yourself," I smirk, gasping when his finger comes to rest on the edge of my pussy. "Mmm . . . and your canvas is my body."

"My Angel," Jake growls, sitting down on the couch, letting me straddle his lap. I can feel the bulge of his cock pressing into me through his suit pants, and I can't take it anymore.

"I fucking want you," I snarl, yanking his tie down and ripping his shirt open. "Now!"

I'm torn between trying to get his pants open and the hungry, passionate kisses we're exchanging, but my body is burning, needing him. I don't know where the fuck Hannah went, but right now, I don't care if she walks in while I'm impaled on Jake's cock!

"Come on," I growl in frustration, fumbling with his belt buckle. "Get them the fuck off!"

Jake chuckles, grabbing my wrists before I rip his pants open. "Damn, you're acting even more cock hungry than the night we first met."

I growl demonically, staring into his eyes. "You ain't seen nothing yet. Your Angel's gone. Just a cock hungry devilslut is left."

"Bring it the fuck on!" Jake moans into my lips, his hands getting his belt open and his pants undone. I can see it in his eyes. Tonight, I'm going to get exactly what I want, when I want it, and oh, my God, what I need is—

Bang! The front door to the apartment flies open just as I wrap my fingers around Jake's cock through his boxers, about to pull it out.

"Good lord, I ain't seen something like that since Johnny came back from Vietnam and we got to get down and busy for the first time in a year," a familiar voice says. I jerk my head up to see my grandmother, Ivy Jo, smirking. "You could club a baby seal with that thing!"

I feel like I've been punched in the chest. I can hear Mindy's unmistakable voice calling out, "Grandma, cover your eyes!"

Jake jumps off the couch and pulls his pants up. I rise to my feet in shock, my eyes going wide with recognition at the women in front of me and the barking dog at their feet.

"Mama?" I whisper in horror. "What are you doing here?"

❄

"Layla and Rita couldn't be here," Mom says, sitting on the couch and gesturing at me, "but they send their regards."

I nod, still half numb. I'm not thrilled that my cousin and aunt didn't come, especially Aunt Rita, but I'll live. If I can live through my grandmother seeing me about to yank my boyfriend's boxers off, Rita not being here is small potatoes.

I'm just glad to see Brianna, Mom, Mindy, and Grandma all in the same place. All four women are seated on the couch wearing pleasant expressions with the exception of grandma, who is scowling murderously at Bertha, my mom's dog. She takes her everywhere, it seems. "That's okay, I'm sure I'll see them," I begin to say when furious barking and yowling interrupts me. "Shit."

"Why the hell did we bring that furball with us, Mary Jo?" Grandma complains to my mom while Bertha chases Mr. Felix around the room. Hannah is doing her best to separate the two, but she's giving Bertha looks that says she agrees. "We didn't even bring the grandbabies out of the hotel room, but you bring the dog." She rises to her feet, brandishing her wooden cane as a weapon. "I swear, I'm gonna crucify that ball of fur!"

"I've already told you a million times," Mom says pleadingly. "Leah needed her sleep and the sitter didn't want Bertha to disturb her and Rafe."

"That's why you should have left her at home!" Grandma growls. Instantly, her expression changes like someone flipped a switch.

"Bah gawd, that cat's beautiful. What's his name? Reminds me of my precious Esmeralda."

"Mr. Felix," Hannah supplies before I can answer. She suspiciously had come back with my family and is now standing off to the side watching us, having given up trying to chase Felix and Bertha around. Felix has had enough of the canine, and he turns on her, giving her one good swipe before he jumps on top of his play tower. Grandma is entertained, at least. "Go on, Mr. Felix, box that hoe!"

"Grandma" I say with a gasp, shocked by her words. "Where'd you learn to talk like that?"

Grandma doesn't turn her head away from the soon to emerge Animal Planet smackdown, but she at least gives me an answer. "I'm on Instagram."

"Which reminds me," Mindy says wryly, keeping her voice low enough that Grandma can't hear. "I need to take her phone from her. She's been putting up pictures she has no idea that she's putting on there. I'm scared she's gonna end up with a picture of her bags. And not the grocery store kind either." Dressed in shorts and a floral shirt, Mindy looks like she's ready to step onto a plane for summer vacation in Hawaii, but most of all, she looks happy.

"Get 'em, Mr. Felix!" Grandma crows, cheering them on with her cane in her hand. "WORLDSTAR! WORLDSTAR!"

"Worldstar? What the hell?" I ask.

Mindy facepalms. "Oh, God, yes. She's on YouTube watching those damn videos, too."

"Damn, she's like a ninja with that cane," Jake remarks with a chuckle, and I have to give him an apologetic *sorry, my family is crazy* look. He gives me a small shake of his head, and I feel myself relax just a fraction. After what they walked in on, maybe we needed this to ease the tension.

"Mama, sit down!" Mom pleads. "You're embarrassing Roxy in front of her friends!"

"Oh, don't stop on my account," Hannah says with a laugh. "This is the most fun I've had in weeks. And it explains so much about Roxy."

Mr. Felix lets loose a yowl that comes from the depths of his saber-toothed ancestors, and Bertha whines a little, backing up. "Hannah, please get him! I don't want to have Bertha going to the vet."

Muttering under her breath, Hannah walks over and grabs Mr. Felix and disappears down the hall. I hear the door shut, and Hannah comes back out, minus Felix.

Now that the commotion has died down, Grandma's eyes fall on Jake. "So who's this handsome young man?"

"Ladies, this is Jake Stone," I say, blushing but still proud. "My boyfriend." It feels good to be able to call him that. Glancing at Jake, I can see he feels the same way. "Jake, this is my mom, Mary Jo, my sister, Mindy, her best friend, Brianna, and my Grandmother, Ivy Jo."

"It's a pleasure," Jake says. Getting up, he crosses over and shakes hands with each of them, giving Grandma one of his heart-melting smiles. "I see where Roxy gets both her sassiness and her beauty from. Did she get her voice from you too?"

"My daughters sure know how to pick 'em," Mom says proudly as

Grandma giggles, of all things. "Handsome and a bit of roguish charm too."

"So Jake, what do you do?" Brianna asks. Like Mindy, she's added some weight, but it looks good on her also. I've only met her a few times, but she and my sister are practically inseparable these days.

"I'm the Regional President at Franklin Consolidated," Jake says. "The corporation I work for absorbed it."

"He's Roxy's boss," Hannah adds.

"Hannah!" I protest, but Hannah gives me a look that says *suck it up, buttercup.* She's right.

"Oh, don't worry about it, honey," Grandma says. "Getting down with the boss has been going on since . . . well, long before my time. And I went to school with Abe Lincoln."

I laugh, shaking my head. "Please forgive her," I plead to Jake. "She probably hasn't taken her meds yet."

"I heard that," Grandma growls.

We all pretend we don't notice Grandma as each of the women takes turns asking Jake questions. They ask him what his favorite color is, his favorite food, even what movies he likes to watch. I start to feel warm sitting next to him, and I'm not even the one in the hot seat.

To Jake's credit, he's the consummate gentleman, answering each question with patience and a pleasant smile on his face.

Mindy is in midst of a particularly tricky question when Hannah interrupts. "Uh, excuse me. I don't mean to be rude, but Jake, would you like to give these ladies' husbands a tour of the Club? Gavin, Oliver, and John are waiting at the Pancake House just down the street from Jasmine," says Hannah innocently. "They said they were hungry."

I look at her suspiciously, remembering how she ran out. "You were in on this!"

Hannah manages to look guilty but doesn't say anything.

Jake chuckles. "I'll be fine. I'll meet up with them and let you guys play catch-up."

I cross my arms and scowl. I know what this is. They're gonna interrogate Jake.

"Don't let them intimidate you," I tell him in his ear. "Gavin's huge, but he's actually a nice guy."

"Are you kidding?" he says with a smirk. "I was born in the jungle. I can handle myself. It was nice meeting you ladies. I'm sure I'll see you again?"

"You sure will," Mindy says. "We've got nowhere to go, and if we do, I'm going to be back."

When he's gone, I place my hands on my hips and scowl at everyone.

"Now, which one of you is going to tell me just what the hell you were thinking, surprising me like this?"

CHAPTER 23

ROXY

I pace back and forth, nervous energy filling my legs as I try to clear my head. I came to Club Jasmine early just for this purpose, to try and get my head right.

It's not working. "Come on, this is just another performance, just another performance," I mutter to myself for what has to be the thousandth time.

"Roxy."

I don't pay the voice any attention as I keep trying to go over stuff in my head. "Quick little talk with the crowd, then *Shake It Off* . . . no, shit, we decided to change the lineup to show my range . . ."

"ROXY!"

I stop as two hands grab my shoulders and I look up to see Mindy shaking me, staring into my eyes. "What?"

"You're freaking out," Mindy says, giving me a smile. "Come on, you've been going over this for an hour now. You know your set backward and forward. Even that old school track you're putting in for Mom."

"Hey, I'm not old school!" Mom complains. "I mean, Madonna's still touring!"

"Yeah, and looking more worn out than I do!" Grandma adds. "Roxy, your sister is right. Sit down. If you keep this up, you're going to wear out your legs!"

I take a deep breath and sit down, Brianna moving over quietly to help with my hair. While she does that, Mindy sits down in front of me and starts doing my makeup. "Okay, now listen," Mindy says quietly. "I can see what's going through your head. You've been trying to give yourself a pep talk, saying if this goes badly, it's no big deal. But you see, you don't need that talk. It isn't going to go badly. Look to your right. Let me get your cheek."

I turn, seeing Grandma. She's gotten herself dressed up in an outfit I can only call geriatric hoochie mama. Mom looks a bit more conservative, but Mindy herself looks like she's about ready to tear up the stage as one of my backup dancers . . . if I had backup dancers.

"All of us here know you're going to knock them dead. All the men know it, which is why the only one sweating is Nathan, and that man seems to sweat everything."

I chuckle. She's right. "He's made his money being a worrywart."

Mom gets up and comes over to me, kissing me on the forehead. "I've always been proud to have two wonderful, beautiful daughters. And I've never been prouder of you than tonight, Roxy. You look amazing, but most all, you're showing the world your heart. Do that, and they'll love you just as much as I do."

I blink, moved. "Mom . . . don't make me cry. Mindy just got my makeup done!"

"She's right, Roxy," Grandma says. She gets to her feet, coming over. "You look beautiful, and you're going to be the hottest thing since Brenda Lee."

There's a knock at the door, and Brianna stops messing with my hair long enough to open the door to my dressing room. She gives a low whistle, and I turn around to see Jake step in the room. He's dressed to the nines, a full tuxedo with bow tie, looking like he's ready to be the next James Bond. "Well, well, you dress up nicely."

"Thanks," Jake says, giving Hannah a wink. She's been a godsend, playing it cool at the office as I've gone through ten days of absolute performance boot camp. She even did the laundry the past two weekends.

Jake comes up to me, looking me in the eyes with those soulful, love-filled eyes that make my life complete. "You look beautiful."

"Second-best looking girl in the room," Mindy teases, fixing the last crystal on my face. "There. Now you look like a superheroine."

"I feel better," I admit, looking up into Jake's eyes. "So the guys are ready?"

It was Jake's biggest gift for this important performance, flown from Summerfield last Sunday, my old backup band from Trixie's, The Roxxers, Jeff, Gregg, and Wes. We've been rehearsing together for the past week, getting back in sync just like we used to be. "They're ready."

"Then it's time to go," I say, giving Jake a kiss on the cheek. "We'll kick some ass out there. You get these bitches to their seats, okay?"

I head backstage, where I see Jeff, Gregg, and Wes already in their performance gear. I smile, but Gregg, who is rail-thin with short hair, looks concerned as he gestures at Jeff, a tall blond with spikey hair. "Dude, I'm worried about the pyro."

"What? We've worked this to the bone!" Jeff complains. "Practices were great with it."

"Yes, but that was in an empty house with half the security staff standing by with fire extinguishers," Gregg retorts. He's always been the more level-headed one while Jeff wants to blast out. "With a packed house, if things go wrong, it'll be a nightmare."

"Nothing's going to go wrong," Jeff says dismissively, getting a little heated. "Rox needs to impress the record exec tonight, don't you, Rox? And pyro's part of that. We had it perfect from the first rehearsal. There's nothing to it."

I place my hands on my hips, biting my lower lip. I want to use the props, but now that the heat of the performance is on, it's only adding to my anxiety. "Let's just not use them," I decide. "It's too risky and we don't need it."

"But . . ." Jeff starts to protest.

"No pyro, and that's final!" I snap, harsher than I intend to.

Gregg grins as Jeff looks like he wants to argue, but he looks away when I scowl fiercely at him. "All right, Rox, it's your show. No pyro."

"Thank you," I say, feeling butterflies flitter in my stomach. "I'm sorry, guys, I didn't mean to be bitchy. I'm just nervous, and I really didn't need the bickering right now." I motion to my band-mates, and we huddle, saying a quick prayer. Just like old times.

We're just finishing when I hear Nathan take the mic on stage. "Club Jasmine . . ."

The DJ, who's going to be taking over after the concert, hits my 'introduction music', and the crowd starts to roar. Nathan lets the sound build for a few moments, and I can see through the side curtain as he grins. "Tonight, we've upped the ante for you. First, let's give a hot Club Jasmine welcome to The Roxxers!"

There's a roar of applause as my bandmates take the stage.

I feel like I'm going to faint as Nathan's voice booms.

"And now, the woman you've all been waiting for. The hottest sensation to hit this part of the country in a decade. She puts the pop in pop princess, the work in twerk. Ladies and gentlemen, and special guests . . . she's baaaaa-aaaaaaack!"

The crowd's roar is like a physical wave, and I can feel it filling my body with energy. *You can do this, girl. Everything's going to be fine.* "ROXY!"

Nathan walks off stage, and as he passes by, I grab his arm. "Nathan!"

"Yeah?"

"Nix the pyro! Tell them, no pyro!"

I don't have time for more. The crowd is chanting my name, but I see Nathan give me a nod, and I feel a bit of relief. The moment I step out on stage, I'm swept away. I grin, all of my nervousness falling away as I wave to the crowd. "Club Jasmine, let's get Roxed!"

The crowd roars again as Wes starts the synth notes for *Toxic*, and I stalk toward the front of the stage, my ass swaying side to side as I start.

Everything goes perfectly. I have them in the palm of my hand by the chorus, and I work it, spinning and twirling while singing my heart out. I've been training *hard* for this, and all those morning runs and dance practices after work have paid off. I'm not winded at all when the final notes hit, and the crowd eats it up.

"Thank you!" I cheer, not even pausing as Gregg switches over to the percussion introduction to *Rockabye*. This is a new one for me at Club Jasmine, and the crowd loves it, especially as Jeff does his reggae-style verses while jamming on the bass guitar. I planned this song for the fact that it is a duet. It gives me a chance to catch my breath before going high-energy for the next few songs.

It's the performance of my life.

I walk to the center of the stage, blinded by the spotlight, sweat trickling down my forehead and sides. Despite being sweaty as hell, I feel more alive than I've felt in a long time, energized by my performance. "Club Jasmine, are you having fun tonight?" A resounding *yeah* roars back at me. "I can't hear you!" I yell, cupping my ear. "Can I get a hell yeah?"

"Hell yeah!"

I laugh. "All right, this next song is for some very special guests tonight," I tell the audience as I look out into the crowd. Through the glare, I can make out the women I love, all of them looking at me with pride in their eyes and smiles on their faces. "I won't embarrass them by saying their names, but they know who they are."

I turn my back to the crowd and raise my mic hand in the hair. "Hit it!"

The song starts, and I start jamming, dropping it low to the floor and bringing it back up again, pumping myself up for this high-energy song. Just as I'm about to sing the opening bar, I'm surrounded by a shower of sparks that blots out the entire stage, and a loud popping noise assaults my ears.

Followed by the blaring of a fire alarm.

"Everybody OUT!" the DJ screams, and suddenly, I realize someone used the pyro anyway and started a fire! I'm frozen in shock as I watch the audience descend into chaos.

Flames are racing up the curtains and there's a rush of screaming people trying to get out the doors. I let out a cry when something falls near me, flames whooshing from it. Almost numbly, I see Gregg, Jeff, and Wes abandon their instruments to head for the fire exit on the side of the stage.

After a moment, I shake off my shock and start to head that way. But before I can cross the stage, one of the speakers falls, sparks and flame erupting in front of me as it hits the stage. Crying out, I hurl myself out of the way just in time.

I roll off the stage to land in the middle of what feels like a stampede, people kicking me, and I can feel someone stumble, stepping on my back as they rush for the exit. I scream, worried that the next step is going to be someone breaking my leg or worse, when suddenly, strong arms are around my body, lifting me up. It's Jake, and he pulls me toward the exit as the flames continue to grow.

We get outside, Jake setting me down as thick, black smoke rolls out the doors of Club Jasmine. I look around, trying to find my family, and at first I'm panicked. I see Mom and Mindy at first, then everyone else. Except Grandma. "Where's Grandma?" I look around frantically, my heart pounding within my chest like a jack-hammer, growing dread twisting my stomach.

"I'm here!" a familiar wavy but powerful voice crows. "It'd take more than this to knock me out! Now set me down, you big gorilla!"

I see Oliver, Mindy's husband, with Grandma in his arms. "Sorry, I took the other exit. Everyone was headed to the same one."

"What the fuck was that?" calls a fresh voice, hacking. "Honestly, what the fuck were you thinking?"

I turn to see an older man, his eyes ablaze in fury. "Who—"

"I'm the person you were trying to impress," the man hisses, coughing. "I came to watch you sing, and you try to put on a pyro show like you're a goddamn pro wrestler? Fucking amateur hour!"

I can see Jake wants to say something, but Nathan comes up, grabbing him, and he's running back into the building, Gavin and Oliver on his heels. I want to rush after them. They're trying to save the building, I guess, but I'm frozen as the man rants. "I swear, between the bad stripper dancing and the horrible cater-wauling . . . I didn't think it could get any worse!"

"You know what, you bastard? Take your bullshit and shove it!" Mindy yells, getting in his face. "It was obviously a fucking accident!"

The man gives her a look and turns on his heels, stomping away. He disappears into the crowd just as the sound of fire engines approaches, and Mindy holds me as I feel like I just destroyed my life. Everything was going great. Until that.

"Oh, my God, Min, I can't believe this," I sob into her shoulder. I'm too weak to look over to see which one of my bandmates looks guilty, though I have a pretty good idea which one it is. But it doesn't matter. I feel like I'm responsible for this. "This is all my fault."

"Shh," Mindy reassures me, stroking my hair until a new set of arms wraps around me. It's Jake, and he drops a fire extinguisher on the pavement before he pulls me into a hug.

"We got everyone out. The fire's mostly under control and it looks like no one is hurt," he says, coughing lightly. "But the roof . . . the roof . . ."

"The club?" I whisper, and Jake shakes his head slowly. I feel my heart break. I'm sure he hates me. I burned down his dream! "Jake, I'm so sorry. I didn't mean to—"

Before I can finish, Jake's phone rings and he pulls it out. He listens, his face going white underneath the streaks of black. "No . . . no!"

"What is it?" I ask as Jake hangs up, and he starts to walk away. I follow him, grabbing his arm. "Jake! What is it?"

"There's been a . . ." he whispers, seeming to lose his voice, his eyes unfocused. "Sophie . . . she's been in an accident."

CHAPTER 24

*T*he cabin of Hannah's car is silent as we make our way to the hospital. I'm riding in the back because, as a heaping helping of extra suck on tonight, my car was parked in the back of Club Jasmine . . . right where a back window blew out and turned my Maserati into a wreck.

This night has been something nightmares are made of. It started off with so much promise, with the chance for a brighter future for Roxy, for Club Jasmine. Now, the club's a wreck and from what I hear, Roxy's career might have gone up in flames right along with it, and to top it off, I'm terrified about how Sophie is doing because they wouldn't tell me much on the phone.

"Jake, I'm so sorry," she says quietly. After getting the call, I turned over everything at the club to Nathan while Hannah drives Roxy and me to the hospital. "You must hate me."

The guilt in her voice tears at my fucking heart. She's said it about a half dozen times as we ride, and each time, I haven't responded.

To be honest, I don't know what to say. Instead, I look out the window, wishing that Hannah could drive faster.

"Jake . . ."

"Don't worry about what happened right now," I tell her quietly, reaching out and taking her hand. "Everything is going to be okay."

Even as I say it, my stomach twists in knots. Things aren't going to be okay. The club being burned hurts on a lot of levels. We're going to lose a lot of money over it. Sure, we had insurance, but that will cover repairs, maybe. It won't cover the operating losses, the fact that nobody's coming through the door, or that I owe the staff something during the time the club's closed. And there's no insurance in the world that's going to cover the damage to Club Jasmine's reputation. There's no guarantee that even if we do get it repaired quickly, people are going to come back.

I just hope Nathan won't lose his shit. He's really taken personal pride in it, and it's the first business venture he's done that bears his real fingerprints and isn't just transactions being shuffled around on a computer.

Honestly, though, my number one concern right now is Sophie. If something bad has happened to her . . . I feel like hell. I said I was going to start spending more time with her. But outside of breakfast and our school rides, we haven't had a lot of time. Now she's in the hospital after an accident of some kind, and if something's happened to her, I'll never forgive myself.

We reach the hospital, and before Hannah's even got the engine shut off, I jump out of her car, storming toward the doors and practically charging through them. The safety glass slides open at what seems like a snail's pace, and I turn sideways to slide through as narrow a gap as I can, crossing the reception area to the desk. I barely notice that Roxy's caught up as I plant my hands on the desk so loudly that the guy on duty jumps slightly. "Where's Sophie Stone?" I pant, knowing I look like a dirty, crazy man. "I'm here to see her."

"Are you of relation?" asks the staffer. The logical side of my mind tells me that he's just doing his job, but there's another side of me, the scared, instinctive brother side, that wants to grab him by the scrubs he's wearing and jack him against the wall.

Instead, I bite down on my words and reach into my tuxedo jacket, finding my wallet. "I'm her brother," I say, showing him my driver's license. "And I'm her legal guardian. Now where is she?"

The guy looks, then nods. "She's in the ER, one of the exam rooms. I'll have someone come to escort you."

"I'm not waiting," I growl, rushing down the hallway, Roxy hot on my heels. I see a sign for the ER and turn, sliding slightly in my dress shoes on the linoleum. I see the doors up ahead, and as I reach them, a nurse steps out.

"Mr. Stone, come with me," she says, not fazed at all to see a man in a soot-stained tuxedo come running down the hallway. She leads us through, not saying much until she stops outside an exam room. "She's in here. We're waiting on some tests."

I nod and slide the curtain back, relief sweeping through me as I see Sophie. Thank God she's awake, leaning back on the exam table as another nurse finishes wrapping up a gauze bandage around her head. She's got the bandage and a bruise on the side of her face, but other than that, she honestly doesn't look all that bad.

"Okay, Miss Stone, just lie back and wait for the docs to come back with the results of the tests," the nurse says. Seeing me, she gives me a professional smile. "Just a precaution. The doctors had your sister do some head X-rays. They should have them back shortly."

She leaves, and I walk over to the side of Sophie's exam bed, worried. "What happened?" I ask, wincing inside at the anger in my voice. I don't want to sound angry. I'm just worried. "Sophie?"

"I got into an accident," she says, sulking. I reach for her hand but she brushes me away. "I'm fine, they say I just hit my head pretty good. The doctor thinks I might have a mild concussion. They're letting me go if the X-Rays look okay."

"Shit, I'm so sorry," I whisper, wanting to hug her but not wanting to be rejected again. Instead, I'm forced to cross my arms over my chest to keep from reaching out. "I'm just glad you're okay. How'd it happen?"

Sophie turns her head and stares at me tight-lipped. With each passing second, the dread in my stomach grows. "Please don't do this. Tell the truth, Sophie. Were you driving? Were you . . . drinking?"

Sophie's lip curls, her eyes flaring in hurt anger. "No, but Jax was," she admits. "It was just one beer though!"

Her admission hits me like a punch in the gut. "What?"

"Jax!" Sophie half yells. "We were going out. He took a wrong turn and hit a pole."

Anger flares in my chest. I can't believe this. A dark thing twists deep in my heart, an evil thing that I can't control, and I grab the railing on Sophie's bed, squeezing the metal so tightly that it starts to creak. "I thought I told you not to see him anymore!"

"Yeah, well, you also told me you were going to spend more time with me, remember that?" she shoots back. "So sorry, Jake. I got bored when you kept going out all the time. You're never around lately," she says, not looking at Roxy but making her point. "He was giving me the attention I want. He at least would listen for longer than the ten minutes it takes to make eggs and hash browns!"

I almost see red, and my hands pull harder, the railing on Sophie's bed whining in protest. I hear Roxy gasp in hurt, and I stare at Sophie, my jaw clenched so hard my teeth ache. I could've lost my sister because of this fuck nut. I warned him last time, and then he goes and drinks before taking her out? I want to choke him with my bare hands.

"I don't give a fuck . . ."

"Hey," Roxy says softly, trying to place a calming hand on my shoulder, but I shrug her off, my temper on the edge of losing control.

"That guy doesn't give a shit about you!" I hiss at Sophie. "I could've lost you tonight!"

Sophie stares at me coldly, unmoved. She looks at Roxy, then looks away. "You have a woman in your life. You don't need me anymore."

Her words hit me like a ton of bricks. And it fucking hurts because lately, it's true. I've been putting everything first but Sophie. "You know that's not true," I whisper. "You're one of the most—" I catch myself. "You are the most important person in my life."

Sophie snorts. "Don't lie to yourself, darling big brother. I'm at least number four or five on your list. But it's okay, I know I'm a burden."

I open my mouth, about to yell at her, but Roxy tugs on my arm desperately. "Not here, Jake. This isn't the time or the place for this conversation."

She's right. Fuming, I spin on my heel and stalk out of the room. When I get out, I slam my fist against the wall, Sophie's words echoing around in my head. She can't understand. All of this has been for her, too!

I turn to storm down the hallway. I need a drink, and I saw a Coke machine on the way here. Roxy is on my ass though, and I can hear her rushing to catch up with me. "Hey, wait up!" She grabs me by the arm, and I stop. "I know you're mad and upset after everything that happened, but your sister has a point—"

"That I put you before her?" I growl, staring at Roxy. "Yeah, she has a point. That I've just risked everything, rolled the fucking dice on my future, her future, Nathan's future, everyone's future on some stupid fucking fireworks. And I watched it all go up in smoke. I risked it all because I let my dick overrule my brain. Everything's all fucked up right now. We're all fucked up. I'm all fucked up. And to be honest, I don't want to hear any shit about how terrible of a brother and guardian I am!"

Roxy's face goes white, and I hate myself for what I just said. I shouldn't be talking right now. There's so much emotion running through me that I don't even know what I'm saying. "If that's how you truly feel."

She turns and runs down the hall, bursting through the double doors and knocking an orderly out of the way. "Roxy," I yell, trying to chase her. "Wait!"

"Mr. Stone?" a voice calls behind me, and I turn to see a doctor with an obviously concerned expression on his face standing outside Sophie's exam room. "Is everything okay?"

I can see that the doc wants to talk about Sophie, and as much as it tears my heart out of my fucking chest that I can't run Roxy down, I turn and slump against the wall. "No, everything's not okay," I whisper, rubbing furiously at my watering eyes. "But what's going on with Sophie?"

The doctor starts talking, but I'm having trouble focusing on what he's saying.

I shouldn't have said what I said.

Now both of the women I love most hate me.

CHAPTER 25

ROXY

"It's all my fault," I wail, my eyes burning as I rock back and forth on my bed in my sister's arms. "I nearly got you guys killed."

Mindy brushes my hair out of my eyes and gives me a comforting look. "Hush, baby girl, we're all fine. I think Grandma even had fun."

"But I wrecked the club!" I cry. I don't bother telling her that it was one of my band members who caused the fire, because it had been my idea to practice with the pyro in the first place.

Mindy rubs my back, shaking her head. "So? They've got to have coverage. Nathan strikes me as the kind of guy who'd make sure of that."

"And Jake hates me!" I sob, collapsing as I ignore her attempt at practicality. I feel warm arms wrap around me, and I turn, burying my face in my sister's chest as hot, bitter tears scald my eyes. "He practically said that I've wrecked everything!"

"Hush," Mindy says, stroking my hair. I have to hand it to Hannah. She knew exactly what I needed when I fled from the hospital, nearly sobbing already. She sent a few text messages, and less than ten minutes after we got home, there was a quiet knock and Mindy was there, changed out of her club wear. Without a word, she bustled me into my room, stripped me down, and helped me into my fuzziest, fluffiest pajamas.

Now, she's doing what she does better than anyone in the world—comforting me. "It's going to be okay, Roxy."

Mindy hugs me tighter, and I hold her close. "He hates me though. I'm sure Sophie hates me, too. I took him away from her, and that's why she was out with Jax."

"Give him some time," Mindy reassures me. "As for Sophie . . . I think we both know she didn't see this Jax just because Jake wasn't spending time with her. An older guy showed her attention and she liked it."

I sob. "I still fucked up everything. I feel so fucking shitty."

Mindy pushes my head back, looking me in the eyes with a stern but loving expression. "Don't you dare put all of this on yourself, Roxy. Sophie's young and was taken advantage of. If anyone is to be blamed, it's that perv Jax. I'm of half a mind to have Oliver and Gavin pay him a visit."

"It'd just make everything worse." I sigh, laying my head back on Mindy's chest. "Min . . . I'll never get another chance. I thought that this was going to be my big break. I'm so sorry, Mindy."

"Sorry for what?" Mindy asks.

"That you came out here to see all of this mess."

Mindy chuckles and kisses me on the cheek. "Roxy, I seem to remember dragging you through a nest of lies for an entire week, all the way to the altar of a wedding, only to tell you that the whole thing was a charade. If that's not an absolute mess, I don't know what is."

"True, but you didn't burn anything down," I protest. "And you still ended up marrying Oliver."

Mindy laughs softly. "Baby, I don't care if you blew up half the city. You're still my baby sister and I fucking love you. You hear me? I fucking love you. And if Jake really loves you, he'll get over his anger. He'll realize that he's wrong and come here crawling on his hands and knees to apologize for talking like an ass to you."

"I just don't know . . . I really don't," I whisper. "It feels like my life is over."

"Well, if it is, then I'm ending your life in style. I noticed it before —you've got some Chocolate Cherry Garcia in your fridge, and I'm thinking the two of us need to carb up before catching some Zs. Oliver already knows I'm going to be staying the night, so you can't chase me out."

I swallow my fresh tears, nodding. "Okay . . . if you say so."

"I do. Now let's go get some chocolate."

CHAPTER 26

JAKE

"What?" Nathan yells into the phone. "Listen, you stupid bitch, I already fucking told you four times that it was an accident. You know what? I'm done talking with you. Put your fucking supervisor on the line." He shakes his head, growling deep in his chest. "What do you mean they're unavailable? I don't care if you have to route this to the fucking CEO. And yes, I'm saying it's a fucking accident! Huh? Go fuck yourself."

Nathan slams down the phone, shaking his head angrily. "Jesus, and I thought those assholes at the SEC were bad. These insurance pricks make the SEC and IRS look like Mr. Fucking Rogers goes to Sesame Street."

I sit in my chair, gripping the glass of mineral water I've been sipping, wishing it were something stronger. We're sitting in the back room of the club on two of the smaller couches that were saved from the mess that was the VIP section.

The fire gutted a lot of the main room of Club Jasmine. The bar is a total loss, the marble top cracked and soot-streaked. As Nathan put it the first time we walked in yesterday, "Holy shit, there's a fuckton of damage."

We've already started, financing everything through our own names and funds. It's not much right now. I can hear the workers out front, a half-dozen guys clearing out the mess. While they do that, Nathan and I are back here, running numbers and trying to get the insurance company to get off their asses. If they don't, a good chunk of our fortune is gonna go down the tubes and it's all going be because of . . .

A hard, bitter lump forms in my throat at the thought. I won't let that angry, stupid fucking idea enter my head again. It's not true. I'm just grateful that Nathan isn't playing the blame game. Still, despite Nathan being my bro, despite all we've been through, I'd happily tell him to go fuck himself if he tried. I'm dealing with enough between Roxy and my sister.

"Shit, man. I really hope they come through," Nathan says after a moment in a calmer tone. When I don't say anything, he glances at me and sighs. "It's gonna fuckin' hurt if they don't."

"Did they?" I ask, already knowing the answer. I'm just still in a haze. I should be at Franklin Consolidated, but I talked with Elena this morning. She's going to send all the files I need to look at electronically and keep me up to date on what I need to be there for. Right now, that place is the least of my damn worries.

Nathan snorts. "Fuck, no. They're dumb as hell. They're saying they want the fire marshal's report, and I told them five times I don't have it. For fuck's sake, I talked with the guy this morning, and he said that even a rush job would take him another week to

226

get together. In the meantime, I've given them the video footage. We just need to get the fucking repairs underway."

I rub my face, feeling the unfamiliar rasp of stubble. I forgot to shave this morning. My head is pounding with a headache that should be in the fucking *Guinness Book of World Records*. Looking around the room, I sigh at how depressing it all is. I don't even know why I came in. There's nothing for me to do. At least Nathan can do his trading with his tablet. I can't do half of my fucking job sitting back here.

But while Franklin is my job, Club Jasmine was my dream. My way out. It was the thing that said I was working for myself, not for some nameless, faceless mass of shareholders and some board of rich assholes who wouldn't understand what I've had to do to get to this point. Club Jasmine might have been just a nightclub, but it was magical when it was open. It's my baby, and I feel compelled to check on it. Every day we're closed is like a knife in my chest . . . and other than bleed money, there isn't a damn thing I can do about it.

"How's Sophie holding up through this?" Nathan asks after a moment. "I mean, the situation between you two."

"She's not talking to me," I say. "I was making progress before the accident. I mean, I thought I was. Sure, I'd spent a lot of time with Roxy and getting this place ready, but . . . now she's down again. Maybe I said some things I shouldn't have. I got so mad when I found out she was with the same asshole who brought her in here."

"You want to pay the fucker a visit?" Nathan asks. "I gave him a little speech before I let him go, but maybe he needs a little more convincing."

I think about it, then shake my head. "No. I'm still debating on it, but if I do, I'll handle it myself."

Nathan snorts, shaking his head. "Teenage girls, man. Shit, even when we were teenagers, I preferred them older. I wouldn't wish that death sentence on anybody. All hormones and Lifetime Channel bullshit."

Despite my sour mood, I have to chuckle at his crude way with words. "Sophie's actually not that bad. In fact, up until now, she's been practically an angel. I guess it was gonna catch up with me sooner or later."

"Actually, I'd say you've done pretty damn good with this."

I turn to Nathan, so exhausted and hurting that I speak my mind. "Nate, about the fire . . . I mean, you've gotta blame me some."

"Bullshit," Nathan says with a harsh laugh. "I'm not a damn child. I agreed to the fucking pyro idea. Hell, I've spent days kicking myself over it, too. Roxy told me as they were getting on stage that they wanted to nix the pyro. I swear I passed it along. I even talked to the stage tech. He says the same. Nobody can find the damn pyro tech though. Someone didn't get the fucking message."

"Sounds like there's more than enough blame to go around and we all get to take a bite of the shit sandwich," I whisper. "Thank you for telling me."

There's a knock at the door, and I get up, swaying as the room spins. Nathan's up in a flash, patting me on the arm. "Yo, you go home, Jake. I got this shit. You go take care of Sophie."

I nod as Nathan leads me to the door. Opening it, we see John, who's been acting as crew chief. He looks different in his old army pants and combat boots, good for the work at hand. "Nathan—"

"Just a moment, John," Nathan says. "Call Jake a cab, and then tell me what's on your mind."

John nods and disappears, and I give Nathan a grateful but exhausted nod. "Thanks, man. I owe you."

Nathan shakes his head. "Don't sweat it."

✳

WE PULL UP TO THE ADDRESS THAT I GOT FROM SOPHIE'S PHONE, a medium-sized house in what looks like a middle-class neighborhood out in the burbs. Luckily for me, Jax is already sitting out on the porch with a blonde girl on his arm, talking, laughing, and carrying on like he didn't just almost kill my sister. I know I told Nathan I was still thinking about this, but I can't stop myself.

Seeing him laugh and joke around makes me even more mad. I jump out of the car and shut the door just a little too hard before telling the cabbie to wait, stalking up the sidewalk to the house.

Be careful, a little voice warns in the back of my head. *You don't want to do anything that you'll end up regretting.*

"What's up?" I ask casually as I walk up.

Jax's grins slowly fades from his face as he recognizes me, and he turns a little pale. "Nothing much," he says finally, a cool note entering his voice. "Just chilling with my girl, Erica."

I sneer. "Your girl, huh?"

He nods, trying to act hard when I know he's a scared little bitch. "Yeah, my girl."

That little smirk pisses me off and I can't help it. Without warning, I snatch him up by the front of his shirt and slam him against the wall.

"Hey!" Erica cries, getting up from her seat, startled by my violent behavior. "Stop it!"

I ignore her, set in getting my point across. "You might not have been legally drunk, so the cops might be done with you, but you could've seriously hurt Sophie. I'm just going to say this once. Stay the fuck away from my sister or I'm going to come back here, and next time, I won't be so nice. You won't need a *girl*, because you'll be missing a set of balls," I growl menacingly in his face. "You understand me?"

Jax gasps, his face turning a dark shade of red as he nods violently. "Yes, I understand! I won't touch her, I swear!"

I hold him in place for a moment longer, letting him feel true terror, then let him go. He comes away with a gasp, grabbing his throat. "Good," I growl. "I don't want to have to come back here again."

"What the hell was that for?" Erica demands as I step away, running forward to wrap her arm around Jax's shoulder as he wheezes.

"Dude's an asshole, and I've had enough of him getting my little sister into things she shouldn't be in," I say. "Ask him about last weekend."

With that said, I turn and walk back to the cab. Behind me, I hear her demand of Jax, "What the hell is he talking about?"

As I get in the cab and he starts the engine, I witness the two arguing, gesturing wildly at each other. The cabbie turns back and gives me a questioning look, but he doesn't say a word. Before we pull off, I see that Erica's had enough. She slaps Jax across the face, spins on her heels, and walks off.

Chuckling, we drive off, and I can't stop the smile that forms on my face.

❄

THE APARTMENT IS SILENT AS A TOMB WHEN I WALK IN, AND EXCEPT for the hum of the fridge in the kitchen, I can't hear anything.

"Sophie?" I ask, pulling off my suit jacket and draping it over the empty sofa. The remote for the TV is untouched, right where I left it this morning to check the news, and I grow more worried. I dropped her off this morning but sent a driver to pick her up after school. I didn't hear anything about a problem, but still . . .

I check my home office. Sophie uses my desktop computer from time to time. Nothing, and I grow more worried. Walking down the hallway, I stop outside her room, relief rushing through me as I hear something inside. I almost decide to let her be, but instead I knock softly. "Sophie?"

There's no answer, and I'm about to turn away when there's a soft reply from the other side. "Come in."

I open the door and see her stretched out on her bed, watching one of the stupid *Real Housewives* shows. Way too much unneeded drama for me. "Hey."

"Hey," she says, sitting up, and to my relief, turning off the TV. "You're home early. For you, at least."

I think of making a wiseass remark, but instead I stop. This isn't the time for it. "I came home because I wanted to see how you were doing. Whatcha been up to?"

Sophie flops back, waving a hand at the TV. "Just watching TV. Jax tried to call me but I didn't answer."

I step into her room, sitting on the edge of the bed and raising an eyebrow. "Why not?"

Sophie looks embarrassed, and deep down, I see a little bit of hurt, too. "I saw him with some chick at a party on Instagram. I know of her. She's a total skank."

"Oh," I say quietly, glad that Sophie figured out that Jax is no good for her but sad that she's hurt.

Sophie reaches over, putting a hand on my arm. "I'm sorry, Jake."

She starts trembling, and I pull her up, giving her a hug. "I'm sorry too, Sophie. Because you're right—you're my sister and I should have given you more attention."

Sophie hugs me back. "I should've listened to you. You were right. He's a piece of shit."

I hold in my grin. I'm happy I paid the little fucker a visit, though she doesn't need to know that. "We all make mistakes," I reply. "I think I've made one or two in my life." It feels good to be hugging her again, like we're back on the right path, the two of us against the world like it's always been.

Sophie chuckles, and I notice that I haven't eaten. "You hungry? How about I make dinner for us?"

"I could eat," Sophie says, letting go. "I'll help."

We go out to the kitchen, where I pull out some kale and bell peppers while Sophie roots around in the fridge. "Pork chops?"

"Anything would be delicious for me," I reply, washing the greens. Sophie nods, and silence falls over the kitchen. I want to make sure everything is smoothed over, but I don't know how to start. Finally, I clear my throat. "Sophie, you've always been my number one priority, and as much time as the club and work take me away, I do it for us so that we can have a good life. I'm trying to do right by Mom and Dad and give you the life they'd want for you. But I don't know what I'm doing, so I need you to help me here. Talk to me because I sure as fuck don't know the first thing about teenage girls."

Sophie takes out the kitchen knife and starts butterflying the chops. "I know you're trying your best, Jake. You've done well by me. I mean, you took me to get my first training bra. How many brothers can say that?"

I chuckle, shaking my head. "Yeah . . . but seriously, Sophie, you are number one to me. Listen, I'm gonna promise you now that I'm going to spend more time with you. Just the two of us, like it used to be."

"But what about Roxy? Have you talked to her?" she asks.

Just hearing Roxy's name hurts, and I shake my head. "After I left your room, I said some pretty stupid shit to her in the hallway. I basically told her that all of this was her fault. I don't think she wants to hear from me."

Sophie sets the knife down, turning to look at me. "You haven't tried to talk to her since? What the hell are you waiting for?"

"Oh, I tried," I say quietly. "She's not picking up her phone, and she wasn't in the office today."

"And you just give up?" Sophie asks, turning back and picking up the knife. She butterflies the other chop, shaking her head. "That's not like you, Jake. You could do more."

I glance over at Sophie. She's dead serious. She puts the knife back down and goes to get the skillets. "You think so? And you're okay with that?"

"Me?" Sophie says, looking down. "Of course I am. I said some things I didn't mean, too. I was talking out of anger and I'm sorry. I'm turning seventeen soon, Jake. I've got a year and some change of high school left, then hopefully I'm going to college. You need someone you can spend the rest of your life with. If you think she's it, stop wasting time. You deserve it."

She's right. No more waiting for her to answer the phone.

CHAPTER 27

ROXY

"Get up, Roxy!" I hear someone say. In the near week that I've been calling off work, I've rarely left my room, preferring instead to spend as much time as I can wrapped in the blackness of my blanket and sleep.

I groan from underneath the covers, barely awake. "Leave me alone," I moan. "I took a shower yesterday!"

"No!" snaps the voice, whom I finally recognize as Mindy. "I'm not going away. I have to leave in a few days and you're being disrespectful to your family. Now get up!"

I look at Mindy, but my tirade dies on my lips as I see her. She's standing there, her hands on her hips, pissed like I haven't seen her in a very long time. "Look at you. You look a hot mess. You've fallen apart. I already checked with Hannah. You won't go to work. You haven't eaten in three days. And why?"

"Because I—"

Mindy cuts me off. "Because you feel sorry for yourself! I know

235

you feel bad about what happened, but you can't let it control your life."

Her words hit me hard, and I look down, catching a whiff of myself. I *am* a fucking mess. I feel so horrible, guilty and ashamed that my family came all this way to see me, and here I am avoiding them because I can't deal with the shame and hurt I feel. "Mindy . . ."

Mindy won't relent. "The past five days, every time we called, you wouldn't answer. I called your home phone and even talked with Hannah, trying to get you to come to the hotel. Then I come by today, only to find out that Hannah hasn't even been able to get your ass out of bed? Your room smells like the zombie apocalypse, and I'm not putting up with it anymore!"

I feel like the worst person in the world. I swear I've almost had a mental breakdown over what happened. Starting a fire in the club, feeling responsible for Sophie getting in a crash, the music guy telling me I was done, and I feel like I've lost Jake. I'm just ready to give up. "I'm sorry," I whisper, tears trickling down my cheeks. "I just feel terrible for causing a shit storm."

Mindy reaches down, pulling me to my feet. "Well, we're changing everything starting now. Do you know what today is?"

"What?" I ask, and Mindy wipes a tear from my cheek with her thumb, just like she used to do when we were kids.

"The day you said you were going to the studio to record that song you wrote."

I immediately shake my head, trying to pull back. "No way, not that. What's the point? That's a waste of time."

Besides, the man I love and wrote it for won't even be there. He's never going to hear it. It hurts to even think about Jake. When Mindy says I haven't eaten, that's why. I think about Jake, and my stomach hurts so much that I can't even imagine food.

"Yes, you are. You're going to shower and eat, and we're heading downtown to record that song."

"There's no point!" I protest. "You heard that asshole. That was my one and only chance!"

Mindy grabs me by the shoulders, looking into my eyes. "The point is, you owe it to yourself. Do it for you. Fuck everything and everyone else. You go in there, and you put that thing on disc for you. Or so help me God, I'm going to introduce you to realms of pain you can't even imagine!"

Her corny line breaks through, and I smirk. "Oh, how's that? I've already heard you sing."

"Yeah, but you've never heard Gavin sing," Mindy says. "Don't make me get ugly on you."

❄️

You better bring it, boy,

I've only got tonight

I'm leaving town tomorrow, I can't stay the night

Have places to go, Catching an early flight

If you want me to stay, you gotta come correct

My heart's almost yours, take that final step

Heartstopper, Heartstopper

Can you feel it in my chest?

Heartstopper, Heartstopper,

Fingers on my breast

Your touch is electric,

Has been from the start

Give it to me, baby,

Or I'ma stop your heart.

I let out a breath, gasping for air as I sing the last note and the club banging beat plays in the background. I don't know how they got the music mixed so perfectly so quickly, but it's amazing.

Maybe I'm wasting my time. Maybe this is nothing more than a final middle finger to anyone who's doubted me. But for the past hour and forty-five minutes that I've been in the recording booth, I've felt a change coming over me. All the worries and pains I've been going through fell away. It was just me, the music, and my heart.

"That's the one!" Oliver shouts in elation to the studio engineer, a nerdy looking blond guy with tiger-striped wide-rim glasses sitting beside him in the system room. "You got what you need. Get to work!"

I tilt my head, watching as Gavin and Oliver start chatting together excitedly while the studio engineer gets his computers together. Scowling, I pull off my headphones and talk into the mic. "What the hell are you two so excited about?"

I seriously don't know what these two are up to. They're nearly buzzing as they come into the studio.

They both grin at me like a pair of mischievous school boys, not saying a word.

"Spit it out!" I beg as their smiles become infectious. "Or I'ma make Mindy come up in here and sing Barney."

They both laugh at me, but Oliver is the one to speak. "Gavin and I have decided to invest a little in you using what I like to call 'fuck you money'. Tomorrow, in ten different time slots on the local radio, *Heartstopper* is going to be played."

"Yeah," adds Gavin. "Not only that, but we're going to release it on iTunes, Amazon, all that. You don't need a label to self-publish."

I blink, shocked. "You two . . . you're batshit crazy!" I exclaim heatedly. "You realize this isn't going to sell shit, right?"

"Who cares?" Gavin says with a shrug. "This isn't about the sales."

"I care!" I protest. "Guys, I tried iTunes already. I put a whole album on there. It sold exactly one hundred copies, and I suspect five of them were you guys!"

"Seven," Gavin says matter-of-factly. "I wanted it to be a round number."

"See!" I say. "You prove my point!"

"Girl, stop with all that fussing. You're amazing," Mindy, who's been out in the hallway and talking with the sound guy, says, coming in. "It's going on there or so help me God, I'm going to turn into Iggy Azalea and treat you guys to my first rap song."

I throw my hands up in immediate surrender. "Oh, hell no. You win!"

Everyone in the studio laughs and Mindy says, "Girl, I promise you, Leigh's going to be singing all the lyrics and copying her auntie's twerk routine by lunch tomorrow."

I grin, the first one I've had in awhile. It feels unfamiliar on my face—that's how down I've been over the past few days. "Well, someone has to teach your daughter some life skills."

Everyone laughs while we close up the studio, turning in the keys to the front desk.

"Mindy," I say as we leave the studio. "Wait up."

"Sure," she says, waving Oliver and Gavin on. "You two go. We'll see you at the hotel." The guys leave, and she turns to me, smiling. "What's up?"

"I can't go back to my job," I say, shaking my head.

"Is it the job or is it Jake?" Mindy asks, and I shrug. She pulls me in for a hug, and I gotta admit, it feels good. "I see. Well, if you find that you can't, why don't you quit your job and come back home with us?"

"After what happened, I feel so guilty. I can't face Jake. I just can't. Not only because of the club, but it will just be so awkward after what we had going."

Mindy nods. "We can help you back on your feet. Hell, I might even have a job for you in the cafe."

When I think about it, what is here for me if there's no Jake? Work is going to be so awkward. I just can't imagine it. I want to go to Jake, but now I can't bear to look at him, not after destroying his hard work and his relationship with his sister.

"I think I might take you up on that offer. Give me the weekend to think about it."

CHAPTER 28

JAKE

*C*oming into the office Friday morning, the first thing I do when I get off the elevator is look over at Roxy's desk.

Empty.

Again.

I sigh and go into my office, setting my briefcase down on my desk before slumping into my chair. I rub at my temples. It's only eight forty-five and I've already got a headache. I know why, too. Sure, Sophie's talking to me and the club's cleaned out now, but there's an aching hole in my chest. The same hole that's in a cubicle just outside my office.

Elena drops off something for me to look over. I don't really give a damn. A familiar figure goes by the office, and I look up, but it's just Hannah. I can't stand this any longer. I pick up my phone. "Elena?"

"Yes, sir?"

"Have Hannah Fowler report to my office immediately, please."

"Of course, sir," Elena says in that tone of voice that says *Great, he's doing something crazy again. FML.*

Still, Elena's a professional, and fewer than five minutes later, Hannah knocks on my office door. "You wanted to see me, sir?"

I nod at the chair. "Relax, Hannah. I think you know what this is about. How is she doing? I haven't seen her all week and she isn't answering my texts. I miss her."

"There isn't much I can tell you," Hannah says. "Mindy dragged her out of the apartment Wednesday, and she hasn't been back since. Honestly, I'm sort of glad she's out for a while. Her room was getting funky."

I nod, and it breaks my heart to hear that. "Do you have any idea what she's doing?"

Hannah shakes her head. "Sorry. She sent me a text last night saying to keep my ears open and that she'd have more information for me today, but that's it."

I swallow, leaning back. "Okay. Well, if you see her, talk to her, whatever . . . tell her I'd like to get in touch?"

"Of course," Hannah says. "Will that be all?"

"Yes, thank you," I say, when suddenly, my office door opens, and Elena's there.

"Turn on the radio!" Elena says, running over to the old-fashioned FM radio that came with my office. "You have to hear this!"

She switches on the stereo, punching in 97.3, the local pop station. She cranks the volume and turns, giving me a look as the DJ goes on. " *. . . so after the recent fire, Roxy decided she needed to say she was sorry for the incident. And as a thanks to her fans from Club*

242

Jasmine, here's the song that she was going to debut a week ago. Heart-stopper."

I jump to my feet as the background track that I'd heard only once before starts bumping and thumping on my stereo. Seconds later, Roxy's pure, sensual voice fills my office.

> It's been too long, gotta get out
> Hittin up the new spot with my girl
> Lookin' sexy as hell, workin' the floor
> Hoping to give this place a whirl
> Nothin' working so far, I'm getting desperate
> I can't stand this creep, where is my Superman?
> He's late, but I don't give a damn.
> One glance in his eyes, and I know what I need.
> Gimme mouth to mouth, because he's a total
>   Heartstopper.
> Heartstopper, Heartstopper
> Can you feel it in my chest?
> Heartstopper, Heartstopper,
> Fingers on my breast
> Your touch is electric,
> Has been from the start
> Give it to me baby,
> Or I'ma stop your heart.
> We head to the back, his lips on my neck
> My knees shaking, my eyes rolling back
> I feel like I'm drugged, everything's a blur,
> And I can't believe when I grab his . . .
> The bed's right there, he pushes me down,
> I bite my lip, I'm not like this,
> But I won't stop, can't stop,

I have to have his kiss.
Heartstopper, Heartstopper
Can you feel it in my chest?
Heartstopper, Heartstopper,
Fingers on my breast
Your touch is electric,
Has been from the start
Give it to me baby,
Or I'ma stop your heart.
He's looking at me, and I know he's feeling the same
This isn't a dance, this isn't just one night.
Somehow it's become more than a game,
He pulls off his shirt, I can't believe the sight.
I'm leaving town tomorrow, I can't stay the night
Have places to go, catching an early flight
If you want me to stay, you gotta come correct
My heart's almost yours, take that final step
Heartstopper, Heartstopper
Can you feel it in my chest?
Heartstopper, Heartstopper,
Fingers on my breast
Your touch is electric,
Has been from the start
Give it to me baby,
Or I'ma stop your heart.

The final notes fade away, and I stare at the radio as smooth silence drifts over the radio for a few seconds before the DJ comes back on. *"Wow. You know, I've been in the radio game for a long time, going on twenty years now, and I haven't heard a song this hot from a new singer in—well hell, I'm going to get in trouble with my bosses, but fuck it, let's play that every hour!"*

"That's Roxy?" Elena says. "I mean, I heard she was a singer but . . ."

Suddenly, my cellphone rings and I pick it up. It's Nathan. "Nathan, not now."

"What the fuck do you mean, not now?" Nathan says in my ear, sounding as breathless as the rest of us. "Roxy was just on the radio."

"I know," I gasp, looking around my office. My body is burning, my chest tight and my stomach twisting. I know what I need to do. "But I need to think."

"Look, just listen up for a moment," Nathan says, laughing. "I just got off the phone with the insurance company. They got back to me, and they're cutting us a check. All of it, full policy value."

"That's great, Nathan, but right now, I need you to do something else," I say, grabbing my suit coat and pulling it on. Elena and Hannah are still staring at me, trying to figure out what the hell I'm doing. "Is there anything we can do to escalate the cleanup? Triple the amount of workers if we need to, get the club cleaned and patched up. If we can't do that, then we're doing this thing in the fucking parking lot in front of the fountain. That still works, right?"

"Uh, It works, but what are you talking about?" Nathan asks.

"I've got a woman I need to win back. And she's got a concert to put on. Roxy's going to sing *Heartstopper* live for her fans. No matter what."

I hang up my phone and head for my office door. As I reach the handle, Elena calls out. "Sir!"

"What?" I ask, turning back.

"There is a board meeting in forty-five minutes," Elena says. "You're supposed to be there."

I button my suit coat, nodding, and head back, grabbing my laptop and briefcase before I turn back around. "I forgot, but I'm still leaving. Tell them I had something very important to attend to. If they don't accept it . . . well, they can fire me."

CHAPTER 29

ROXY

"*And now, that local artist who's shooting up the charts. She's reached number twenty-five on the iTunes download charts already . . . here's Roxy with* Heartstopper!"

I look over at the radio, shaking my head as I reach over and turn it off. While I'm amazed and shocked that my song has gained so much traction, I don't need to listen to it again. I suspect that most of the buzz in downloads is from locals who saw me at the club, but it still feels good.

Mr. Felix is sitting in my lap, purring. It helps, even though I still feel a little down. Looking around the apartment, it's hard. In packing my stuff up, this place just doesn't look at all like the apartment I've shared with Hannah.

Some of the things are the same, the voice in my head says. *This sofa is the place you and Jake first had sex.*

I run my hands along the cushion, sighing. Setting Felix aside, I glance at the clock. It's nearly five thirty now, and Hannah said she'd be home around six. I promised her that I'd get some delivery Chinese food for us to share. I feel like hell, running out on her, but she said that she's already got people lined up to share rent with her. I think she's trying to make me feel better about it, but I hope it's true.

There's a knock at the door, and I set Felix aside. Going over, I look through the peephole to see that it's Mindy, and I open up. "Hey, Min, what's up?"

"What's up?" she asks, grinning. "I just heard you on the radio again, and you ask what's up? I see you've got the jaded pop star act down already."

I smile slightly, letting Mindy in. She looks around, whistling. "Wow, you got packed quickly. Is Hannah upset?"

"No, she says she understands, and we're going to have some girl time later. I mean, I still haven't turned in my resignation to the office. I've got another three days of vacation time built up."

"That's good," Mindy says. "So where is your stuff, anyway?"

"I packed up what I'm going to take. It's in my room. Feels strange to be living out of a suitcase again. Well, partially. I gave Hannah a lot of my office clothes. If I ever have to put on a professional pencil skirt and those damn heels again, I'm going to scream."

Mindy chuckles, nodding. "The advantages of owning a cafe. I wear New Balances to work most days. The only heels I have I wear when Oliver and I—"

"TMI!"

Mindy laughs. "Come on, let's get the hell out of here."

"Where?" I ask. "I mean, I promised Hannah dinner!"

"Send her a text. She'll understand. And if she is upset, tell her Oliver Steele will pay for her to go out to dinner tomorrow anywhere in town."

I can't help it. I smirk. "More of his 'fuck you' money?"

"Something like that. Come on, the whole family's waiting for you."

❄

I WAKE UP WITH A START, SURPRISED THAT I DOZED OFF. PART OF IT was that I've been getting over my depression, and part of it has been that my body clock is still so screwed up. I blink, looking around. "Where are we?"

Mindy, who's driving, glances over. "Ha, you don't recognize it?"

I sit up some more, looking out the side windows. Unfortunately, Mindy's got some of those dark tinted windows and it takes me a minute. "We're heading downtown. I thought you said we were getting together with everyone. The hotel's out near the airport, right?"

"Right both times, but I didn't say that the rest of the fam was at the hotel."

I'm immediately suspicious, my shock growing as we make a right turn and I see Club Jasmine. "What the hell are we doing here?"

"Trust me," Mindy says, parking out front. The amount of work that's been done is amazing. There's still some scorch marks on the front, but all of the fire smell is gone. Mindy leads me up the steps, opening the door. It's dark inside, and I blink, trying to adjust to the gloom. "Well, here we are."

"Mindy, this is so not cool," I complain. "I mean, why remind me . . ."

"She's baaaa-aaaaaack!" an electronic voice booms out of the darkness, and suddenly, stage lights blossom. The floor is still a mostly scarred wreck, but they've swept and cleared out an area in the middle, where the bare concrete is surrounded by lights.

Hannah steps out of the shadows, grinning. "Our guest of honor has arrived. Have a seat."

"Mindy, what is going on?" I ask as the lights come up and I see Mom, Grandma, Brianna . . .

"Hit it!" Hannah says as Mindy leads me over to a chair and sits me down. Hannah moves out of the light as bumping dance music starts up. There's a silly little curtain, nothing more than a rope with a sheet hung over it, and Hannah giggles as she gets on the mic again. "Welcome to the Club Jasmine Gentlemen's Revue!"

Suddenly, the curtain twitches, and Bertha comes running out, yapping furiously. "Goddammit, Mary Jo, if you don't stop dragging that thing with you everywhere, I'm not going with you anywhere anymore!"

Mom gets up and chases Bertha down while I lean over to Mindy. "What the hell is this?"

"Just enjoy. Think of it as more fuck you money," Mindy says, patting my shoulder. "Trust me, you'll enjoy it."

Mom gets Bertha under control and sits down, grumbling to Grandma. "You know, you've had pets too."

"Whatever," Grandma says. "Bring on the flesh parade!"

"Up first," Hannah says, trying not to laugh, "is our very own superstar, former All-Pro running back, Gavin 'Anaconda' Adams!"

Brianna, of course, claps the loudest as Gavin emerges, clad in what I can only call a stripper's version of a Navy uniform. Skintight white pants are underneath his cheap white tunic as he adjusts the bill of his cap. Lifting a microphone to his lips, the music changes, and I groan.

Gavin starts to sing *Up Where We Belong* by Joe Cocker, and even Brianna has to clap her hands over her ears.

"I love you, but never again!" she screams as Gavin shrugs and drops his microphone. Ripping off his tunic top, the music changes into a techno/club remix of the classic Joe Cocker song, and he gives his wife a lap dance that leaves Brianna in a fit of laughter before he sashays offstage.

Mindy's laughing her ass off as Brianna wipes her forehead with a hand towel. She looks over at Mindy and me, chuckling. "I didn't marry him for his singing."

Hannah chuckles, shaking her head. "And now, for our second act . . . Oliver Steele!"

Oliver comes out, and my jaw drops as he comes out dressed in perhaps the most ridiculous outfit I've ever seen him in, a leather set of hot pants and a motorcycle vest. "What the hell do you and he get up to?" Grandma asks. "That sure as hell ain't what I expected!"

Mindy's beet red as Oliver picks up the mic and starts singing *Do You Really Want To Hurt Me?* As he sings, he dances, and he's even worse than Gavin, Mindy blushing and laughing uproariously as he caterwauls his way through the song. "Brad would love this!" I laugh as Oliver peels off his vest to show off his chiseled torso.

Mindy's flushed herself as Oliver retreats behind the curtain, and Hannah takes a minute to laugh. "Don't quit your day jobs. Either of you."

"So who's next?" Grandma asks. "I love those men, but damn if my ears aren't bleeding."

"Next . . . a very special performance," Hannah says. The music slows, not the silly club mixes, but I've heard this in clubs before.

The voice I hear next shocks me. I've never heard it like this before.

I watch in pure amazement as Jake comes through the curtain, stripped to the waist, his body gleaming under the lights as he approaches me with pure love in his eyes, singing *Take My Breath Away* by Berlin.

The song finishes, Jake saying nothing as he lowers the microphone, and I feel tears in my eyes. "Jake . . ."

"HIT IT!" a booming voice comes from the back, and suddenly, Gavin and Oli are back, having changed clothes, thank God, this time with Nathan joining them as they suddenly break into the Backstreet Boys' *I Want It That Way.*

"My fucking ears!" Mindy screams in laughter as Gavin and Oliver both sing their parts. Nathan's even worse, but he's a good sport as he swings his hips in front of Grandma and Mom.

I barely notice, my eyes on Jake as he sings, reaching out for me. I lift my hand to his, not even realizing it until he pulls me to my feet. I look in his eyes as he sings the final lines.

The music fades away as the other ladies clap, but I can't do anything but look at Jake. "Roxy, my sweet, beautiful Angel," he says softly, wrapping his arm around my waist. "I can't live without you. When I heard your song . . . I'm sorry. I was wrong. I was an idiot . . . please don't leave. Stay here. Stay with me. I need you. I love you. I didn't mean what I said. You were blameless. I was angry and scared for Sophie and took it out on you."

I nod, putting my arms around his neck and pulling him into a soft kiss. His tongue caresses mine, and I hear cheering behind me. I turn to see Mindy and Brianna in their husbands' arms while Grandma and Mom wipe away their tears. Even Hannah is wiping away a tear or two, and Nathan looks like he's got some allergies going on.

"Looks like I'm staying," I tell Mindy, who grins and gives me a thumbs-up.

"But what about the apartment?" Hannah mock whines. "I've got two potential roomies wanting to see the place tomorrow!"

"Well, I've got a spare bedroom," Jake says, "and Sophie would love to have you around."

"Deal!" Hannah says, grinning. "Roxy, you've got twenty-four hours to get your shit out!"

There's laughter all around, and Nathan disappears to the back to return with four bags of Chinese food. He starts divvying it out, and I turn to Jake, looking into his eyes. "You'd really want me to move in?"

"I want to start with you moving in," Jake says quietly. "And Mindy already told me you want to leave Franklin. If you still want to, that's fine. You can pay your share another way."

"How?" I ask.

"Next Saturday, we're doing an outdoor concert for Club Jasmine. Know of a hot pop act who can work the stage and has a song that's rocketing up the charts who can sing her ass off for us?"

I blush, giving Jake a raised eyebrow, and he nods. "Only if you want to," he adds.

I nod and jerk my thumb over my shoulder at Nathan. "Talk to my manager," I say, giving Jake a huge smile. "He's the brains of the outfit, remember?"

CHAPTER 30

JAKE

I grin at the happy, exuberant guy looking back at me in the mirror, stunned at the image. I can't help myself and start humming *Heartstopper*, even dancing a little, popping my hips. The world seemed so dark a few days before, and now everything is looking up again.

"Oh. My. God." Sophie laughs quietly behind me, and I turn around. "Next thing I know, you're gonna pull out those hot pants and start doing the YMCA."

For this first time in my life, I think I blush. Sophie comes over and pats me on my chest, grabbing my tie and pulling it around my neck. "Now you're dressing me?"

"You always take forever with your tie," Sophie teases. "And this is your special tie."

I glance down at the cornflower blue tie and lift my eyebrow. "Really?"

"Sure is. You only seem to wear it when you've got stuff planned or you're really happy. So which is it?" she asks as she starts wrapping the silk around itself. "I think I know."

"What?" I ask, and Sophie laughs.

"My big brother is in loooove!" she teases, tugging on the knot that's magically appeared. "Now, fix your collar, and you can fix me some eggs. And I don't want to see that with your hips ever again!"

This is what being in love gets me, I think as I tug at my collar and find myself snapping my fingers as she walks out. *Doing things I would never do. It's pretty awesome.*

I thread my belt, and as I adjust my fly, Sophie sticks her head in again. "Hey, eggs?"

I look up, glad I had things mostly done. "Don't you ever knock?"

Sophie shakes her head. "You leave your door open all the time. Nothing to knock on."

"Huh," I think. Point, Sophie. "Okay, well, how'd you like some bacon in your eggs?"

"Always up for the fine swine," Sophie says with a grin. "I'll help."

❆

THE FIRST HALF OF THE DAY FLIES BY, AND AS I GET READY FOR THE monthly meeting with the advisory board and corporate, I still feel like I'm walking on clouds. Elena knocks on my door, and I call her in. "Yes, Elena?"

"Miss Price has asked to see you," she says, smiling a little. She knows, but she seems to actually be pleased by the whole thing. Maybe Elena's a romantic at heart. "Shall I show her in?"

"Please," I answer, but before Elena can, she's practically pushed out of the way as Matt bursts into the room, along with Byron and Maria Bennett, the woman corporate sent down to talk face to face with the Franklin Consolidated board today. She's from human resources and was going to talk about the changeover of retirement and health insurance plans next fiscal year.

"There he is!" Matt says, stabbing a finger at me. "I told you he's been breaking Rule 34(b) of the Corporate Code of Conduct!"

I sigh, giving Maria a look. "What's he talking about?"

"Don't try to play innocent!" Matt says, his reedy voice grating on my ears. "They've been carrying on an affair. As the regional president, that's a clear conflict of interest. I've watched them!"

"Watched me do what?" I ask as I see Roxy slide in the back of the office, her eyes blazing. I hold up a hand, and she nods, keeping her peace. "Have any of you seen me or Miss Price do anything unprofessional in the office?"

Sure, it's a gamble—we did have the elevator . . . and the supply room—but nobody was there either time. Matt blusters, then points at Roxy. "She's singing at your nightclub, and you two have been seen cavorting there!"

"Is this true, Jake?" Maria asks. "You know the rule applies regardless of time or place."

Anger burns in me, but before I can respond, Roxy steps forward.

"It doesn't matter," she says, staring Matt in the eyes. "I was just asking to see Mr. Stone so I could personally turn in my resignation. This was my last day here. So you see, no conflict. On the other hand, I can think of some people in violation of Rule 72(f) . . ."

I don't even know what the rule is, but Matt and Byron, who's just been a spectator, both immediately look guilty. Maria gives them a once-over, then she shakes her head. "Matt, I think you and I need to have a talk later about wasting HR's time with baseless accusations. Jake, I'll see you in the boardroom in fifteen?"

"Sure," I say, giving Matt and Byron a raised eyebrow as Maria turns on a heel and walks out. "You two . . . I suggest you both start polishing your resumes. I think Franklin Consolidated could use some manpower reductions. Now get out of my office."

They leave, Elena laughing softly as she watches them. She gives me a nod and leaves as well, closing my door behind her. Roxy looks adorable as she shifts from side to side, giving me a shy smile. "Sorry, I hadn't really planned on doing that. But since we talked about it, I figured I'd drop the bomb a little more dramatically."

"Well, that's how you divas are," I tease, crossing my office to take her hand. "So, you get invited to move in, and now you're going all Hollywood on me. What's next, gonna want that condo in Beverly Hills?"

Roxy laughs, stepping in closer. "No, I want to sing for love. Jake, I'm gonna sing at Club Jasmine because I love it. You and my family are the number one priority in my life, and singing is number two. I don't care if I get a Grammy or sell a single CD. I'm going to sing because I love it, make the music I like, and sing the music I want. Whatever happens, happens."

"So, me and your family are tied at number one?" I tease, and she lifts my hand, kissing my knuckles.

"Mindy likes you, so yeah, you're tied. She already asked me when you'll officially join the fam."

I blink and grin. "Tell her we'll see, but it might be damn soon."

Roxy grins back. "Well, then, you go do your executive ish, and I'll go clean out my desk. See you later at home?"

Without waiting for an answer, she turns and walks out, swaying her ass and humming *Heartstopper* under her breath. I grin and would probably still be grinning if Elena didn't knock on my door again. "Sir? The meeting?"

"Oh, yeah," I say, grabbing my report folder. "You have everything prepped?"

"Of course. Have a good meeting, sir."

❄

I STARE AT MY COMPUTER, WISHING THE MEETING HAD GONE MORE quickly. Everyone and their brother on the board had questions about the new retirement system. Of course they would. Most of them are over fifty-five. I'm surprised they didn't ask if that came with a golden ager discount at the local steakhouse.

Everyone left—even Elena said goodbye as the sun went down— and now I'm left trying to handle this last bit of busy work before I go home.

"What are you still doing here?"

I look up, seeing Roxy at my door. "Just wrapping up a last email. What about you? Figured you'd be out the door long ago."

"Cleaning my stuff out took longer than expected," she says. "Hannah insisted on running out and getting red velvet cupcakes for the floor to share as a parting gift. Everyone but Matt and Byron got one. So . . ."

She pulls the plate out, and I see a pair of red velvet cupcakes with what looks like vanilla frosting on top. "You want to share?"

I smile as I click and send off my last email, shutting down the system and closing up. "Looks delicious."

She brings the plate over and sets it on my desk. As she crosses my office, I watch her seductive smile and the way her hips sway as she walks in her high heels. "I thought you said you hated pencil skirts."

"One more day won't matter," Roxy says, handing me a cupcake. "A toast. To the future."

"May it be as sweet as this," I say, touching cupcakes with her. I take a bite, but I'm distracted as Roxy's sensuous lips wrap around the soft, rich cake and she bites down, crumbs dropping down onto her chest and a smear of frosting staining her lips and cheek. "You missed some."

I lean in, kissing Roxy and licking the sweet vanilla frosting off her mouth before pulling her closer, letting our kiss deepen more. "Mmm, well, it's almost the fantasy," she teases when our lips part. "I've wanted to be seduced by my boss ever since seeing you."

"Well, isn't it lucky for you that your resignation form won't get turned into HR until tomorrow morning then?" I reply, reaching up and cupping her breast through her blouse. "So you still work for me, *Miss Price*."

Roxy moans as I squeeze her left breast, massaging the soft flesh as she presses herself up against my body, my cock quickly hardening in my pants as she grinds against me, and I growl, kissing down her neck as I feel the few crumbs of leftover cupcake smear against my dress shirt. To hell with it. I need her now, and I turn her around, pushing her against my desk as I lift her up to sit on the edge. "Oh, sir," she whispers as she runs her fingers through my hair. "God, I'm glad I'm quitting this job. I'd need this every night if I stayed."

"I'm glad too," I growl as I pull open her blouse, buttons flying everywhere. Fuck it, someone will clean it up later. Roxy's breasts rise and fall with her gasping breath as I feast my eyes on her flushed skin, and a naughty thought comes to me. Reaching next to her, I take the uneaten half of my cupcake and smear the frosting over her breasts and bra. Roxy grins as she realizes what I'm doing.

"Hungry, sir?" she asks, her words torn from her throat as I lick and suck at her skin. The sugary frosting adds to the sweetness of her skin, and I suck her nipples clean through her bra, biting and pulling on them as Roxy cries out gently, her fingers pulling at my hair as she fights the sensations swirling through her. "Sir . . . oh, fuck, Jake . . . oh, God."

I kiss back up to her lips, stroking her hair and looking in her eyes. "Roxy, I love you."

"I love you too . . . but my fantasy isn't done yet," she jokes, pushing me back. Taking me by the hand, she leads me over to my office chair and pushes my shoulders down, making me sit before she sinks to her knees. "Now, Mr. Jake Stone, sir, I think I need to show you just how devoted I am to my boss."

My hands tremble as Roxy has me grip the arms of my chair and pushes me back, leaning back as she undoes my pants and takes out my throbbing cock, cooing as she takes it in. Turning around on her knees, she grabs the other cupcake and lets the tip of her tongue swirl through the frosting for a minute before she scoops the rest of it off with her fingers and traces them down my cock, covering my pulsing skin with the creamy white sweetness.

"An appetizer before dinner," Roxy says, reaching out with her tongue and tracing up the whole length of my cock. I moan. Her touch is electric as she swirls her tongue all around my cock, licking it glistening clean before spreading her lips and swallowing me.

"Oh, God, baby," I moan as she slowly sucks my cock deeper and deeper between her magical lips, rolling my balls between her fingers as she scratches her other hand down my chest. Feeling Roxy work her lips up and down my thick cock, I lean back, relishing the warm, wet prison of her lips as she pleasures me. "That's it, show me what you love, Roxy."

She bobs her head up and down, soft whimpers and moans coming from her chest when I put my hand on her head and force more of my cock down her throat, taking over. I don't jam myself down her throat. I just don't let her up until she's gagging, choking on my cock before I pull her off and pick her up, kissing her lips hard and lifting her.

I put her down on the edge of my desk, pulling her skirt down hard enough that I hear fabric rip. Fuck it, she didn't want to wear this thing again anyway. Roxy gasps as I pull her panties down and rub the head of my cock between the wet, pink lips of her pussy. After all the teasing and erotic torture of her lips and tongue on my cock, I can't hold back, and I thrust into her with a single long thrust. I bury myself deep into her, and Roxy grabs my forearms, hissing in pleasure and digging her fingernails into my skin. The pain is delicious, and I grind against her, feeling her clit rub against the base of my cock as I stare deeply into her eyes.

Pulling back, I lightly put my hand on Roxy's throat as I thrust again harder, our hips slapping together as she wraps her legs around me. I don't squeeze. I just pound her pussy harder with the throbbing heat of my cock, both of us soon gasping and crying out as our hips slap together sharply.

"Fuck me, baby, oh, fuck, yes," Roxy groans as she squeezes me, massaging my cock as she tries to give it back to me. I thrust harder and faster, long strokes as I swirl my hips, grinding inside her tight body until I'm trembling, lost on the edge again. Roxy sees my eyes roll back and scratches my forearms again, digging her thumbs in and pulling me back from the edge.

I grunt my thanks as I let go of her throat and push her knees up and apart, hammering her body on top of my desk as hard as I can. Sweat runs between our bodies as our hearts race, and I give everything I can to my angel, shuddering as she starts to tremble.

"Roxy . . ." I barely get to gasp before I'm on the edge again, and this time, there's no holding back. With a hard gasp and a scream that I'm sure can be heard all the way to the parking lot, I slam my cock as deep as I can into her as I come, filling her. Roxy wraps her legs around me and throws her head back, crying out her own climax as her pussy squeezes me tighter, drawing out my orgasm.

When I can focus again, I gather Roxy into my arms, holding her trembling body as my cock softens before slipping out of her. I kiss her soft lips again, Roxy wrapping her arms around my neck and burying her head in my shoulder. "I'm going to miss this office."

"Yes, but now we have a whole apartment to explore," I remind her.

Roxy thinks, then starts laughing. "An apartment, huh? We've never had sex in bed at your place."

I laugh, holding her close. "Nope. Weird, isn't it? I hear some people actually like it that way."

"Fucking perverts," Roxy jokes, unwrapping her legs from around my waist and standing up. "Next thing you're going to tell me is that you're going to want to actually start naked too."

"It does happen."

Roxy shakes her head, laughing. "What sort of weird shit are you getting me into?"

The day is exactly as I'd dreamed it'd be for the past six months. It seems impossible that I could have such a picture perfect day, but I do. The sky is blue, the weather warm but with a light breeze off the ocean for our ceremony, and now . . . now comes the cherry on the sundae.

"You ready?" Mindy asks me as we wait in the back of the hall. She can't believe that I'm doing this, but ever since Jake got on his knee in front of all of Club Jasmine and asked me to marry him, it seemed like there was only one way that I could start off our reception.

"I'm almost ready," I say, adjusting my top. Sure, I'm singing a pop song on my wedding day, and sure I'm doing it in front of a ton of people who have seen me shake my ass in a lot less, but that's what's going to make this special. I fidget with the long skirt, tugging on my garter. That'll come after the song, and I've already promised Nathan that I'd have Jake try to toss it in his direction. He is my business and investment manager, after all. "How are Mom and Grandma?"

"Grandma's happy as hell that you banned Bertha from the church and the reception," Mindy says with a laugh. "John's consoling Mom, but she'll be fine. Hey, you sure you want to do this before the cake cutting and all of that other stuff?"

"Why?"

"Well, it is kind of untraditional," Mindy says, turning red when I give her a raised eyebrow. "Okay, okay. I know, I'm the last person in the world to talk about non-traditional. But a musical revue before the reception begins?"

"The reason is simple," I say with a chuckle. "Once that cake is cut and the champagne starts to flow, I plan on dancing my ass off with my husband and then seeing if we can get to some baby making."

"Planning kids already?"

I nod. "You know that Jake and family are more important to me than my singing. Although, Club Jasmine would flip the fuck out if I made an announcement that I'm pregnant."

Mindy laughs and kisses me on the cheek. "I'm so happy for you, Roxy. I'll go take my seat."

Mindy leaves, and I quickly warm up my voice. There's no need to stretch out. This performance is like only one other, and I'm quickly ready. I nod to John, who gives me his quiet little smile and nod before he opens the door and I enter the reception hall.

All the lights are off, the only illumination coming from dual spotlights, one on me, one on Jake as he sits in a chair in the middle of the dance floor. The tune is familiar but slowed down, acoustic as I start singing. "It was too long, I had to get out, hitting up the new spot with my girl."

Of course, I adjust the lyrics just for this performance. Jake smiles as I serenade him, and there's a few whistles when I straddle his waist, the high slits on my skirt allowing me to do so. "Heartstopper, Heartstopper, can you feel it in my chest? Heartstopper, my husband, showing me the best, your touch is electric, I was yours from the start. You gave it to me, baby, and now you have my heart."

Jake pulls me closer and kisses me tenderly, his fingertips just resting on the curve of my jaw as our assembled friends and family applaud. I can hear my old friend from Trixie's, Brad, in the background blowing his nose, his distinctive lisp reaching out over the crowd as he cheers me on, "Yaass bitch! Work it!"

The reception starts, and true to my promise, Nathan catches the garter and Hannah gets to catch the bouquet. Later, I'm stunned as the caterer brings out a five-foot-tall cake. "What is this?"

"This is your stepfather insisting that he gets to do something for you," John says from the far side of Mom, smiling. "Enjoy."

There's enough cake for triple the amount of people who are there, and I make the caterer promise that they're going to send large chunks home with everybody who works at the hall today. I just can't imagine seeing this much cake go to waste.

Speeches are hilarious, as everyone from Grandma on down has something to toast me with, and I'm quickly left red-faced as Brad tells everyone about my first time in Trixie's. "So here was this sassy little thing getting up there and doing the world's worst twerk and singing her ass off. Thankfully, she had two things going for her. First, she could actually sing. Second, and more importantly, she had me to show her how to move her ass. Jake, you can thank me later, and Nathan, I want my one percent!"

The dancing starts with another surprise, as Jake says he's got something special for me too. Oliver and Gavin get up as well as they set up three chairs in the middle of the floor in a wide triangle. "My bride, will you, Mindy, and Brianna have a seat, please?"

I glance at Mindy and Brianna, but they're clueless as we sit down. Jake, Oliver, and Gavin disappear for a minute, and I start to get worried when the lights dim again and the music starts.

"Oh, my God," I groan as I hear the familiar grinding electronic bass beat. "They're not."

"They sure as hell are!" Brianna says as Jake, Gavin, and Oliver come out dressed as male strippers. They've got the moves down pretty well too, and *Magic Mike* is left in the dust as Jake grinds on me, turning around to rub his ass in my lap before taking my hands and making me grab his crotch. My body's on fire by the time he moves off, and I feel sweat trickling down my neck to disappear between my breasts as the three guys reach for the waistbands of their banana hammocks before stopping and giving the three of us naughty smiles. Jake shakes his head, and the three of them dance for us a little more, Gavin actually hitting the splits. "Whoa, I didn't know he could do that!"

"It's useful," Brianna says, her voice sounding breathy as Gavin bounces back up. The song comes to an end, and while the three of us heartily applaud, Brad is having a fit behind us. I bet he's thinking he's died and gone to heaven watching the three handsome men.

Dinner starts, and as we eat, I lean over to Jake. "So tell me, my husband, just what inspired that?"

Jake chuckles. "Well, the guys knew you were going to sing for me, and they wanted to return the favor. Unfortunately, we all know that Gavin and Oli—"

"Those two boys can't sing to save their lives!" Grandma cackles.

After dinner, the dancing starts, and I feel like I'm in heaven as Jake takes me in his arms and we have our first dance as husband and wife. "So when did you know?"

Jake thinks, then smiles. "I knew I wanted you long-term the first time you sang *Heartstopper* for me. But marry you? When I first heard you on the radio. It was like from that instant, it wasn't just about giving you your dream. That was when I realized you are *my* dream. I'd do any and everything possible to stay by your side, to have you with me. I knew I wanted to be more. I wanted to be your husband."

"You waited another two months to ask me, though," I tease as we slow dance.

"I wanted to have a chance to ask you on stage," he says, grinning. "Took the workers that long to complete the repairs."

"I—" my eyes are drawn over to a commotion where someone's trying to teach Grandma how to breakdance.

Jake takes my chin in his fingers and turns my eyes back to him. "Hey, I thought I was doing a good enough job of dancing?"

I feel the thick bulge of his cock press up against my hip, and I tremble, grinning. "You do more than enough to keep my attention."

"Cheers, you two," says a voice behind us, and I turn to see Hannah standing there with several glasses in her hand, one of which she holds out to me.

"What's that?" I ask, taking the glass from her.

"A little surprise," Hannah says behind a little sip. She gives Jake a look. "Can I talk to your bride for a moment? I know y'all were getting your bump n' grind on, but it will only take a sec."

Jake chuckles, stepping away. "Sure."

Hannah winks at him as I give her a playful scowl over the rim of my drink. "This had better be good for sending my husband away like that."

"I've decided to quit my job at Franklin," Hannah announces suddenly, causing me to gawk in shock. "I just . . . watching you, Roxy, I realize I want to be more than an office drone too. And with you gone, it just isn't fun anymore. I've already talked to the landlord. I'm gonna move out and downsize to something more affordable, chase my dream."

"What is it?" I ask, and Hannah grins.

"Not too sure yet, but I've always wanted to travel the world and take pictures. Maybe I'll figure it out along the way. I've managed to square away a little nest egg until I get it sorted out, I think."

I raise my glass, and we toast each other. "Well, then, to Hannah Fowler, who's going to be the sassiest bitch traveling the globe."

"And to Roxy Stone, who's the baddest bitch on stage. I love you, babe."

I sip my drink and look across the floor. Jake has already found a new dancing partner in his sister, Sophie. She looks gorgeous in her pink gown, her arms wrapped around her brother's neck, staring up at him with love. I can't hide the smile on my face. I'm never going to be her mother, but big sister? I feel like that already.

"I love you too, babe," I say, returning my gaze to Hannah. "And hey, don't be a stranger, okay?"

"Damn right. I'm couch surfing with a pop star!"

I laugh and take a longer sip of my drink. "Yeah, well, this pop star is going to finish her drink and then find her husband so she can go consummate this union. You'll never guess what we're taking to the honeymoon."

"What?" Hannah asks, and I grin.

"I'll send you pics," I say, giving her a wink.

At that moment, the music cranks up. Unlike the normal moldy mix of old pop classics that are 'safe' for some of the older crowd to listen to, Jake and I flew in our DJ from Club Jasmine, and as the bass fills the floor, we've got plenty getting down and dirty. This is my wedding, after all, and I give absolutely zero fucks if someone doesn't like it.

Laughing, I stand there, bobbing my body to the music, watching the room as Hannah waltzes off in search of a dancing buddy. I'll let Jake get in a few more moments with his sister, knowing that after they're done, he's mine for the night.

For the next several minutes, my heart is filled as I take in all the people I love under one roof, having the time of their lives. Mom is dancing with John, Brianna with Gavin, and Mindy with Oliver. Even Hannah has finally found a guy to grind on, Oliver's younger brother, Tony. It's weird. They don't even know each other, but they look like they're having a good time together.

All feels right with the world.

Feeling like it's time, I make my way over to my husband, desire heating my core. Jake looks up and separates from Sophie as I approach, a giant grin on his face.

"Hey, Jake, you big stud," I say softly, wrapping my arms around his neck. "Take me to bed or lose me forever."

"Your wish is my command."

Jake pulls me closer, growling lightly as he sweeps me off my feet, and to the hoots, hollers, and cheers of our family and friends, he carries me from the reception hall and into the rest of our lives.

Want the deleted scenes? Sign up to my mailing list to receive them!

Irresistible Bachelor **Series (Interconnecting standalones):**
Anaconda || Mr. Fiance || Heartstopper
Stud Muffin || Mr. Fixit || Matchmaker
Motorhead || Baby Daddy

PREVIEW: STUD MUFFIN

LAUREN LANDISH

Hannah

"*I*'m so done with men!" I declare over the phone to my six months pregnant bestie, Roxy. "Finished! I swear to God, I'm going lesbian!"

I'm at work, sitting at my desk, doing everything but my job. I know I should be working, but I'm in too shitty of a mood. It certainly doesn't help that the rat bastard's portrait is sitting right in front me. That smooth golden skin, those suave brown eyes, the looks that made me ignore all of his bullshit. The picture of the asshole who used to make me smile now only seems to piss me off. "I don't care if he looks like Ryan Gosling with a ten-inch cucumber in his pants and says that he wants me to have his babies all while promising me the pleasure of a thousand orgasms," I growl. "I don't care. I'm turning him down."

Roxy laughs. "It must be bad! What the hell happened this time?" She pauses, chuckling. "Or do I even want to know?"

"Screw this shit!" I snatch the portrait off my desk, taking it out of the frame. Snarling, I rip up the picture of the two of us and crumple it into a ball. "Roxy, it's the craziest shit you'll ever hear." I toss it into the wastebasket with one hand. "Score! LeBron ain't got shit on me!"

"Enough fucking around. Tell me!" Roxy commands immediately. "Now you have me curious."

I take a deep breath, anger twisting my stomach as I think about last night. "You won't believe it. He has mommy issues!"

"For real?" Roxy gasps. "What does that even mean?"

My eyes go big even though Roxy can't see them. "I mean, he's got legit Mommy issues, girl! We were going at it, and suddenly, he starts asking if he's been a bad boy and if I would punish him!"

Roxy laughs in disbelief. "Seriously? That's nuts!"

"I shit you not. I thought the whole time he was calling me *Mami*, like Latino style? I mean, he's from Miami, right? No, the guy literally meant Mommy, as in . . . he even asked if he could put on a diaper!"

"No way!" Roxy chokes with laughter.

"Way! After I heard that, I was like, fuck this, I'm outta here!" I shake my head in disgust. "Seriously, Rox, this is five in a row who've turned out to be either a jerk, a freak, or a damn pervert. I'm starting to think there's not a man out there for me."

Roxy laughs. "Come on, Hannah, don't become jaded. The right guy will come along and knock you off your feet eventually. You'll see."

"Ha! That's easy for you to say, Miss I-Just-Got-Nominated-For-

A-Kids'-Choice-Award. Let's see here," I say, starting to count on my fingers. "Lance was a drunk jerk, Hank was a cheater, and Troy never could keep it up without drugs or closing his eyes . . . talk about a boost to your self-esteem. And then there was that prick To—" I stop short of saying his name. We were never dating. But he still adds to the line of terrible luck that I have. I shake off the thought of him. "Meanwhile, the right guy came along for you and you just fucked him to death to make him love you."

"I did not!" Roxy protests. "We didn't even get our clothes off on the first try!"

"I'm just kidding," I say with a mirthless snort. It's not what I remember her telling me, but that's beside the point. Still, Jake's a good catch. While my life has been on replay, Roxy's gotten out. Not a superstar yet, but at least she's got a man she loves and has every weekend to do what she always dreamed of—singing.

I feel like I'm going through the motions. Since quitting my job at Franklin Consolidated, I tried out photography for a little while, and while I enjoyed it at first, I quickly realized it wasn't for me when I was taking a lot more pictures than I was selling. Besides, with Roxy moving on to be with Jake, I was starting to drain my savings, even if I did downgrade my living situation. So I picked up this job at Aurora Holdings and have been here since.

Aurora's a good job, and it does allow me to travel, which is something I've always wanted. Real estate research and scouting for rich investors is actually fun. And I do still have my camera, even if the only people who see my work are my Facebook friends. Still, it's not where I want to be.

"Yeah, well, you don't have to be angry about me and Jake," Roxy says, and I can hear that she's not really hurt, but still a little peeved.

"I'm sorry," I say. I'm coming across as bitter and I don't mean to. "I don't want to seem like I'm being Princess Pissy Panties over here. I'm happy for you, Rox. It's just that . . . I thought I might have had something special with Josh." I bite my lower lip. "While I felt creeped the fuck out about the whole thing, at least I hadn't invested a lot of my time into the relationship. What's that saying, better now than later? I'm more upset about another failed venture. Another waste of my time."

"Oh, honey, I understand," Roxy says emphatically. "But you'll get through it. As you like to remind me, you're that bitch who turns bad boys into choir boys."

"Girl, I feel more like 'that dumb trick who gets nothing but shit' right about now."

"Oh, stop it," Roxy says before burping loudly. "Sorry, I'm blaming that on the baby."

I laugh, having heard Roxy let loose some wall rattlers before. "Seriously. I've decided I'm cursed when it comes to men. So maybe I'm going to hang up my coat for a while. Hell, I'll even break out the granny panties and let the garden grow since no one will be breaking and entering any time soon."

"I don't believe you. You'll be back to riding dick in a week." Roxy snorts a laugh. "You need it like the rest of us need water."

"Just watch me. I'm serious."

Roxy giggles, unconvinced. "Well, other than dicks with dicks, how are you doing? Liking the job?"

I shrug, though she can't see me. "It's good. I like my boss, I directed some good sales last quarter, and most importantly, I still get to travel and take pics. Especially awesome that I get to do that on someone else's dime."

Sharp voices interrupt my words, and I hear footsteps approaching from outside.

"Shit. Okay, boss coming. I got to get off quick."

Roxy tries to get out a quick, "Bye, Mommy—" in a baby voice.

I hang up before she can finish, vowing I'll get her back the next time I see her, and pretend to start working. Bringing up my desktop screen, I pull up a recent property on my computer along with a few websites about the area. As I do, the two voices become clearer.

"Just give me the chance, Mrs. Sinclair," I hear Cassie White, my twenty-one-year-old, relatively new coworker say as the two women walk into view. My boss, Myra Sinclair, is dressed sharp as a tack, as usual, in a slim-fitting white pantsuit, her grey-white hair cut into a trendy side bob. She has money, and I gotta give it to her—she built it the old-fashioned way. She's used her own sweat and genius to become the head of the property division of Aurora Holdings. Now, she's always wanting the world to know it. Cassie, in perfect minion fashion, has on a grey pantsuit, her dark blonde hair pulled back into a sophisticated ponytail. It's not that Cassie doesn't have skills. She's smart when she wants to be. She just seems to still be in the 'make a good impression' stage and hasn't quite figured out that she needs to move on.

Sinclair spins sharply on Cassie, causing her to nearly stumble back and fall to the floor. "Absolutely not! I told you already that you're too inexperienced. There's too much riding on this, and I wouldn't be comfortable with only you there."

"But I can do it," says Cassie enthusiastically, flashing her dimple-filled smile that I'm sure melts the hearts of men but does nothing for Myra.

"Funny you say that when you nearly botched your last assignment. I seem to recall your spilling coffee into Mr. Balding's lap. He had second-degree burns on his balls and we narrowly avoided getting sued."

Cassie bites her lip, looking guilty. I remember that day. It had been my quick thinking—and a nearby pitcher of iced tea—that had stopped the burns from being worse. "That was an accident."

"That's one of the main reasons I don't want to send you alone. You lack grace and experience." Cassie scowls at Myra's insult, but she pretends not to notice. Myra shakes her head sadly. "Besides, my bosses have someone else in mind . . ." Myra goes silent and looks my way, and I pretend to be preoccupied with the paper I'm scribbling on.

"Hannah," says Myra in an almost singsong voice.

I look up from my computer. "Yes, Mrs. Sinclair?"

"Our quarterly report just came in," she says, brandishing the stack of folders in her hands. "And do you know what it says?"

I beam with pride. Damn right, I do. That, at least, I can take pride in. "That we're doing great, better than we expected."

Myra lets out a laugh. "Oh, dear, that's a good one!" Her smile fades fast, leaving me confused. "Apparently, Aurora Holdings has lost its holdings, pun intended. The shedding of our properties in

Puerto Rico and Europe has hurt our shares, and several divisions are under threat of becoming extinct."

She doesn't have to say which divisions she means. I was responsible for the selling of the European properties, but the market was crashing, the properties were old, and there was no way we were going to get a better price. It was the right thing to do. Still, my mouth goes dry. I thought we were doing great. "We had that company conference call," I protest, thinking of last week's call. "The CFO was talking a good game."

Myra snorts, flipping a dismissive hand. "Jason Randal is a braggart used car salesman and nothing more. The damn fool wouldn't know his asshole from a hole in the ground. It was all talk, Hannah. That's what it was, designed to keep our shareholders appeased and the company from panicking. We've already taken a pounding in the market. We start a shareholder revolt, and we're in deep shit."

I gulp. I've never heard Myra be this brutal before. "Mrs. Sinclair . . ."

"The truth is, our company is close to bankruptcy," Myra says, a note of doom entering her voice.

Her words hit me like a semi-truck in the chest and the office goes totally silent. I clutch the edge of my desk as Cassie turns white in the face, dread gripping my insides. I thought for sure we were doing amazing things. I just secured a contract on a property in a new market that's going to be super hot within ten years. Even Myra said I'd done a great job in closing the deal.

Ugh. This couldn't have come at a worse time.

I was so confident after the last deal that I signed a new lease for an upgraded apartment. There's no way I can afford to lose this job. I don't care if I have rich friends. I'm not asking for a handout.

"So what's going to happen?" I ask, feeling slightly nauseous.

Myra shrugs. "If we don't get a few things falling our way . . . it's not looking good."

I bite my lower lip as I watch Cassie grab herself by the arms. She looks like she's about to cry.

"But," Myra says, giving me the eye of the tiger, "there's an opportunity."

"What's that?" I feel both motivated and frustrated at the same time.

Myra tosses the folder on my desk. "Hawaii. We've tried to secure this in the past, but the man never seemed ready to sell."

I flip through the papers, skimming the details. "Wow," I say as I look at the photos that are included. They're not professional, but still, the property is so impressive it doesn't need pro photography. "This could be big."

Myra nods. "And it could be the thing that saves us. I just need someone competent to go seal the deal. I've worked hard and told the suits that this division can handle it. They were impressed by how you secured the Hastings deal. They want you on the task."

"Me?" I say incredulously. "I'm not sure I'm the one for the job with so much at stake."

Myra clucks her tongue reprovingly. "They won't be happy to hear that. But if you insist, I'll tell them."

"I'll do it," I say immediately. It's my ass on the line too, and if it goes south, at least I can't blame anyone but myself. I try to regain my confidence, squaring my shoulders. "I'll take care of it. I know the island market . . ."

I go silent as Myra gives me a bemused and worried look. "It's not what you think. You see, the owner is an eccentric man by the name of Wesley Mobber." Myra picks up the folder off my desk and flips through it, turning pages until she pulls out a glossy photo with a page paperclipped to it. She hands me the photo of a middle-aged white man smiling through a week-old beard with a twisted knot of dreadlocks on top of his head. "He's not going to let just anyone have the property."

I stare. The guy looks like something out of a parodied Internet meme or something. "What's that supposed to mean?"

Myra sighs. "Wesley is not a motivated seller. From what I gather, he'll sell, but first, he has to like you. Like I said, people have been trying to secure this property for a while. He's not doing anything with the land, so he's basically losing money. But he doesn't give a shit. He's got enough to sit on the damn thing until your grandchildren are geezers. And so far, his eccentric ways have proven quite . . . difficult. He's granted us a meeting though, so you have to work your magic and seal the deal."

"I can handle eccentric," Cassie boasts immediately, as if she knows exactly what that means. I damn sure don't. "I'll do my Cassie Charmer and have his head spinning so fast that his dreads are going to—"

"I don't think so. You can stay here," I try to say. If it's this important, I can't risk Cassie screwing this up. Besides, the first surfer hottie she sees, she's going to be distracted for the rest of the stay.

"But this will be good for me!" Cassie pleads, turning to Myra. "You say Hannah is great at her job, you've mentored her yourself. Let me learn from her, maybe she can mentor me?"

Myra bites her lips, thinking thoughtfully. "Maybe..."

I shake my head gently, "Myra, if this contract is do-or-die for the company, I need to focus 100%, not spend time teaching Cassie."

Cassie ping-pongs her head between the Myra and me, finally settling on Myra. "That's the best time to learn."

Myra scowls, and coalesces, "I'll give it some thought, Cassie." Myra turns her gaze back to me. "I need you to go through the report, do your research, and then get back to me asap on your plan of attack so we can book your trip."

"Right away—" I begin to say.

Cassie cuts in quickly. "How am I supposed to get the experience if you don't give me the chance? Please, Myra, I won't let you down. I'll just watch, learn, and follow Hannah's instructions."

Myra pauses, staring at Cassie thoughtfully.

Seeing a hole in Myra's armor, Cassie presses her advantage. "I can play fetch, help her with research . . ."

Myra holds up her hand. "Okay, you know what, Cassie? You're going, but you're going to be Hannah's assistant. Whatever she needs, you do, and nothing more."

"Thank you!" Cassie lets out a squeal of delight, coming forward to give Myra a hug, but stops dead in her tracks when Myra fixes her with a frosty scowl.

"Don't thank me. Just do your job well," Myra growls. She turns and nods at me. "Report to me when you're done. I'm counting on you." She walks out of the room and enters her office, closing the door behind her.

I let out a groan and mutter under my breath, "Just great . . . she's saddling me with the motor mouth from hell."

"Oh, come on, Hannah," Cassie says, flashing her dimples at me. "You've got the wrong impression about me. You'll see."

I point a stern finger at her. "I'm serious, Cass. I don't want you to even breathe without my approval. We can't screw this up."

Cassie's smile only widens. "You got it, boss."

"And no fetching coffee!" I have to add, remembering the narrowly avoided lawsuit. "I don't want any more fried balls on my watch."

Cassie salutes me. "Got it. No more fried ballsacks!"

Staring into her smiling face, I can see disaster just over the horizon, but I'm hoping I'm wrong. If Myra says for her to go and watch, I'll go with it.

Want to read the rest? Get Stud Muffin HERE or visit my website at www.laurenlandish.com